romance author with widespread appeal. This engaging and sweetly romantic story is just too delightful to miss."

—*New York Times* bestselling author Lisa Kleypas

"Clever, fun, and fantastic!"

—*New York Times* bestselling author Suzanne Enoch

"Ms. Bowman is quite the tease. How I love a good society scandal. The hero is absolutely yummy!"

—Award-winning author Donna MacMeans

"Bowman's engaging sense of characterization, gift for creating sexual chemistry, and graceful writing style give her debut romance a splendidly satisfying emotional depth."

—*Booklist* (starred review)

"This fast-paced, charming debut, sparkling with witty dialogue and engaging characters, marks Bowman for stardom."

—*Romantic Times Book Reviews*

"Bowman's cast of intriguing, well-developed characters— particularly smart, sensible Lily—makes this an engaging debut that will have readers seeking future installments."

—*Publishers Weekly*

"*Secrets of a Wedding Night* is positively enchanting. It became impossible to put down after reading just a few pages. I was up very late finishing this wonderful tale of love and second chances." —*Romance Junkies Book Reviews*

The Accidental Countess

VALERIE BOWMAN

St. Martin's Paperbacks

This is a work of fiction. All of the characters, organizations, and events portrayed in this novel are either products of the author's imagination or are used fictitiously.

THE ACCIDENTAL COUNTESS

Copyright © 2014 by Valerie Bowman.
Excerpt from *The Unlikely Lady* copyright © 2014 by Valerie Bowman.

All rights reserved.

For information address St. Martin's Press, 175 Fifth Avenue, New York, NY 10010.

ISBN: 978-1-250-04208-8

Printed in the United States of America

St. Martin's Paperbacks edition / November 2014

St. Martin's Paperbacks are published by St. Martin's Press, 175 Fifth Avenue, New York, NY 10010.

10 9 8 7 6 5 4 3 2 1

For my sister and brother-in-law,
Sandra Morgan and Matt Morgan,
two of the only people I know who love dogs as
much as I do and who just happen to be
living their very own happily ever after.

I love you guys.

CHAPTER ONE

London, early October 1815

"How can one attend the country house party of a person who does not exist?" Cassandra Monroe sat in her cousin Penelope's drawing room, sipping tea and staring at the slightly older woman who had clearly lost her mind. Cass set her teacup aside and rubbed her temples as she spoke. The headache that had begun minutes ago was slowly turning into a full-blown megrim.

Lucy Hunt, the newly married Duchess of Claringdon and Cass's best friend, sat next to her, also eagerly awaiting Penelope's answer. The entire story made absolutely no sense. Neither of them was having much luck getting Pen to answer their questions about her elusive friend Patience.

"Yes. Tell us again exactly *who* Patience is," Lucy prompted.

Penelope popped another bit of teacake into her mouth and slowly wiped each finger clean with her napkin. She rolled her eyes. "That's precisely what I've been trying to tell you." Penelope's voice took on a beleaguered tone, as if she were speaking to a pair of imbeciles. "She doesn't exist."

Lucy tapped her finger on her cheek. "Yes. That's what I thought you said, dear. Which is why we think it makes no sense."

Cass nodded and looked back to Pen for yet another answer. Thank heavens Lucy was here. Pen often confused Cass to no end, but it made her wonder if she were the mad one, this particular instance notwithstanding. Lucy, with her penchant for bluntness, would get to the bottom of it all posthaste.

Pen shrugged and yanked up her puce-colored bodice with both hands. "I made up Patience, as an excuse."

Cass tilted her head to the side and eyed her cousin carefully. "But didn't you tell me just last week that you and Patience went shopping together on Bond Street?"

"Exactly!" Pen replied.

"Exactly what, dear?" Lucy's brow remained furrowed, and she gave Cass a look that indicated that she finally understood what Cass had been talking about all these years when she'd mentioned that Pen was an egg short of a dozen.

Pen stood and wandered over to the large bay window that overlooked the street. She traced a finger along the pane. "It's quite simple. Patience Bunbury is someone I invented to get out of doing things I do not want to do."

Cass narrowed her gaze on her cousin. "Get out of things you don't want to . . . ? So, you're saying you did not want to go to the theater with me?"

Pen nodded. "Exactly."

"You invented Patience and told me you had already made plans with her?" Cass continued.

"Precisely," Pen agreed, another smile spreading across her round face. "To be quite precise, I didn't invent Patience to get out of going to the theater. I invented her last summer. But I invoked her when you asked me to go to the theater. That's what I love about Patience. She's the perfect excuse for everything!"

Cass frowned at her cousin. The headache was worsening by the moment. "Why exactly are you telling me now?"

"I'm telling you now because I need your help," Pen answered simply.

Cass tilted her head. "Help with Patience?"

"No. Well, yes. Sort of," Pen replied.

"I'm afraid I don't follow at all, dear," Lucy said.

Cass bit her lip to keep from smiling. Lucy had begun calling everyone dear now that she was an old married woman. Cass thought it was quite charming.

Pen turned away from the window and stamped her foot. "I asked you to come over today because I need your help with Captain Swift. I expect him to arrive at any time."

Cass sucked in her breath. *Captain Swift? Julian? Arriving at any time*? She smoothed her hair, sat up a bit straighter, and tugged on the ends of both her gloves.

Captain Julian Swift was the man to whom Penelope was nearly betrothed. He was also the most perfect, handsome, wonderful gentleman in the entire world and Penelope didn't even want him. Julian had been severely wounded at Waterloo and had spent the last three and a half months recuperating. He'd nearly died, and Cass had been alternately praying for him and writing to him. While Pen didn't seem to care much one way or the other. Cass had known that Julian was expected to return from the Continent any day now. She just hadn't quite expected it to be today. She gulped.

Without looking at her, Lucy quietly moved her hand over and squeezed Cass's. "I don't think she meant that Captain Swift is expected right *now,* dear," she whispered. Cass let her shoulders relax a bit. Lucy knew how much Julian meant to Cass. She'd always known.

It wasn't that Cass had any intention of taking her cousin's intended, never that. Why, that would be detestable.

She merely wanted to see him. Just once, to ensure that he truly was alive and well. And then . . . she would let him go. Wish him and Pen well on their nuptials and try her best not to think of him again. Not like *that,* at least. Perhaps she'd join a convent. A sigh escaped her lips.

Pen shook her head at Lucy. "No. You're wrong. That's exactly what I mean. I expect him to arrive quite literally at any moment."

Cass pressed her hand against her throat. "I cannot breathe."

Lucy half turned to pat Cass's knee through her skirts. "You'll be fine, darling." She pointed a finger toward Pen. "Just a moment. You're saying you called your cousin over here on the same day Captain Swift is expected to arrive to tell her something about a young lady who doesn't even exist?"

Pen nodded, her fat brown curls bobbing against her equally plump cheeks. "Yes."

Cass still struggled for breath. Julian was coming? Expected at any moment? Her mind couldn't process the information. She'd been waiting for this for so long, imagined it, dreamed about it. But now that it was here, she was in a panic. If she were the type of young lady who swooned, surely she would have swooned by now. Thank heaven for small favors; at least she wasn't a swooner.

Her gaze dropped to her clothing. Why had she worn this unremarkable light blue gown? It had seemed lovely enough when she'd picked it out this morning, but now it just seemed drab.

Her hand flew to her coiffure. Why had she allowed her maid to fix her hair in such a plain fashion, a mere band around her head? It wasn't sufficient to greet Julian. Oh, it was all wrong. All wrong, indeed.

"Take a deep breath, dear," Lucy whispered from beside her.

Cass did just that. She was dizzy. That was a sign of imminent swooning, was it not? Oh, good heavens. Perhaps she was a swooner after all. Anyone might become a swooner given the correct set of circumstances, mightn't they? Her mind raced. Her palms were sweaty, as were her underarms. Oh, wonderful. She would see Julian for the first time in seven years smelling like a barnyard animal. She sniffed at her sleeve.

"Isn't that right, dear?" Lucy asked, turning to her.

Cass froze. "P-pardon?" She hadn't heard a word the other two ladies had said. She worried her bottom lip.

"I was just telling your cousin here that I believe she owes you some sort of explanation for all of this."

Pen plunked her hands on her hips. "That's what I've been trying to tell you."

"Then out with it, dear, and do try to be a bit more clear this time," Lucy retorted.

Pen took a deep breath. "Captain Swift will be here at any moment, and I need you to greet him, Cass, and tell him all about Patience."

Cass blinked at her cousin. Now she was entirely certain she was on the verge of a hysterical fit. Why was Pen babbling on about some nonexistent young lady when Julian was about to walk through the front door at any moment?

"What about Patience?" Cass nearly shouted at her cousin. She clapped her hand over her mouth at her impertinence. She took a deep breath and shook her head. "That is to say . . . what in heaven's name has Patience got to do with Juli . . . Er, Captain Swift?"

Both ladies raised their brows. Lucy quickly filled the silence. "My question exactly." She turned her attention back to Pen.

Pen gave them both another I'm-speaking-to-imbeciles look. "I wrote to Captain Swift. I told him I'm leaving town, going to visit my friend Patience for the next fortnight at her country house party."

"You're leaving town? With Captain Swift coming?" Cass's voice was high and thin. She shook her head. It was official, this entire story had been invented by a loon.

Pen sighed long and deep. She crossed her arms over her middle and paced in front of the window. "No, I'm not *actually* leaving. Well, I will be, eventually, but the point is that Captain Swift is arriving sooner than I expected. His letter was in this morning's post. He'll be on the next mail coach. Apparently there wasn't enough space on the last one so he sent the letter instead."

Lucy rolled her eyes. "Pen, dear, I'm still not exactly certain what you're talking about."

Cass twisted her hands together. "Yes, Pen, what do you mean?"

Pen stomped back over to where they were sitting and plopped back down in her chair, a huff escaping her lips. "I'm talking about needing an excuse—a good one—to miss seeing Captain Swift when he arrives."

"And a house party is a good excuse?" Lucy asked, treating Pen to her own I'm-speaking-to-an-imbecile look.

Pen waved a hand in the air. "I told him I'd already committed. Not to mention, dear Patience needs me. She was recently jilted over the summer by Mr. Albus Albatross, and this house party is just the thing she needs to lift her spirits."

"What? Who is Mr. Albus Albatross?" Cass rubbed her temples again. The headache had not abated with all this nonsense.

Lucy cleared her throat. "I believe Mr. Albatross doesn't exist, dear, because Patience does not exist."

Cass curled her hands into fists on her knees. She never got angry. Never. Frustrated perhaps, unhappy at times, even irritated. But angry? No. Anger wasn't exhibited by proper young ladies and Cass was proper if she was any-thing. But as she stared at Pen—who was still making abso-lutely no sense whatsoever—anger, white and hot, rushed through Cass's veins. Pen was toying with Julian and he didn't deserve it.

"I swear, Pen, if you don't explain exactly what you mean this minute, I'm going to walk out that door and never speak to you again!" She jabbed her finger in the direction of the exit.

Lucy and Pen exchanged amazed glances.

"Why, Cass, I don't believe I've ever heard you raise your voice before today," Lucy remarked.

Cass was shaking, her fists still clenched. She glared at Pen. "What I still do not understand is why. Why don't you want to see the man you're supposed to marry?"

Pen had the grace to bow her head a bit, then she shrugged. She yanked at the top of her gown with one hand. "I just. I can't. It was so difficult when I thought he was dy-ing . . . and now. Oh, I don't know. I need some time to think about things."

"What things?" Cass prodded. She crossed her arms over her chest and stared down her nose at her cousin.

"You know. He will want to plan the wedding and choose a date and I'm—I'm simply not prepared."

Cass pressed her lips together. Oh, yes. Why should she be prepared? She'd only had *seven years* to prepare. And this entire farce was so like Pen. She was always asking Cass to do outlandish favors for her, nothing quite *this* out-landish to date, but it still shouldn't have surprised her. And Cass, good proper young lady and steadfast cousin and friend, had always agreed, always done whatever her cousin asked. But not today. Not with Julian. She couldn't. She wouldn't.

Lucy shifted in her seat and took a sip of tea. "So, you're saying that in order to evade your intended who is just back from the war and whom you haven't seen in years, you've invented a friend whose fictitious house party you'll supposedly be attending until such a time as you deem fit to return and see him?"

Pen smiled and nodded happily. "Yes. Exactly."

"And what does your mama think of this?" Lucy wanted to know.

"Oh, Mama doesn't know. I hid Captain Swift's letters, and thankfully she and Papa are both out this afternoon." She turned to face her cousin. "That's why I need you, Cass. Julian knows you. He likes you. You've been writing to him all these years, haven't you? You are friends, are you not?"

Cass nodded. She couldn't meet her cousin's eyes. *Yes. We're friends, but I'd like to be much, much more.* Oh, she was the worst cousin on earth, the very worst. Pen would order her from the house if she knew how much Cass coveted her would-be bridegroom. At the very least Pen certainly wouldn't ask her to do this mad favor for her.

Lucy set her teacup aside and dabbed at her lips with her handkerchief. "I have one more question."

Pen nodded a bit impatiently. "Yes?"

"Have you completely lost your mind?" Lucy asked, a serene look on her face. "Or just a part of it, dear?"

Cass had to sharply turn her face away to keep her cousin from seeing her smile.

Pen blinked at Lucy. "I don't know what you mean." Pen stood again and made her way back over to the window with her teacup in her hand. She glanced outside. "I just need—"

The teacup dropped to the rug with a solid thunk, spilling its contents on the expensive Aubusson carpet. "Oh, my goodness. He's here!" Pen called.

All the anger drained from Cass's body, replaced with

sheer, freezing-cold anxiety. She pressed her hand to her belly. "I think I may cast up my accounts."

Lucy squeezed Cass's hand and raised her voice to address Pen. "Who's here?"

Pen whirled to face them, a look of panic in her blue eyes. "Captain Swift! He's here! Now!" She rushed to the drawing room door and opened it before turning back to the other two ladies. "Cass. Cass, please," she begged. "You must do this for me. You must tell Captain Swift I've gone to see Patience in the country. You must."

Cass's teeth chattered. She shook her head. She couldn't do this. She could not. "But I haven't even seen him in seven years, Pen. I was a child when last we met. And besides—"

"Please!" Pen nearly shrieked. "I must go. I'll sneak up the back staircase so he won't see me. Cass, please do this for me. Please!" And with that, Pen was gone from the room in a sweep of puce skirts.

Cass sat dumbly staring at the empty teacup lying haphazardly on its side on the carpet. She blinked, replaying the last few moments again and again in her mind. A log snapped in the fireplace. The smell of burnt wood filled the room. "This cannot be happening. It simply cannot," she murmured.

Lucy took a deep breath and pushed her hands down her legs, smoothing her skirts. "It appears it is happening," she said just before Pen's butler arrived at the door to the drawing room.

"Captain Julian Swift," the butler pronounced.

"Show him in, please," Lucy replied in a commanding voice, as if she were the lady of the house. She turned quickly to face Cass and grasped her shoulders. "Cass, look at me."

Cass managed to meet her friend's eyes. Her headache

had been replaced with a strange buzzing sensation and a dazed feeling. She grasped at the smooth satin of Lucy's sleeves.

"You look frightened half to death." Lucy squeezed her shoulders and gave her an encouraging shake.

"I *am* frightened half to death. Oh, Lucy. What am I going to say? What am I going to do?" She searched Lucy's face. Lucy was always sensible, always rational, always so good with words. Lucy would know what to do. Wouldn't she?

Lucy nodded, a determined look in her eye. "Don't worry, Cass. I'll handle it. Leave all of the talking to me. I have an idea."

CHAPTER TWO

Cass had heard of people being overcome by fits of un-
even breathing. She'd even seen it a time or two at the
odd, overly crowded crush. Once Lady Sarah Marking-
ham had delicately fluttered to the parquet floor in the
middle of the Thorntons' ball, only to be carried away by
two footmen and followed by her mother who declared
that smelling salts were in order and she just so happened
to have a vial of those useful little pebbles in her reticule.
But Cass had never expected such a dramatic turn to happen to *her*. Today was certain to be the first. Spots danced
before her eyes. The room seemed to be closing in on her.
For a strange moment, she thought she smelled oranges.
She braced a hand against the arm of the sofa.

Lucy had said to leave all the talking to her. Of course
Cass meant to leave all the talking to her. That was Lucy's
strength, after all, talking. And a duty Cass was more than
grateful to relinquish to her friend at the moment. She
doubted she could utter a word if she was prodded with a
hot poker.

Yes, Lucy would talk. As it should be. In fact, Cass,
Lucy, and their third close friend, Jane, had all agreed at

a ball last June that they would use one another's strong points to help each attain what they wanted in life. First, Lucy had chased away Cass's unwanted suitor, the Duke of Claringdon. It turned out in the chasing, however, that he'd actually been the perfect suitor for Lucy all along.

Next, they had promised to help their bluestocking friend Jane convince her parents to stop constantly pestering her to marry. Jane wanted nothing more than to be left in peace to study and write and stop being forced to attend all those hideous balls and routs.

It was Jane's turn, yes, but here Lucy was, using her skill with words to help Cass in her time of need yet again, and Cass was infinitely grateful to her friend. In the moments it took for the butler to show Julian into the drawing room, Cass pulled her hand away from the arm of the sofa and set it in her lap. She swallowed hard and straightened her shoulders. Then she concentrated on not sliding off the settee in a fit of wrong breathing.

"You look absolutely breathtaking, dear," Lucy said with a small, encouraging smile. "Captain Swift is certain to be amazed at your beauty."

"I was quite serious when I said I may cast up my accounts," Cass answered.

"Don't do that, dear," Lucy replied quickly.

Cass took a small gulp of air and nodded shakily just before the door to the drawing room swung open again and Captain Julian Swift strode into the room.

A funny little noise flew from Cass's throat. A whimper? A sigh? Both, perhaps. She turned her face up to him and just . . . stared, her eyes, no doubt, wide as saucers.

Julian was there, not the dream of him, not the memory, but the flesh-and-blood man. He was even more dashing and handsome than she'd remembered. She'd been barely sixteen the last time she'd seen him. Julian had been three and twenty. Now she was three and twenty. She gulped.

She'd been a child back then, really. She hadn't matured at a fast pace. She'd had straggly blondish hair, unremarkable blue eyes, and freckles on the bridge of her nose. She'd also been far too thin and all knobby-kneed. She hoped she'd grown into the swan her friends always told her she would. But at this moment, facing Julian, she could only remember herself as an awkward young girl. Weren't friends always telling one another how beautiful they were even if it was entirely untrue?

Staring at Julian, she was rendered completely speechless. Her gaze swept from the tips of his boots to the top of his head. He wore his army uniform. Oh, my, he wore it well. A deep red coat with epaulets, dark gray trousers, and black Hessians. Julian was two inches over six feet tall, had blond-streaked hair and broad shoulders and the most amazing gray eyes she had ever seen.

He flashed a smile as soon as he saw the two women sitting on the sofa. Cass sighed again. His teeth hadn't suffered any ill effects from his service to the Crown, still straight and white and perfect. And while he had a few small crinkles at the corners of his eyes and he looked a bit older and more distinguished, for certain, he was still as handsome—more so—than Cass remembered from her vivid dreams.

And he was standing directly in front of her.

The look on his face was a bit of astonishment mixed with confusion. His gaze remained fixed on Cass. He'd barely glanced at Lucy. Lucy looked back and forth between the two of them, and Cass forced herself to pull her gaze away from Julian and turn her attention to her friend. There was a gleam in Lucy's eye, the type of gleam Lucy always got when she was up to one of her schemes. But Cass had no time to consider it. Instead, she stood to greet Julian. Did he recognize her? The look on his face told her he must. Didn't he?

"Ju . . . Julian?" she barely whispered.

Lucy's hand on her arm stopped her and Cass promptly snapped shut her mouth. Oh, yes, Lucy had told her to leave the speaking to her.

Lucy stood, too, and executed a perfect curtsy. "Captain Swift."

"My lady?" Julian said in a tone that clearly indicated he had no idea who she was.

"I am Lady Worthing," Lucy offered.

Cass let out a small gasp. Why had Lucy given him a false name?

"Lady Worthing," Julian repeated, bowing over her hand. "A pleasure."

Cass waited with bated breath to be introduced. Julian had to know who she was. She couldn't look at him. What if disappointment lurked in his eyes? She couldn't bear it.

"And this is . . . ?" Lucy paused deliberately, sweeping her hand in Cass's direction.

Cass held her breath again.

The silence seemed to last an interminable amount of time but it was probably only seconds. Cass glanced up at Julian. Her name would fall from his lips any moment now. Should she curtsy? What was appropriate under such circumstances? This was the man she'd written to nearly every day for the last seven years. She knew more about him than Pen did. She thought about him, dreamed about him, had cried endless tears when she'd believed he would die. And now, here he was, seeing her again. All grown-up.

His brow was furrowed and he stared at her as if seeing a ghost. "Penelope?" he asked in a voice that was half awe, half disbelief.

Cass's mouth fell open. He didn't recognize her. And he apparently didn't remember Pen, either. Pen had been eighteen that last time they'd seen each other. She hadn't changed much, other than the addition of a bit more girth.

"No," Cass breathed, shaking her head.

Lucy swiveled on her heel and gave Cass a deadly glare. "Allow me," she said with a clenched jaw in a voice that clearly told Cass to stop speaking.

Oh, good heavens. Whatever Lucy was up to, it was going to be both messy and complicated. It always was.

Lucy turned back to Julian, a wide smile on her face. "Oh, heavens no, though we are here for the same purpose you are. To see Penelope."

Cass remained silent and motionless at Lucy's side, but her mind was shrieking, *What is Lucy doing*? Why wasn't she introducing her? It was beyond awkward.

"Please have a seat, Captain Swift." Lucy gestured to the chair across from them.

Julian reluctantly sat, though his gaze remained on Cass, clearly still wondering about the identity of the other occupant of the room.

"Would you care for some tea, Captain?" Lucy asked next in the most nonchalant voice in the world, as if she wasn't entertaining a man in someone else's drawing room with an unnamed lady at her side. Cass wanted to expire from embarrassment, but Lucy kept a perfect hostesslike smile pinned to her face.

"No, thank you. I don't drink tea," Julian replied.

Cass glanced at her lap and tugged at the ends of her gloves. Oh, good heavens. He was going to see the teacup on the rug and wonder why it was there. Then, he'd piece the entire idiotic scheme together. Very well, perhaps *that* was unlikely.

Julian leveled his furrowed brow on Lucy. "Is Miss Monroe—Penelope—here?"

Lucy sighed. "I'm afraid not, Captain Swift. Though

my friend and I were just looking for her, too. Seems we stopped by at an inopportune time."

Cass kept her gaze trained on her lap. Her *friend*? That's all Lucy was going to say?

"I don't understand," Julian replied. "The butler said—"

Lucy leaned forward and lowered her voice to a whisper. "Just between you and me, Captain Swift, the Monroes' butler is a few pence shy of a pound these days." Cass glanced up to see Lucy frown and shake her head as if it was a sad bit of news, to be certain.

"Oh, I see." Julian nodded as if he completely understood.

Cass bit the inside of her cheek. Lucy was egregious. How long could Cass remain silent?

"I'd sent Penelope a note this morning telling her I was to be here this afternoon. I suppose she didn't receive it," Julian continued, obvious disappointment marking his features.

Cass longed to reach out and squeeze his hand, run her fingertips along the strong jut of his jaw. She should say something, blurt out her name. But she was having the best time just watching him, staring at his beloved face, beyond relieved to have the chance to see it again.

Lucy sat forward and poured a bit more tea for herself. "It seems we got our days confused and Miss Monroe has already left," she informed Julian.

Cass took another deep breath. Obviously, Lucy was going to go along with Pen's madcap scheme. She was actually going to do it, tell Julian that Pen was at her fictitious friend's house party. This whole thing was ludicrous.

"Already left?" Julian's burnished brows snapped together again.

"Yes, and the silly thing is that she is on her way to the same place we are." Lucy took a small sip of tea.

"Where's that exactly?" Julian asked.

"Why, Miss Bunbury's house party, of course," Lucy replied.

"Miss Bunbury's house party?" Julian asked.

"Yes. Patience Bunbury is one of Penelope's dearest friends. Hasn't she mentioned her to you in her letters?"

"I . . ." Julian cleared his throat and shifted a bit uncomfortably in his chair. "Miss Monroe rarely writes me letters."

Lucy's eyebrows shot up. "Rarely writes you letters? Oh, I must be mistaken as to your identity then, Captain. I was under the impression that you and Penelope are all but engaged." Lucy turned her face so only Cass could see and gave her a quick wink.

Cass wanted to stamp on Lucy's foot, but at the moment, all she could do was smile and nod. She wasn't at liberty to speak since she still hadn't been introduced. Just the way Lucy preferred it, no doubt.

Julian looked away again and tugged at the collar of his coat. "Yes. We're supposed to be betrothed . . . eventually. But I was about to say that she did mention Miss Bunbury to me in the last letter I received."

Lucy took another tiny sip. "Ah, so you know all about her then." Lucy sighed dramatically. "At any rate, it seems Penelope has left prematurely for Miss Bunbury's house party, and in addition to missing us, she's missed her intended, back from the war. Such a pity."

"You said you are going there," Julian replied. "I assume that means you know where this house party is?"

"Oh, yes. We know precisely where it is," Lucy replied serenely.

"Could I trouble you to give me the direction? It's imperative that I speak with Penelope as soon as possible."

Lucy's smile didn't quite reach her eyes. "Eager to see your future bride, Captain Swift?"

He tugged at his collar again. "Something like that."

Cass had to look away. This was excruciating. She couldn't listen any longer. And what possible address could Lucy give him? It was preposterous. She'd have to come out with the truth now that he'd caught her in her lie.

"I'd be more than happy to share the address with you, Captain Swift." Lucy set her teacup on the table in front of her and folded her hands on her lap. "In fact, I can do even better than that."

"Better than the address?" Julian tilted his head in inquiry.

Cass's insides went hot and cold. Suddenly, it all came together, the sly look Lucy had flashed, the failure to introduce her, the questions she'd asked Julian, the things she'd said.

"Yes." Lucy turned to Cass and splayed her hands in front of her as if displaying her for the first time. "Because this is Miss Patience Bunbury right here and we would be delighted to invite you to her house party."

CHAPTER THREE

As soon as the front door closed behind Julian, Cass forced herself to count to fifty. She ensured he was well gone from the property before she jumped up, spun around, and bore down on her closest friend.

"Lucy, how could you? How could you!"

Lucy remained serenely seated and calmly pressed her hands to her coiffure as if smoothing her dark locks. "Cass, if you'll only sit down and think about this reasonably, you'll see—"

Cass turned and paced back and forth in front of the fireplace. She pressed her hands against her cheeks. "Reasonably? Reasonably! I believe reason left this room over an hour ago, right around the time Pen started speaking nonsense about a person who doesn't *exist*!"

Lucy merely raised a brow. "Sit down, Cass. Allow me to explain."

But Cass couldn't sit. All she could do was pace the carpet and tug at her gloves. How in heavens would she ever extract herself from this situation? Julian hadn't said where he was going, but it stood to reason that he'd go visit his older brother, the Earl of Swifdon, in Mayfair. He would probably stay with his brother until he secured his own lodgings. Either that or . . . "Lucy, did you even stop to consider that Julian may now be on his way to see his closest friend, *your husband*?"

Lucy pushed up her chin. "Of course I'd thought of that."

"And yet you still did this?"

Lucy nodded. "Yes. That's precisely why I didn't tell him my real name. I thought of that and several other things, and if you'd sit down and be calm for a moment, I'll tell you exactly how this will work."

Cass tossed her hands in the air. "It can't work. It won't work."

Lucy stood up, stalked over to where Cass was pacing, grabbed her arm, and dragged her back over to the settee. "Sit!"

Cass did as she was told, then she dropped her head into her hands. "Very well, tell me. Tell me all about this addle-brained scheme of yours."

"First of all, I take extreme exception to the fact that you just referred to my brilliant plan as an addle-brained scheme—" Cass lifted her head and opened her mouth to retort, but Lucy pointed a finger in the air. "Allow me to finish." Cass snapped her mouth shut. "And secondly," Lucy continued, "this is going to work perfectly."

"You've just invited Julian to a nonexistent house party, given by a nonexistent person," Cass pointed out.

"Not nonexistent, not now." Lucy flourished a hand toward her. "You're Patience."

A strange strangling noise came out of the back of Cass's throat. "That is so mad I don't know where to begin."

Lucy took up her teacup once more. "Don't you see, Cass? This is the perfect opportunity. You've been waiting for seven years to see Julian again. You wrote him a letter telling him how much you love him, for goodness' sake."

"A letter I never sent," Cass replied.

"That's not the point. Do you or do you not love him?"

Cass took a deep breath. It was true that when she'd heard that Julian was going to die from his injuries, she'd written him a letter. Lucy, with her domineering insistence, had convinced her to. But Cass had never been able to post the letter and now she was heartily glad she hadn't. Oh, why hadn't Julian recognized her? Was she truly that different-looking from seven years ago? If he had recognized her she wouldn't be caught in this awful predicament right now.

She didn't answer Lucy. She didn't need to. Lucy knew how much Cass loved Julian. It was hardly a secret. She'd loved him since she was a girl.

"Penelope, Lord Julian's coach is coming up the lane. You'll want to meet it." Penelope's mother's voice rang through the house. It was Cass's parents' manor house. And it was Cass's sixteenth birthday. Her cousin and aunt had come for the celebration. Julian Swift, Penelope's intended, was soon to be leaving for the Continent with the army. He had decided to visit the party to say his good-byes to Penelope.

Cass's stomach filled with nervous knots. Julian? Julian Swift? Here? On her sixteenth birthday? It was a dream come true. She would never have thought to invite him, would never have imagined he would come. But apparently, he could not delay his journey any longer and he wanted to say good-bye to his intended before he left for God only knew how long. Perhaps forever. But Cass refused to think about that. Not today.

She hurried over to the looking glass that hung on the wall of her bedchamber and took a good look at her reflection. Her eyes were too big for her small, pale face. Her hair was lanky and a nondescript color. Her lips too

wide, her nose too small. And those freckles weren't helping anything at all. She was a fright, a sixteen-year-old
fright. Perhaps she would be beautiful one day, but today was not that day. Today she was too thin and too
scrawny and too everything. Too nervous, also. Mustn't
forget too nervous. The only good thing was her gown. It
was ice blue. It brought out the bit of color in her eyes
and didn't make her skin look too, too pale. Her mother
had had the gown made specifically for her birthday celebration and Cass looked good in it. Well, as good as
she was going to look with the rest of the fright to go
along with it.

"Must I speak with him, Mother?" Penelope replied in
what could only be described as a petulant tone.

Cass swung around to stare at her cousin. All she
could do was blink. "You do not wish to see Lieutenant
Swift?" It made no sense to her. How could her cousin
not want to see her intended?

"He's not even a lieutenant," Pen shot back. "He's a
second lieutenant, just received his commission."

Cass didn't see how that mattered. "But he's . . .
he's . . . your intended." Not to mention he was handsome,
kind, strong, sincere, and absolutely wonderful. All of the
times Cass had been in his company, she'd been positively mesmerized by him. Pen was a lucky, lucky young
woman.

"He is not," Pen retorted, crossing over the thick carpet and staring at herself in the same looking glass that
Cass had recently abandoned. "He's not my intended
yet. Nothing is settled definitely."

Pen's mother plunked her hands on her hips. "I don't
care if he's a cadet. He's going to be your husband one
day and he's made the trip all the way out here to say
good-bye to you before he leaves. You'll do him the cour-
tesy of speaking with him."

Pen rolled her eyes and stuffed a fat brown curl be-hind her ear. "If you insist, Mother."

"I most certainly do. Now, I'll go and greet him. You come down to the rose salon in ten minutes, miss."

Pen's mother strode from the room, giving her daugh-ter a stern stare.

"I wish she wasn't so set on my match with Julian Swift," Penelope said, after her mother had vacated the room. "For all I know he'll be gone for five entire years. Five years! Can you imagine?"

Cass shook her head. In part because she truly couldn't imagine Julian being gone for such a long time and in part because the thought brought tears to her eyes and she was already desperately fighting them. "No," she murmured. "I cannot."

"He might not even return at all," Pen pointed out.

Cass could only nod, but her cousin's words stung her heart.

"I may never see him again," Pen added.

Cass walked silently back over to the looking glass and took her cousin's hand. "Is that why you don't want to speak to him, Pen? You're afraid of getting close. In the event that he . . . d-dies." She closed her eyes on that last word. Unthinkable. Unimaginable.

"Not really," Pen replied, tugging her hand from Cass's grasp. "I just cannot bear to think of myself growing old and ugly waiting for a man who might not be coming back. It's completely unfair, don't you think?"

Surely Pen didn't know how harsh her words sounded. Surely she didn't mean them the way they came across.

"I'm sorry, Pen," Cass said simply. "It must be quite difficult for you."

"You've no idea," Pen replied. "And I'm sorry, too. Sorry that Mother and Father chose a second son with a target on his back to be my groom. I know I'm not the

best catch of the Season, but surely they could find me someone who isn't about to go cavorting all over Europe. They only want this match so that they can be connected to the Swifdon title."

Cass couldn't disagree with her cousin. It was true that the Swifdons were an illustrious family. But how could Pen not want Julian? Tall, handsome, kind Julian? Why, Cass had been in love with him since the day she'd first seen him.

"What are you going to do, Pen?" Cass smoothed her hands down her skirts.

"What can I do?" Pen asked with a sigh. "I'm going to have to go speak with him. Say good-bye." Just then, Pen's eyes lit with fire. "Do me a favor, Cass. Come and save me in five minutes."

Cass blinked rapidly. "Save you?"

"Yes. Come down to the rose salon and interrupt. Tell me you're about to begin the celebration or something. Anything. I cannot bear to stay there and endure an awkward discussion with Lieutenant Swift for Lord knows how long."

Cass shook her head. She couldn't imagine not wanting to savor what might well be her last moments on earth with Julian. "Oh, no, I cannot—"

"Of course you can. Do it, please. For me?" Pen squeezed Cass's shoulder and flew from the room saying, "Thank you, Cass, you're such a dear," on her way out as if Cass had agreed.

Shaking, Cass turned slowly and took another look in the mirror. She'd gone white as a ghost, whiter, even, than she had been before if such a thing were possible. Perhaps she'd turn translucent next. Translucent with freckles, what a lovely combination. She sighed. What was she to do? Pen was expecting her to barge in on her last private moments with her future husband and interrupt them. Cass paced in front of the mirror, pondering it all for a moment. There was one good thing to consider.

If Cass did it, in the end she'd be alone with Julian. Possibly.

Very well, she would do it. It was her birthday after all, wasn't it? What better birthday present could she ask for than a stolen moment with the man she loved?

Cass waited the interminable five minutes before carefully making her way down to the rose salon. The door was shut. She bit her lip. Oh, surely she'd be interrupting something. Then she remembered that was the entire point.

She glanced down at her pretty dress and a bit of confidence flooded through her. She straightened her shoulders and knocked.

"Come in!" Penelope's overly eager voice rang out.

Cass pushed open the door and tentatively made her way into the room. Pen was there, sitting on a settee in the center of the room. Julian stood across from her with his back to the fireplace, his hands folded behind him. He wore his uniform and the sight of him in it was amazing, but it also brought tears to Cass's eyes. He looked so handsome and noble and . . . Julian was an officer in His Majesty's army. He would be in harm's way in a matter of days.

"Yes, Cass? What is it? Are you all right?" Pen stood and Cass got the distinct impression that her cousin would have run from the room already were she not waiting for Cass to voice the reason why she must. She stared at Cass with hope brimming in her dark eyes.

"Good afternoon, Lady Cassandra," Julian said, bowing to her.

Cass fought her blush and curtsied back. "Lieutenant Swift. So good to see you again."

"What is it, Cass?" Pen asked, a note of petulance back in her voice.

"I . . . uh . . . er . . . *Mother wanted to see you, Pen,*" Cass murmured. As excuses went, it was particularly weak, but Cass had been preoccupied with the thought of seeing Julian. She hadn't spent a moment of the last five minutes planning what she would say to extract her cousin from the room.

Penelope obviously didn't need a better excuse. "Oh, dear. I must go and see what she wants. Do take care, Lieutenant Swift. Safe travels."

Julian held out a hand to her. "Penelope, wait—"

She was gone from the room without a backward glance and Cass was left alone with a crestfallen Lieutenant Swift. She was a bit embarrassed by her cousin's behavior. "I . . . I'm sorry," she said, not quite knowing what else to offer him.

He stared at the empty space that Penelope had just occupied, a chagrined look on his face. "I was going to ask Penelope to write to me."

Cass pressed her hand against her middle, trying to quell the nervous flight of butterflies there. "Pen isn't much of a writer, I'm afraid. She rarely answers my letters from the country."

"She didn't seem quite eager to . . . Still, it would be nice to get a letter now and again."

"I'll write to you." The words flew from Cass's lips before she had a chance to examine them. She nearly clapped her hand over her mouth for her impertinence.

He turned to her with a bit of hope in his gray eyes. "You would do that?"

She tilted her head up to face him. He was so tall, so tall and—"Yes. I adore writing."

"You do?"

"Yes. I can tell you what Pen is up to, keep you informed," she offered.

He smiled at her, his white teeth flashing, making Cass's

insides feel all squishy. "I'd like that very much, Lady Cassandra."

Cass blushed and glanced away. Had it been horribly forward of her to volunteer to write to her cousin's intended? Would her mother be angry? Would Pen? Would her aunt? Cass tried to summon the requisite shame, but all she felt was an overwhelming sense of happiness. Contentment. She grinned like a fool. She would have a connection to Julian while he was gone. They might merely trade the usual bits of information, but it would be something, better than nothing, better than waiting to hear the odd piece of news from her cousin. Yes. It was just perfect.

"Thank you," Julian finally said, and Cass dared to meet his gaze.

"Think nothing of it, Lieutenant Swift," she replied, digging the toe of her slipper into the thick carpet.

Julian scrubbed a hand through his hair and pointed toward the door. "I suppose you'll want to get back to the party."

"It is my birthday." Cass glanced toward the door as well. She hesitated. She couldn't very well tell him that she'd rather spend the entire day alone in here just staring at him rather than set foot out the door again. That would be entirely inappropriate. Wouldn't it? She nearly laughed aloud at her own thought.

"Happy birthday, Lady Cassandra," he said. "I must admit I don't have a gift for you. Please accept my apology."

She smiled at him. "No apology necessary, Lieutenant."

Cass turned to the door and stepped toward it. Unless. A voice stopped her, a clear undeniable voice. The voice of a devil, a devil who had not heretofore made his presence known to her. But now he was undeniable and he was standing directly on her shoulder, whispering in her ear. She'd never been so bold, had never even considered it.

But somehow the devil nudged her with his fiery little prickly pitchfork and she turned back to face Julian Swift.

"Unless . . ." She murmured the word the devil had whispered in her ear.

Julian's eyebrows shot up. "Unless?"

"There may be something you can give me for my birthday."

His brows furrowed. "Indeed?"

It was as if she was no longer in her own body. Instead she was floating somewhere high above it, near the ceiling of the drawing room, staring down at the plucky little freckled blond sixteen-year-old whom she'd never met before. The same little blond sixteen-year-old who walked back over to Lieutenant Swift, stared up into his impossibly handsome face, and said, "You could give me my first kiss."

If Lieutenant Swift was shocked or horrified by her request, he did not betray himself by word or deed. Instead, he let his hands fall to his sides and blew out a long breath. "You've never been kissed before?"

Cass shook her head. "No."

"No, I don't suppose you have at your age."

Cass had promptly closed her eyes and puckered her lips, lifting her chin to meet his mouth.

The touch was feather light. But it was not his lips on hers. It was the back of his fingers against her cheek. He softly rubbed her skin. He was standing so close to her that she could smell the scent of his wool uniform, the barest hint of his soap, the spicy tinge of his cologne. A scent she would cherish and remember for years. *Still, she remained in that position, her lips tightly puckered, waiting, waiting, for a kiss that never came.*

Instead, the light sweep of his fingers against her cheek turned into a flicker near her ear. He pushed a soft curl behind her lobe. Cass opened her eyes, blinking. She didn't understand. Wasn't he going to kiss her?

"Happy birthday, Lady Cassandra." He leaned forward and the warm brush of his lips against her forehead nearly singed off her eyelashes. She would never wash her forehead again. All right, perhaps that was a bit too much. Was it?

"I look forward to your letters," he said softly. Then he turned on his heel and strode from the room, the sharp click of boots against the marble floor resounding in Cass's soul.

Cass had never forgotten that moment. At first his refusal to kiss her on the lips had stung but over the years she'd come to realize that he couldn't have done anything else. It would have been entirely inappropriate and ungentlemanly of him to kiss the sixteen-year-old cousin of his future wife even if it was a birthday request. And frankly, the kiss on her forehead had been enough to hold Cass over for the last seven years.

Lucy's voice penetrated Cass's memories. "Haven't we always talked about how you wished Captain Swift would come back safely from the war and you would have a chance with him?" Lucy said. "Don't you see? I'm giving you that chance."

Cass leaned her head against the back of the settee and groaned. "I *wished* that but I never expected it. Julian and Pen have been all but engaged since they were children. Their parents decided on the match years ago. They've only been waiting for Julian to return to officially announce it. A *chance* with him is not possible."

"Not with a thought like that, it's not," Lucy continued, completely undaunted. "Besides, we've always known Pen isn't exactly in love with the man. She's run away from him, after all. Hardly the actions of a besotted future bride."

"That's beside the point. It's just not right for me to . . . to . . ." Cass rubbed her hand against a temple. The headache had returned and this time it was wielding a scythe.

"To what? Be in love with him? You can hardly help that, dear." Lucy smiled and patted Cass's hand with her free one.

Cass slumped her shoulders and sighed. "Oh, Lucy, you know I would never do anything to hurt Pen, or Julian. I must go to him. I must tell him the truth immediately before this gets any further out of hand. I—"

Lucy set down her cup with a clatter and turned to face Cass. She plunked both hands on her hips. "No one will get hurt. It's nothing more than a lark. We'll have the house party at my parents' country estate. They've gone up to Scotland for the autumn. The servants adore me. They'll play along. I'll explain everything to them."

Cass shook her head, pressing her fingertips to her temples. "No. It's madness. Simply madness."

"Why? What could go wrong?" The look on Lucy's face was pure innocence.

Cass's mouth fell open. "What could . . . ? The fact that you would even ask such a question is evidence of what a lunatic you are. What about your husband?"

Lucy's grin widened. "Derek is leaving for the Continent soon. He'll be gone for at least a fortnight. It's perfect timing. He'll never know."

"Fine. What about my parents?" Cass continued.

"We shall tell your parents you're at Miss Bunbury's house party. Chaperoned by me, of course." Lucy's smile was unrepentant.

Cass tightened her grip on the arms of her chair. Lucy had an answer for absolutely everything. Lucy always had an answer for absolutely everything. The worst part of this entire thing was that somewhere in the back of her mind, Cass was actually beginning to consider it. A lark, Lucy had said. No one will get hurt, Lucy had said. Was that possible? Truly?

Cass concentrated on breathing, breathing and thinking. It was as if the devil was back, sitting on one shoulder whispering, "Do it, Cass. Say yes!" While an angel had made her home on the other, whispering, "I cannot believe you're even considering this, miss."

Cass buried her face in her hands. Why was it becoming increasingly difficult to come up with reasons to say no? "My parents still haven't forgiven you, Lucy," she offered lamely.

Lucy shrugged. "They may not have forgiven me, but they very much appreciate that I am a duchess and can introduce you to eligible gentlemen."

Lucy had her there. Cass's parents were still distraught because Cass had allowed a duke to slip from her grasp, but they were mollified a bit knowing the new duchess was Cass's closest friend. They hoped the alliance would help to secure a fine match. But still, Cass mustn't allow Lucy to confuse the issue. "Fine. But what about the fact that you just told Julian that Penelope would be at the house party? Do you expect Penelope to arrive at a party if she knows Julian will be there, and play along with this farce? She made it up to get away from him."

"Of course I don't expect Penelope to attend." Lucy rolled her eyes. "That would ruin everything."

Cass splayed a hand in the air. "Then why did you tell Julian she would be there?"

Now Lucy was giving *her* an I'm-speaking-to-an-imbecile look. "So he would come, of course."

Cass shook her head. "This makes no sense."

"It makes perfect sense. We'll tell him Pen was waylaid along the road or had to turn around because she forgot something. Who knows? I'll think of something."

"That's your plan? Are you jesting?"

"Yes, it's my plan. And no, I'm not jesting. Honestly, Cass, you act as if we've never done anything like this before."

Cass groaned. Oh, she remembered only too well. "If you're speaking about your little stint behind the hedgerow last summer, might I remind you that that didn't work?"

Of course Lucy was speaking about the hedgerow incident. When the Duke of Claringdon had returned from battle last June, he'd taken an immediate interest in Cass. Alarmed, Cass had asked her blunt friend Lucy to be her voice and discourage the duke. That had ended with Lucy hiding behind a hedgerow in a garden and feeding Cass lines to say in an effort to discourage him. Later, Lucy had hidden atop a balcony pretending to be Cass, and, well, there had been a great deal more egregious behavior before it had all ended in the obvious conclusion that Lucy was perfect for the duke herself.

However, as usual, Lucy remained undaunted. "Yes, but it all worked out in the end, dear, and that is what's important. Be bold!"

There they were, Lucy's two favorite words. Cass had known her friend would say them before long. Lucy used *be bold* as her reasoning for doing everything she shouldn't do. In fact, the tenet had got them both into a great deal of trouble. Cass sighed. Yes, boldness spelled mischief. Though Cass couldn't deny that her friend was now happily married and madly in love with her duke of a husband as a result of being quite bold, indeed.

Cass placed her hands back on her hips. "What precisely do you think will come of this little scheme, Lucy? What do you hope to be the result after it's all over?"

Lucy grinned. "Now who's being ridiculous, Cass? Why, I expect that Julian will fall madly in love with you, of course."

Cass closed her eyes and pinched the bridge of her nose. "Even if that were true, are you forgetting that he'd be falling in love with Patience, not me?"

Lucy nodded. "Yes, Patience whom he is already very much infatuated with."

Cass gave her a look that indicated she was quite certain the duchess had lost her mind. "What are you talking about? He was in my company for only a few minutes."

Lucy crossed her arms over her chest and tapped her fingers along her elbows. "There is one thing you've failed to realize, my friend. I saw the way Captain Swift looked at you when he walked in the room, the way his face fell when he realized you weren't Pen. That's when I made my decision. I had to wait to ensure he didn't recognize you first, though, of course. I'm telling you, Cass, he's half in love with you already."

Cass bit her lip, gazing at the pattern of the carpet. "It would be nice to visit with him, dance with him, and pretend. For just a day or two."

Lucy's smile grew even wider. "That is the spirit."

"But what if—?"

"Oh, Cass. Don't worry so much. You've always been a worrier."

Cass wrinkled her nose. "That's quite funny, actually, because I don't think you worry enough."

"Nonsense. Besides, you worry enough for both of us. We'll have this party and you'll pretend to be Patience. It will all work out in the end. You'll see. Be bold!"

Cass groaned.

CHAPTER FOUR

Fifteen minutes later, Julian was ushered into Derek Hunt's town house. His encounter with the two ladies at Penelope's parents' house was still replaying itself in his mind. Lady Worthing? He'd never met her before, but she seemed a lovely young woman. She was pretty, high-spirited, and had the most unusual eyes he'd ever seen; one was blue, the other green. But the other young lady, Patience Bunbury, why, she'd nearly taken his breath away. He'd never been so instantly physically attracted to a woman before.

It was as if lightning had struck him in the head the moment he saw her. He'd never quite been at a loss for words before, either, but he'd been unable to coherently form a sentence. He'd been immediately enchanted by her dark honey-colored hair, her bright blue eyes, her high cheekbones, and long dark lashes. Nothing in all his experience had prepared him for the reaction he'd had to her. He'd obviously been away at war and without the company of a woman for far too long. And like a complete idiot, for a moment, a horrible, confused moment, he'd actually wondered if she was Penelope.

Fool. Of course she wasn't Penelope. His memory of Penelope was of a stout, short young woman with dark curls, dark eyes, and a bit of a turned-up nose. No. The blond woman had not been Penelope. He didn't even know why he'd said it. It was nonsense. Or perhaps it had been desperate hope.

Worse, for a crazy, haphazard moment, one that had made his heart nearly beat out of his chest, he'd wondered if the beauty was . . . Cassandra.

Hunt's butler pushed open the door in front of him and showed Julian into his closest friend's study, tearing Julian from his thoughts.

Derek Hunt sat behind a huge mahogany desk. As soon as he saw Julian, he tossed down his quill, stood, and strode around the desk to greet him.

The butler bowed and took his leave, just before Hunt clapped Julian soundly on the shoulder. "Swift," Hunt said. "I cannot tell you how good it is to see you safe and sound and back on English soil."

Julian returned his friend's embrace. "Thanks to you."

"Nonsense." Hunt gestured to Julian to take a seat in front of the desk in a large leather chair. Hunt scrubbed a hand through his dark hair and eyed his friend carefully. His face was grim. "I never got over having to leave you after the battle."

Hunt had seen Julian ensconced in a makeshift hospital outside of Waterloo before he'd been forced to follow orders to return to England immediately and report to the War Office.

"You had a job to do," Julian replied. "I would've done the same." He meant that. Hunt had done everything he could have for him at the time. Hunt had saved his life. Hunt had frantically searched for him after the battle and when he'd found Julian lying on the field, he'd leaped from his mount and pressed his own kerchief to Julian's wounds to staunch the flow of blood from the bullet that had torn through his chest.

Julian took a deep breath. It was difficult to think about even now. He'd been certain he would die that day. They both had. What Hunt didn't know, however, was that Julian had wanted to die that day. Intended to. Planned on it. And so he'd made Hunt promise him something, promise him to return to England and marry his good friend Cassandra Monroe.

"Did you arrive in town today?" Hunt made his way over to the sideboard.

"I did. This afternoon."

"And was this your first stop?" Hunt asked, splashing brandy into two glasses.

"No," Julian replied. "I went to the Monroes' house first."

Hunt lifted both glasses and turned to face his friend, a furrow in his brow. "Cassandra's?"

"No." Julian shook his head. "Penelope's."

Hunt crossed over the thick rug and handed Julian one of the glasses. "Ah. The woman you're bound to marry?"

"Not precisely. Not yet. Hopefully not ever."

Hunt resumed his seat behind the desk and gave Julian an inquiring stare. "Not ever? What do you mean?"

Julian took a long swallow of his drink. "I'll tell you something, Hunt." He stopped and grinned. "My apologies, *Your Grace.*"

Hunt waved away the honorific. "There will be none of that between us. You're practically my third brother."

Julian nodded. "I'll tell you something. When you think you're dying, you take a long, hard look at your life. I made some important decisions while I was recuperating. I thought a great deal about my future over there."

Hunt arched a brow. "Sounds like it. And your future doesn't include Penelope Monroe?"

"No. I must speak with her as soon as possible and let her know. She wasn't home today."

Hunt took a long swallow. "There's something I have to tell you, Swift."

Julian eyed him carefully. "That you didn't marry Cassandra?"

Hunt nodded once. "How did you know?"

Julian smiled again. "For one thing, Cassandra wrote to me and told me, and for another, I see a ring on your finger."

Hunt laughed a long, loud laugh. "I did my best with Cassandra, believe me. But she was entirely uninterested in me. It seems she—" Hunt hesitated, then he shook his head. "It seems she is in love with another man."

Julian's breath caught in his throat. He narrowed his eyes on Hunt. "Cassandra's in love with someone? She never mentioned that in her letters."

Hunt coughed into his fist and glanced away. "Be that as it may . . . she rejected me quite thoroughly."

"And in the meantime, Cassandra and Jane Lowndes, and everyone else realized that you were perfectly suited for their friend Lucy."

"Yes, Lucy Hunt now, my duchess."

Julian raised his glass. "Congratulations, my friend, and very best wishes to your new bride."

"I'd introduce you to Lucy but she's gone out to visit with friends this afternoon."

"Another time, then. I look forward to it."

Hunt let out a long breath. "You don't want to pound me to a pulp, then?"

"No." Julian smiled. "I asked you to marry Cassandra when I thought I was dying. Everything's changed now."

He glanced away, out the window, watched a coach rumble down the dusty street. *Everything's changed.*

Hunt cleared his throat. "Which has led to your decision about Penelope?"

Julian pulled himself from his thoughts. "Precisely."

"I see. Have you gone to visit Cassandra yet?" Hunt asked.

"No. I intend to go there next." Julian shifted in his chair. "Which brings me to the other reason for my visit."

Hunt nodded. "Which is?"

"Have you heard anything more about Donald?" Julian asked.

Hunt rubbed a hand against the back of his neck. "Damn it. We were trying to keep you from knowing about that."

"I know. When your brother came to see me in hospital, he would barely mention it. I had to pry the smallest bit of information out of him."

"Collin and I didn't want you to worry. We wanted you to concentrate on recovering."

"I understand," Julian replied. "But now I need to know. Do you know anything more?"

"Unfortunately, no. According to the War Office, Donald and Rafe are still missing in France. I'm leaving for Bristol soon for a debriefing on the latest and hope to learn more. Wellington finally agreed. Collin and I are returning to the Continent to search for them."

Julian shook his head. "I tried my damnedest to get Wellington to allow me to stay on the Continent and help search."

"You nearly died, Swift. You deserve to be back home. Rest."

Julian clenched his jaw and glanced out the window again. "I've been resting for months."

"It was that or permanently rest six feet under."

Julian bowed his head. "He's my brother, Hunt."

"I know."

And Hunt did know. His own youngest brother, Adam, had been with Donald and their friend Rafferty Cavendish on the Continent. But they hadn't been in battle. They had been doing something far more dangerous . . . spying on the French. Why his steadfast brother would agree or even attempt to be a spy, Julian had no idea. At this point he had more questions than answers.

Hunt's second brother, Collin, had already led one trip to the Continent where he'd managed to locate Adam and bring him back to London, but Rafe and Donald were still missing. Apparently, Wellington had finally consented to allow Derek and Collin to return for another look.

"I'm coming with you," Julian said. "As soon as Wellington approves my latest request."

Hunt cracked a smile. "Not a chance. You just returned. You'll stay here. Enjoy yourself a bit. I'll write and keep you informed. You have my word."

"Thank you for that," Julian said softly. "I still wish I knew why the hell Donald would have volunteered to be a spy. Why would he have risked his life to go over there like that?"

"You mean because your father's dead and Donald's an earl and he has no heirs?"

"Especially because my father's dead and Donald's an earl and he has no heirs. That and the fact that I wasn't expected to return, either. There's only Donald, and Daphne, and me. I don't understand why he would take that risk."

"I don't know, either, but I did learn that he volunteered."

Julian's gaze snapped to Derek's face. "Volunteered? Why would he do that?"

"The War Office was looking for someone like him, a member of Parliament, the House of Lords. They wanted someone no one would suspect, someone who merely appeared to be traveling through. Uninvolved."

"But Donald's not cut out to be a bloody spy. We both know that."

"He had Rafe with him." Hunt cleared his throat. "He still does. Rafe's one of the best. If there's any chance of survival, Rafe will have found it. Trust me, Swift."

Julian stood and paced over to the window, shoving his hands into his pockets. "Damn it, Hunt. I should be the one still in France, not Donald. Only you wouldn't be looking for me, you'd be looking for my grave."

Hunt's voice was sharp. "What the hell are you talking about?"

Julian shook his head. "It doesn't matter. I've already asked Wellington to reconsider and then—"

"I can't allow you to come with us," Derek said, his voice taking on the tone of the war general Julian had known in battle. "You know that. Your orders are to stay here for now."

Julian clenched his jaw. "Yes, for now. But if you don't find anything—"

"We'll talk about that if and when the time comes."

Julian nodded reluctantly. He intended to change that, of course. Get new orders. Hell, ignore his orders if he had to. Donald, his brother, the boy who was raised to be earl, couldn't be lost in France. He just couldn't be. His father would be spinning in his grave.

Julian prayed to God that Derek and Collin would find them. If anyone could, it was the capable Hunt brothers. Julian would stay here for now, just as Hunt had said. And if he must stay in England and pretend to be enjoying himself, he would settle things with Penelope Monroe first.

"Will you be staying at Donald's town house?" Hunt asked. "If not, you're welcome to stay here."

Julian leaned back in his chair. "No, actually. I'm going to the countryside. To Surrey."

"Surrey? What's in Surrey?"

"When I went to visit Penelope this afternoon, I was told she was on her way to a friend's country house party there."

Hunt arched a brow. "Seems odd. She's left town knowing you were coming?"

"Apparently she left before she received my letter informing her that I'd be here this afternoon."

"Damn the luck."

Julian smiled slightly. "Yes, well. I'm going to follow her there. We cannot become engaged. She needs to hear it from me in person. It's only right. The sooner I speak with her the better, and if I can't go with you and help you find Donald, at least I can do right by Miss Monroe."

Hunt nodded. "I wish you well, Swift. How long will you be gone?"

"The house party is for a sennight and as luck would have it, I've been invited. I'm not certain how long I'll stay, however." Not that he'd mind being in Patience Bunbury's presence for a bit.

"What do you plan to do after that?"

Julian met his friend's stare. "I intend to travel to France and help you find Donald and Rafe."

Hunt squinted. "I'm to be gone for a fortnight. I hope to hell I find them, Swift, and that it's all settled by the time you return from Surrey. I'll see you back here in London in two weeks' time. One way or another, I intend to have news."

Julian returned to his seat and tossed back the rest of his brandy. They both knew Hunt might well be on a mission to find Donald's and Rafe's bodies. Julian couldn't think about that now. He wouldn't think about it now. He stood and shook his friend's hand. "Good luck and safe travels."

Hunt walked him to the front door. "I look forward to introducing you to Lucy. She's a spitfire to be sure, a troublemaker, some would say, but her heart is very much in the right spot."

Julian raised a brow. "A troublemaker?"

"As troublesome as she is beautiful, I'm afraid," Hunt added with a laugh. "I'll have to tell you some of the stories about her antics when she was trying to dissuade me from my courtship of Cassandra."

Julian laughed. "It sounds as if Her Grace is someone I'm quite looking forward to meeting."

CHAPTER FIVE

The devil on Cass's shoulder had won. It was that simple.
The devil came to her sometimes, the pesky little beast,
after their first meeting on her sixteenth birthday. How
well she remembered his awful insistence that day. His
advice had been surprising, to be sure, and ultimately futile.
But in the matter of Lucy and the fictitious house party, in
the end, Cass had listened to the horrible little fiend. From
his perch on her shoulder, he had enticingly told her she
might have a bit of fun at a house party with Julian, regardless of the outcome and the hopelessness of the entire
situation. Oh, she had doubts, scores of them, worries and
doubts and outright anxiety, but she'd managed to push it
all aside and pretend.

Pretend. That's what Lucy said they were doing. It was
a lark, like acting in a play. And they so adored plays. The
servants would pretend, too. Lucy had simply told them
all that they were having a sort of playacting house party,
something like a masquerade, but without the feathers
and dominoes. Lucy could be so persuasive.

"Haven't you been telling me that you want to change?
Be different? Stand up to your parents more?" Lucy had

prodded, knowing exactly how to prod. "Now's your chance. Be bold! Do the things you've never imagined you could do. You'll surprise yourself, I'm certain of it."

She'd surprise herself? Cass had liked the sound of that. She'd spent her childhood and young adulthood following every rule to the letter. She'd painted and sung, and played the pianoforte. She'd curtsied and danced and said all the right things to all the right people. She'd been demure as if she invented demureness. She'd listened to her mother and father, been kind and understanding to her older brother. She'd asked after all the servants, seen to all of her friends, and now, now, just what if it was her time? Her time to be a bit scandalous, her time to finally break a rule or two instead of just daydreaming about doing it.

"For the next sennight, you are Patience Bunbury," Lucy had announced. And somehow that had given Cass permission to go ahead and break rules. She wasn't demure Cassandra Monroe any longer, she was Patience Bunbury and she'd already decided . . . Patience Bunbury was quite wicked indeed.

And so Cass had jotted off a letter to Pen, informing her that she'd done just as her cousin had asked and told Captain Swift that Pen was attending Patience Bunbury's house party. Cass just happened to leave out the part that she herself was en route to that same house party and, oh, pretending to be Patience, as well. Instead, she'd told Pen that she and Lucy were retiring to the country for a bit. Cass had been certain lightning would strike her as she'd written the letter. It was dreadful of her to continue to lie, first to Julian, now to Pen. But that pesky little devil didn't care.

"Pen started it," Lucy had pointed out with a shrug. That had only served to make Cass feel all the more guilty. That was absolutely no excuse. Was it? Oh, there was that blasted devil again.

Cass traced her finger along the windowpane of the coach as she and Lucy traveled to the countryside. They bounced along in the duchess's new, resplendent vehicle, Cass trying not to bite at her fingernails every time she so much as thought of what she was traveling into: a giant falsehood.

The grand estate of the Earl of Upbridge, Lucy's father, was settled in the quiet countryside of Surrey. A sense of calm settled over Cass when the manor house finally came into sight. She had grown up here in a sense. Her parents' estate was less than three miles away. She sat up straight and gulped. "Lucy, what if my parents get word of this house party and decide to pay a visit to your parents?"

Lucy laughed. "Cass, you're forgetting that your parents are decidedly unhappy with my family at present. It's perfect timing, actually. And didn't you send your mother a letter?"

"Yes. I informed her that I am staying with you in town for the next week."

"Settled, then."

Cass bit her lip. "Only if my parents remain safely over at their estate."

"I anticipate no problems," Lucy replied with a smile, pulling on her gloves as they approached the front of the manor house.

Cass sighed. Of course Lucy was convinced everything would be quite all right. Cass, however, lived in constant fear that her mother would arrive, tell Julian everything, and demand her daughter return home instantly. Her mother had never cared much for her daughter's infatuation with Julian, and it had little to do with the fact that he was marked for her cousin. "He's a second son, Cassandra. He might be good enough for Penelope, but we didn't raise *you* to marry a second son."

That was just it. Her parents had raised her to marry a

man with a title, an illustrious title, the more illustrious the better. The only reason they hadn't completely disowned her for turning down a duke was the fact that somewhere in the back of her mother's mind, she was probably thinking that Cass might marry a duke with a family name that went back centuries and that would be an even better catch than the newly minted Claringdon. That's all she was to her mother, a pawn to be played in the great game of the *ton*'s marriage mart.

When Lucy's coach finally pulled to a stop at the entrance to the estate, the butler and housekeeper were there to greet them with a bow and a curtsy.

"Don't worry about a thing, Your Grace," the housekeeper said as she ushered them into the foyer of the manor house. "The servants, we've all been aflurry preparing for the party. Everything is arranged."

"Thank you so much, Mrs. Prism," Lucy responded, allowing the butler to take her hat and cloak and waiting for Cass to hand over the same. "But you must remember you cannot refer to me as 'Your Grace' during the party. And this is Miss Bunbury." She gestured to Cass.

"Of course. Of course." The housekeeper chuckled. The butler had a twinkle in his eyes. They continued into the house. It smelled exactly as Cass remembered it from childhood, a mixture of lemon wax and silver polish. The bustling of the servants and the smiles on everyone's faces bolstered Cass's confidence. As the day progressed, Cass noticed that true to Lucy's word, all of the servants appeared to be completely at ease with calling their mistress Lady Worthing and pretending Cass was named Patience Bunbury. In fact, they'd already begun. It was quite ludicrous, actually, but Cass had to smile at the willingness of the earl's servants to participate in their mistress's foibles. They did appear to be completely devoted to Lucy.

When the butler stopped by to get Lucy's approval on

the wines to be served with the first dinner, she answered, "Thank you, Merriman."

"My pleasure, Lady Worthing." He bowed before taking his leave.

"Leave it to you to orchestrate such madness, Lucy," Cass said with a laugh.

"They think it's a lark, dear. There's no reason this shouldn't be fun."

"I see." Cass pressed a hand to her belly. Perhaps it would be all right after all. *Perhaps.*

"The servants have done an outstanding job. All we have to do is see to the finishing touches. Come along." Lucy turned in a swirl of yellow skirts.

Cass spent the rest of the day following her friend through the cavernous rooms as they made the last-minute plans for the house party's amusements. Mrs. Prism tracked them with a quill and parchment to scribble down their requests.

"I sent word to Captain Swift letting him know that the house party doesn't officially begin until Saturday," Lucy said as they entered one of the drawing rooms.

"What did you say about Pen?" Cass asked.

"I told him that Penelope had been confused as to the start of the thing, hence her leaving London too early. I managed to secure us a few days before Julian appears." Lucy smiled.

"Yes, but you put us in the position of having to immediately explain to him upon his arrival why Penelope is not here when she left for the house party several days earlier," Cass replied.

"Leave it all to me," Lucy said with a simple, confident flick of her wrist.

"You do not have a magic wand, do you?" Cass asked, glancing about under the furniture as if the said wand might be found.

Lucy rolled her eyes. "No, I have a quick tongue, and that is even more useful. Magic wands can be stolen, dear."

Cass shook her head but couldn't help but laugh at her friend's antics. That was it. If she was going to pretend, she might as well pretend on a grand scale. How many times had she thought, what she wouldn't give to have a small bit of Lucy's courage and confidence for a day? Just one day. Though she wouldn't say no to that magic wand, either.

But this was Cass's chance, her one chance. She was courageous. She was confident. She was Patience Bunbury! She nodded resolutely and turned to face her friend.

Lucy spread her arms wide, indicating the entire back half of the drawing room. "And here is where we shall play cards after dinner," she said, turning in a circle and clapping her hands together once. "Of course I shall seat you next to Captain Swift at every opportunity."

Cass turned in a circle, too. "Seems you've thought of everything."

Lucy nodded. "Of course I have."

Cass made her way over to the wall and traced a finger along the edge of a portrait hanging there. "Is Jane coming?"

"Absolutely. She says this is one Society event she's actually looking forward to. In fact, Jane is one of only a few guests I've invited. She's never met Captain Swift, which, of course, is of the utmost importance."

"When did you plan all of this?" Cass asked, shaking her head.

Lucy grinned. "I was in a flurry of writing letters two nights ago after we spoke with Captain Swift."

"Who else did you invite? Garrett?" Cass asked, referring to their fourth good friend, Lucy's first cousin, Garrett Upton. Garrett lived nearby as well. He and his cousin were fast friends and the three of them had grown up together, riding horses and playing games across the neighboring estates.

Lucy's only brother had died of fever when he was a child. So Garrett, her father's only brother's son, stood to inherit Lucy's father's earldom because his own father was dead. In fact, Cass suspected that now that she was without the prospect of a husband again, her own parents had turned their marriage-minded gazes toward Garrett Upton. Garrett, of course, was nothing more than a friend to Cass, but because the Upbridge estate bordered the Morelands' estate, Cass's father had mentioned upon more than one occasion how much he liked the idea of uniting the two families in land and matrimony.

Lucy turned to face Cass and pursed her lips. "No, ah, not exactly."

"Not exactly? What do you mean?"

"With Garrett it's a bit . . . complicated."

Cass narrowed her eyes on her friend. "Why?"

Lucy flourished a hand in the air. "Oh, you know Garrett. Always wanting to do the right thing and tell the truth, et cetera, et cetera. I've told him I'm a bit indisposed." She lowered her voice so Mrs. Prism wouldn't hear. "He thinks I'm with child and stopped asking questions. It's perfect. I doubt he'll come looking for me."

Cass's mouth dropped open. "Lucy! You didn't allow him to think that."

"Yes. I did." She winked at Cass. "What? It's the perfect excuse."

"You're completely incorrigible."

Lucy blinked. "You say that as if I don't already know it." Then she turned her attention to the housekeeper. "We'll meet you in the pantries in ten minutes, Mrs. Prism."

Mrs. Prism nodded and left the room while Cass made her way over and plopped down on the sofa. She pulled a throw pillow onto her lap and hugged it tightly against her middle. "Who else will be coming to the house party?"

Lucy tapped her finger against her cheek. "I invited Lord Berkeley."

"Lord Berkeley?"

"Yes, Berkeley."

Lord Berkeley was one of Garrett's old friends from school. He was a viscount who lived in the north and rarely came down to town. The friends had met him in Bath last summer where he'd unsuccessfully attempted to court Lucy. Apparently, Lucy had remained on good terms with the viscount.

"How did you manage to convince Lord Berkeley to come down for this?" Cass asked.

"I simply informed him that he owes me a favor after shamelessly pretending to write me beautiful letters last summer."

Cass's jaw dropped open. "You did not say that to him, Lucy!"

"I most certainly did. He agreed wholeheartedly and sent his acceptance immediately. And the best part is, he has never met Captain Swift, either."

Cass pulled up the pillow to her chin. "Nothing you do should surprise me but it does."

Lucy had wandered over to the far side of the room where she was inspecting some apples in a bowl. She turned back to Cass and called, "Oh, Patience."

Cass didn't move. She remained staring blindly into the crackling fireplace.

"Patience!" Lucy said more loudly, slapping her slipper against the marble floor.

This time Cass turned her head. "Yes."

Lucy put both hands on her hips. "That was a drill. You must get used to responding to that name."

"Oh, Lucy. What am I going to do? I cannot speak to Julian as if I don't know him. What if I slip and say something only Cass would know?" Cass said, allowing the pillow to fall back into her lap.

Lucy turned over one of the apples and then stared at it as if its precise placement was of the utmost importance. "Hmm. I suggest you keep quiet if you think you might be tempted to do that."

"What if Jane or Lord Berkeley mistakenly call me Lady Cassandra?"

"Pretend as if you didn't hear them and give them a stern look."

"What if Garrett or Owen or my parents arrive?" Cass asked.

"Garrett's not going to arrive and why would your brother have any reason to come here? He rarely leaves London."

"What if—? What if—" Cass glanced around as if searching for another reason to worry.

"What if your head falls off?" Lucy supplied. "Is that what you're going to say? I swear, Cass, there's no need to worry. I expect this week to be enormously successful. You should, too."

"But that's just it, Lucy. I don't see how it can be successful. What can we possibly hope to accomplish here?" Cass bent over and rested her forehead on the pillow in her lap.

Lucy made her way back over to the settee, sat next to her friend, and hugged her, pulling her close with her arm around her shoulders. "Why, we're going to give Julian the opportunity to know you, Cass. See you, speak with you, be alone with you. He can't possibly wish to marry Penelope, after spending time with you."

"But they're betrothed—"

"No they are not. Not explicitly. Not officially. I intend

to see that it remains that way. Besides, you seem to forget, your cousin doesn't appear to be particularly interested in Captain Swift."

Cass rubbed a hand over her forehead. How was it that Lucy always seemed to make sense when she rebutted Cass's concerns? "Yes, but—"

"No. Stop it. Think positively. That is the only way this will work. You must promise me you'll stop worrying."

Cass groaned and squeezed the pillow. "Oh, it's all so . . . so . . . uncertain."

Lucy pulled her close again and gave her a conspiratorial smile. "Ah, the very essence of romance is uncertainty, dear. Never forget it."

CHAPTER SIX

"Well, I for one have never heard of Miss Patience Bunbury," Julian's younger sister, Daphne, said as she sat across the drawing room from him writing a letter, while he and his mother looked on.

"I can't say I've made her acquaintance, either," his mother, the countess, added.

A blond curl flew over Daphne's shoulder as she tossed her head and gave Julian a sly look. "Quite curious if you ask me."

Julian settled into his chair. "What do you mean, curious?" He'd greatly enjoyed spending these last few days with his mother and Daphne. The two women had been beside themselves with happiness when he came striding through the door. His mother had silently held back tears, her eyes brimming with them, and hugged her second-born, while Daphne had clapped her hands and nearly shrieked with excitement.

It was damn good to see them again. His sister, just a girl when he had gone to war, was now a beautiful, accomplished young woman who he quickly learned was always buzzing about the house doing several things at once. His mother had deeper worry lines in her forehead and a few more wrinkles but she still had the same laughing gray eyes he remembered.

They'd caught up on everything from the less gruesome aspects of Julian's time at war, to the frivolities of the last London Season, but neither of the women seemed to know what had possessed Donald to go off to the Continent.

"He said he was going to Italy on holiday," his mother told him. "I don't know why he would leave in the middle of a war. But you know Donald, always so evasive. Never wanting to worry us. Though now I'm concerned because he's been gone for months and we've yet to receive a letter indicating that he's arrived safely."

"I'm certain news will come soon, Mama," Daphne said. "And besides, Captain Cavendish is with him. He'll keep Donald safe."

"Yes, you're right, dear. Captain Cavendish has been an excellent friend to our family through the years and he's an excellent soldier."

Daphne had nodded, but the look she gave Julian made him think she knew more than she was letting on. Especially since she knew Donald was with Rafe. Julian had inclined his head toward his sister, the siblings tacitly agreeing to allow their mother to continue to think Donald was on holiday. But Julian made a mental note to ask Daphne about it later.

Now that he and his mother and sister had had a chance to become reacquainted after all these years, Julian had informed them he was leaving for the countryside and that's how the subject of Patience Bunbury had come up.

"I just mean that it's a bit curious that Miss Monroe is off at a house party hosted by a young lady we've never heard of," Daphne said with a shrug, returning her attention to her letter.

"Perhaps you merely never met Miss Bunbury," Julian suggested.

"Of course I never met her, silly," Daphne replied, shaking her head. "I just thought I knew nearly everyone and I don't know her."

"There's a first time for everything, dear," their mother replied. "I'm certain Miss Bunbury is a fine young lady if Miss Monroe has chosen to befriend her."

Daphne tossed her quill on the desk and turned fully around in her chair to face Julian, her hands braced on her knees. There was a decided twinkle in her eye. "Ooh, speaking of fine young ladies, tell me, have you seen Lady Cassandra Monroe since you've returned?"

Julian cleared his throat. "No. I . . . haven't. I paid a call to her parents' town house yesterday only to discover that the family has already retired to the country for the autumn." At first, Julian had been more than a bit disappointed; however, when he'd learned the address of Lady Worthing's house party, he'd discovered that it was near Cassandra's parents' estate. More good fortune. Once in Surrey, Julian would find Penelope, say what he needed to say, and then he would go to the Monroes' estate to visit Cassandra.

"I'm sorry to hear that," Daphne answered, a crestfallen look on her face. "Tell me, does she still write to you?"

"Yes, quite often," Julian said, a lump unexpectedly forming in his throat. What could he say about Cassandra? She was his best friend. She'd written him for years. She'd begun soon after he left with the army after her sixteenth birthday. He'd thought it would be nothing more than a simple, friendly correspondence. But it had turned into much more. Cassie didn't know it, but she had saved his life.

"Nearly every day?" His mother's eyebrows shot up. "I daresay that's more often than Daphne and I wrote. Did Penelope write you as much?"

Julian shook his head. "No." *Not even remotely close.*
He leaned back in his seat and steepled his fingers over
his chest. Penelope. Over the years, he'd considered re-
signing himself to their marriage. Penelope had been
eighteen when he'd gone off to war. They'd decided to
wait until after he returned—if he returned—to make it
all official. It hadn't been fair to Penelope to make her
wait all these years. Especially when Julian had had no
intention of ever coming back. He was under no illusion
that Penelope loved him or even wanted to marry him for
that matter. The few letters she'd written to him in all these
years had been short and full of inane banter. Nothing
true. Nothing real. Nothing like the letters he received
from Cassandra. Cassandra's letters had been heartfelt and
honest, full of witticisms and intelligence. She made him
smile. She made him laugh out loud, and most of all, she
made him feel as if someone in this great big world, someone other than his mother and his sister, really, truly cared
if he lived or died. God knew his father never had. He was
a useless second son after all. He'd been told that often
enough. His father had purchased his commission and
handed it over with words he'd never forget.

*Julian knocked on the door to his father's study. "May I
come in?"*

His father grunted his assent.

*Julian pushed open the door and strode forward. He
stopped in front of his father's massive wooden desk,
standing at attention. He stared out the window above
his father's head, his hands clasped behind his back, his
new uniform still rough against his skin. He'd get used to
the rubbing eventually.*

*"Julian." His father's voice was deep yet cold, as al-
ways. "Or should I say, Lieutenant Swift now?"*

"Thank you for the commission, my lord. I intend to make you proud."

"You're leaving soon?"

"Yes. I've said good-bye to Mother, Donald, and Daphne. I've leaving for Surrey in a few minutes, to say good-bye to Miss Monroe."

His father snorted. "You might as well tell her good-bye forever. No reason to keep her on the hook, waiting for you."

Julian's brow furrowed. "My lord?"

"Since you won't be coming back."

Julian kept his jaw locked, his eyes still focused out the window. "You've that little faith in me, Father?"

"On the contrary, this is about the faith I do have in you. You said you intend to make me proud."

"Father?"

The earl slammed his fist against the desk, making the papers and ink pot bounce. "Damn it, Julian. Must I spell it out for you? You're meant to die in battle. Honorably, of course. The more honorably, the better. That's why I purchased the commission for you. I expect you to make both me and your country extremely proud."

An icy claw grabbed at Julian's chest. He concentrated on keeping his gaze straight, his jaw firm. A harsh breath escaped him. "Sir." He bowed once to his father, turned on his heel, and left the room.

It was the last time he ever saw his father.

Julian had wrestled with those words during the entire ride to Surrey seven years ago. Would he say good-bye to Miss Monroe for good and let her go, or would he ask her to write to him? He understood what he had to do. Understood what it would finally take to gain his father's love, his approval. And he would do his duty. But it might be weeks, months even, before he died, and he couldn't bear the thought of not having something to look forward to in that time. When Cassie had offered to write to him, he'd had some small glimmer of hope, some small shred of happiness to hang on to.

Julian had left for the Continent with his division as soon as he returned from Surrey. Within the month, word came that his father had died.

The days turned to weeks, the weeks to months, the months to years. And Cassie's letters arrived like clock-work, comforting, uplifting, friendly, and funny. Daphne and Mother wrote to him of course, but their letters were less frequent and meant to distract him with humorous bits of news. Cassie's letters were different. They were heart-felt, meaningful. They were the only evidence he had left that he was still alive. And he'd never been able to write to her—this girl who kept him from a dark abyss—and tell her that he never intended to return. He couldn't do that to her and he didn't want to believe it himself. Cassie's letters were real but they were also the only place he allowed himself to pretend.

Julian glanced around the room, his brother's room, his brother's house. Julian had been back in town for less than a fortnight but already he was seeing to the corre-spondence and acting in his brother's stead. The servants came to him with issues and his mother seemed perfectly content to allow him to run things. Daphne seemed quite pleased with it all, too, probably because he allowed her to get away with more than Donald did.

Donald.

Julian took a deep breath. He and his brother had not been close. Donald was several years older than he and had been raised to be an earl. When Donald wasn't away at school, he was spending time with their father. It had always made Julian envious. How he craved his father's attention and approval for one day, one hour, one minute, even. Daphne had always been close to Mother and that had left Julian alone, alone and unnecessary, a spare to an earldom that didn't require a spare. Father had made that clear enough.

Julian shook his head. None of that mattered now. Not at the moment. He'd done as he was told, gone off to the army, off to war. And in all those long, lonely days and nights, he'd looked forward to Cassandra's letters. Waited for them each time the mail arrived, and while other soldiers were often disappointed to find that the call came and went with nothing for them, Julian could always rely on Cassandra. She never failed him.

"I heard that Lady Cassandra's parents are ever so unhappy with the fact that she rebuffed the Duke of Claringdon's advances," Daphne offered from her perch at the writing desk.

"Yes, but anyone could see that the duke and Lady Lucy make a much more matched pair," his mother said. "Still, I can understand their disappointment."

Julian laughed. "Derek told me himself that he did his best to win Lady Cassandra."

"It's true," Daphne added. "Though he never truly had a chance at winning her heart."

Julian frowned. What did his sister know about it? "Why do you say that?"

Daphne's lips turned up at the corners in a whisper of a smile. "Oh, there's only one gentleman Lady Cassandra is interested in and he's been, ahem, quite unavailable."

Julian sat forward and braced his elbows on his knees. There it was again. Just as Hunt had said, Cassandra Monroe was in love with another man. That's why she'd refused Hunt. But who was this man? And when had it happened? None of Cassandra's recent letters had mentioned a man. Well, any man other than Derek and Garrett . . . Upton. Upton? Could it be Upton?

Why did the thought of Cass with another man make Julian's chest hurt? It made no sense. He shook his head. No matter. Whoever the chap was, he had better be good enough for her. That was all. Cassandra was loving and kind. She deserved to be happy. He wanted only the best for his closest friend. She meant a great deal to him. So much that when he believed he was dying, his first thought hadn't been for himself or even Penelope. No. It had been for Cassandra. Hunt had been there, his face a stone mask, trying his damnedest not to look as if he knew his friend was already dead. He'd pressed his kerchief against the flow of blood from the bullet that had torn through Julian's chest. Hunt had clenched his fist and his jaw and Julian had known right then that his friend would do any-thing he asked. His dying wish. What had it been? Hunt had already promised to tell his mother and Daphne in person, let them both know how much Julian loved them. That would be taken care of, no question. That day on the blood-soaked battlefield, he'd made Hunt promise to re-turn to London and marry Cassandra. Julian had known from her letters that she was still unmarried. She needed someone, someone good, someone strong, someone who would take care of her and treat her well. Hunt was the perfect candidate. Or so Julian had thought.

"Whoever he is, he's a lucky man," Julian said, ab-sently rubbing a hand through his hair.

"And you haven't even seen her yet," Daphne said un-der her breath.

Julian glanced up and narrowed his eyes on his sister. "What was that?"

"Oh, nothing. Nothing," Daphne replied, turning back to her letter.

Julian leaned back in his chair. It didn't matter. He wished Cassandra well in her match, but marriage was the furthest thing from his own mind. He intended to put an end to his almost engagement and then go in search of his brother. Fate had intervened and made a mess of things. His brother was on the Continent in harm's way and Julian was here, safe in London. He needed to right that wrong.

Julian looked across the room at his mother and his sister. He hadn't informed them of his intentions of ending things with Penelope. Better to do it first and then explain afterward. But he knew what he had to do. The weeks of recovery had taught him something he couldn't forget. He couldn't live his life as a lie. Marrying Penelope would be a lie. His sense of honor had warred with his gut instincts, but in the end, he knew he must put an end to their agreement. He didn't even know Penelope, certainly didn't love her. He hadn't been thinking about her as his blood seeped into foreign soil. No. He'd been thinking about Cassandra, Cassandra whom he only remembered as a young girl. She'd asked him for a kiss for her sixteenth birthday. He smiled at the memory. She'd been a scrawny little thing, all arms and legs, knees and elbows, but she'd certainly had the potential to turn into a beauty. Perhaps not one as gorgeous as, say, Patience Bunbury, but a good-looking young woman just the same. What did Cassandra look like today? Once he arrived in Surrey, perhaps he'd write to his friend Owen, Cassandra's older brother, and see if he was in residence in the country, too. It would be good to see both siblings again.

Julian's first goal was to find Pen and end things. His second goal had been to find Cassandra and . . . what? See her? Thank her? Tell her that she'd changed his entire life? It sounded idiotic in his thoughts. He could only imagine how it would sound in person.

His third goal was to return to the Continent, with or without permission, and help in the search for Donald and Rafe.

But first things first, hence his planned trip out to the countryside tomorrow to attend a house party. He supposed it had been fortunate, his running into Lady Worthing and Miss Bunbury. If he hadn't met the two ladies at Penelope's house three days ago, he might not have known where Penelope had gone off to and he certainly couldn't have arrived uninvited. It had been quite fortunate, indeed.

"I cannot wait to hear all about the house party," Daphne said with a sigh. "It almost makes me wish I had been invited. And I detest house parties."

"Why would you say that?" their mother asked, sipping at the teacup the butler had just handed her.

Daphne wrinkled her nose. "Ah, all that country air and tedium. I much prefer town. So much to see and do."

"And trouble to get into?" Julian offered.

"I don't know what you mean," Daphne replied, turning her head and batting her eyelashes at him innocently.

Their mother gave Julian a knowing look over the lip of her teacup. She'd written to him on more than one occasion about Daphne's penchant for, ahem, colorfulness. The countess set down her cup and stood. "I bid you both good night. I'm exhausted." She turned to Julian. "I'll see you in the morning, dear, before you leave on your trip."

Daphne and Julian said good night and Julian stood as his mother left the room. Donald's absence was wearing on her. Julian could tell. After the door shut behind the countess, Julian settled back into his seat. "Don't worry, dear sister. I'll tell you all about the house party after I return."

"Thank you. And you must tell me all about this Miss Bunbury. I'm simply dying to make her acquaintance," Daphne replied.

Julian stretched his legs out in front of him and let his head fall back against the chair. He stared absently at the frescoed ceiling. Miss Bunbury. If he were being honest, he wasn't exactly reluctant to see her again himself. Try as he might, he couldn't seem to get the image of that young lady out of his mind. She was gorgeous. Yes, it had been a long, long time since he'd been with a woman, but he'd seen many of them since returning to England. None of them had affected him the way she had. The way she smiled and flashed a row of bright white teeth that tugged at her full lower lip when she was thinking about something.

"What does she look like?" Daphne asked, shaking Julian from his thoughts. "Perhaps I have met her and I'm thinking of a different young lady."

Julian took a deep breath, still staring at the ceiling "She's tall, blond, pretty."

"Pretty or beautiful?" Daphne asked, a smile in her voice. *Gorgeous.* "Quite pretty."

"And her friend, what did you say her name was? Lady Worthing?"

"Yes, she's got dark hair and the most unusually colored eyes." Julian stood. "I'm going to retire for the evening, as well. I have some letters to write before I go to sleep. Good night, Daphne."

"What's unusual about them?" Daphne asked, just as Julian made it to the door.

Julian stopped. "Unusual about what?"

"Lady Worthing's eyes."

"Oh, one is blue and the other is green." He reached for the door handle.

"Really?" Daphne's voice was sharp and he turned to face her.

He narrowed his eyes on his sister. "Yes, really. Why?"

Daphne pursed her lips. "And you say this house party is in Surrey?"

"Yes."

"Hmm. Perhaps I do know this Lady Worthing after all."

CHAPTER SEVEN

Cass wore her lavender gown. The newest one she had had made for her twenty-third birthday. Her hair was twisted behind her head in a fetching chignon and she'd pinched just enough pink into her cheeks. She might have been ill-prepared to see Julian the first time, but when he arrived at Upbridge Hall, she intended to look her very best. She'd decided to stop thinking about the madness of the plot she'd become involved in. The fact was that she would have a few days with Julian, a few uninterrupted, wonderful days in which she could dance with him and laugh with him and talk to him without having to acknowledge the fact that he was meant for another woman. That's all that mattered. For now.

She would tell him the truth. She would, just as soon as the opportunity presented itself. In her quieter moments, however, she had to wonder. Would Julian know her? Know from her speech, her voice, her mannerisms, her words? Know that she was his dear friend whom he'd been writing to for years? He was certain to guess. How could he not? But then she had only to look at Lucy and see her sparkling, radiant confidence. A certainty she wore like a cloak, a cloak Cass desperately wished she could purchase or borrow.

It was madness, pretending to be Patience, and nothing good could come of it. Lucy was hoping that somehow Julian would fall in love with her and renounce Penelope. Cass already knew for certain that would never happen. It couldn't. Julian, the honorable man she'd come to know and love, would never do anything so callous as toss over his intended for another woman. And of course there was the inevitable day of reckoning, in the background, over-shadowing her happiness. For eventually, Julian would learn her true identity—as Pen's cousin, she couldn't pretend to be someone she was not forever—and then he might well hate her for lying to him. Cass wasn't usually a liar. She wasn't. After all, she was the same young woman who had walked an entire five miles to the vicar's house one sunny summer afternoon at the age of fifteen after discovering that her dog had come home with the vicar's hat in her mouth. It would have been quite easy, preferable, perhaps, to hide the evidence and pretend as if she knew nothing about that bit of wool, but instead, she'd marched down the lane, ruining her favorite pair of slippers, with the soggy bit of material in her hand and presented the facts to the vicar and his lovely wife. She'd profusely apologized and offered to pay for a new hat, but the vicar had graciously declined, though he never did leave his door open so that Daisy could get in again, and knowing Daisy, Cass was sure she'd tried.

No. Cass wasn't a liar, but would Julian see it that way when the truth was revealed?

Oh, she supposed she had lied before, but only when the circumstances truly merited it. Like last summer when she'd told Lucy she was sick with a head cold. She hadn't been sick at all. She'd done it in order to keep Lucy and the duke in each other's company when it was clear to everyone they were meant to be together and were both just being typically stubborn about getting around to acknowledging that fact. Why, if Cass hadn't told that little fib, Lucy might still be on the shelf. Wasn't that a lie for a good reason?

Cass sighed. It wasn't just the lying, though. There was something else to consider: the fact that Julian would no doubt eventually be interested in greeting his old friend Cassandra. No. Regardless of Lucy's confidence, it was absolutely not going to end well. There was no doubt about it. But Cass could pretend. She could act for a sennight. She had little choice. She'd already started down this twisty path . . . with a giant shove from Her Grace, Lucy Hunt.

Lucy stopped at the entrance to Cass's bedchamber and leaned inside. "The butler tells me Captain Swift's coach is on its way up the drive."

Cass froze. She pressed a hand to her belly and breathed deeply. "He's here?"

Lucy nodded, her dark curls bobbing against her cheeks. "Yes. Come with me to greet him?" She held out a hand to Cass.

Cass nodded woodenly. She stood and made her way over to her friend.

"You look absolutely gorgeous, dear," Lucy said. She kept holding her hand as they made their way down the stairs, across the marble foyer, and out onto the gravel in front of the house.

Cass concentrated on breathing normally the entire way. Julian was here. Julian. But she couldn't talk to him the same way she would if she were Cass. She couldn't refer to any of the things she knew about him. She couldn't tell him she remembered how hard he'd worked to earn the respect of his men. She couldn't tell him she knew he'd nearly died of thirst in a desert in Spain. She couldn't tell him she understood why he hated confined spaces after spending night after night in a tent. She couldn't say any of the things she wanted to say to him. She had to feign complete ignorance. Could she do it? Lucy had warned her to say as little as possible about anything in the past. Did she have it in her? Was she even capable of such subterfuge?

Had Julian already been looking for her as Cass? Had he gone to her parents' house to try to visit her and found her missing? Oh, the web they'd spun was already too tangled to sort through. Instead, Cass pasted a smile on her face as the coach rolled to a stop in front of the manor house.

Very well. Enough worrying. Cassandra Monroe was a worrier. Patience Bunbury was decidedly not.

One of the footmen hopped down and opened the door to the coach. Julian emerged soon after, looking like the blond Adonis he was. This time, he wasn't wearing his uniform. Instead, he had on a simple white shirt, cravat, emerald-green waistcoat, dark gray trousers, and black top boots and hat. He seemed every bit a handsome member of the *ton* on holiday, no longer the injured army captain. Cass swallowed hard. It didn't matter. The man looked good either way.

He smiled brightly when he saw the two ladies waiting for him. Cass's heart skipped a beat as she remembered the way his eyes crinkled slightly at the corners when he smiled like that, as if he was holding something—just a bit of himself—back. He strode forward, and she let out her breath. He didn't have any other outward signs of lingering injury. She'd noticed that at Pen's house. Now she confirmed it. Cass had prayed about that, over and over. She'd gone to bed more times than she could count reciting prayers for him in a feverish voice until sleep overtook her. Then she usually slept fitfully, plagued with awful nightmares of Julian being shot and bleeding to death or being run through with a bayonet. She usually awoke, sweating, breathing heavily, and sometimes crying. Then she began the praying all over again.

Julian had been shot in the chest. Apparently, the bullet had just missed his heart. Or so the surgeons told him. It had sliced through him and ripped through the back of his coat. He'd been beyond fortunate to live. In fact, it was a miracle that he was standing here, looking handsome and friendly and making Cass's mouth go dry.

You are Patience. You are Patience. You are Patience. The singsong voice played in her head. Oh, good heavens. This wasn't going to work for five minutes, let alone a sennight. She braced herself and lifted her skirts to turn and flee, the lavender satin clutched in her fists. Lucy's hand came out to capture one of hers, giving it a reassuring squeeze. Lucy knew her so well. Cass let the fabric drop and stood rooted to the spot.

"Good afternoon, Captain Swift." First, Lucy curtsied to him. Then she swept up her skirts to walk toward him. She stopped in front of him and offered him her hand.

"Lady Worthing, thank you for your kind invitation," Julian replied, bowing over Lucy's hand.

"You remember Miss Bunbury?" Lucy asked, motioning for Cass to come stand beside her.

Cass jumped. She'd been so distracted looking at Julian, she'd nearly not heard Lucy's introduction. Trembling, she made her way slowly over to Lucy's side and curtsied to Julian.

"Of course. Miss Bunbury." He bowed over her hand. The warmth of his strong fingers radiating through his glove made Cass forget to breathe.

"Cap . . . Captain Swift," she finally managed.

Lucy clapped her hands. "Do come inside, Captain Swift. The footmen will take your things up to your rooms. I expect you'll want to relax before the ball this evening."

"There is to be a ball this evening?" Julian asked, falling into step behind the ladies, his arms crossed behind his back.

"There is to be a ball this evening?" Cass echoed, turning to look at Lucy, fear clutching at her insides.

Lucy's smile never faltered. "Oh, you know, not a ball actually. More like a small dance. I do love to dance, don't you, Captain Swift?"

The footmen were already busily unloading the trunk from Julian's coach.

Julian cleared his throat. "I can't say I've had much occasion to lately, my lady."

Lucy looked a bit chagrined. "Oh, no, of course not. But I do hope you'll enjoy yourself once everyone is here."

"Yes, as to that, Lady Worthing, I assume Penelope has arrived. It's quite important that I speak with her."

Lucy's eyes went wide with an innocent look she'd perfected for just such occasions when she was up to something. Cass knew it well. "Oh, no, Captain Swift. She's not."

Julian's forehead furrowed. "She's not? I thought you'd said she'd already left to come here."

Lucy waved one gloved hand in the air. "Yes, well. I wrote to her and told her we'd mixed up the dates and the party wasn't to begin for another three days. I believe she returned to London. I thought perhaps *you'd* heard from her and could tell us when she'd be arriving."

Cass winced. It was fortunate that Julian was behind her and couldn't see her face. She was certain it would give away the entire ruse. It was just like Lucy to add that little extra bit about thinking perhaps Julian had heard from Pen. A perfect detail, actually. Lucy was no amateur.

Cass dared a glance back, attempting to keep her face carefully blank. Julian shook his head. "London? You mean to say that Miss Monroe is still in London? Where I just came from?"

Lucy sighed. "I'm afraid so, Captain Swift, but you must stay here with us and wait for her. She's sure to arrive any day now."

Lucy stepped back and entwined her arm through Julian's. She pulled him past Cass, and they walked into the house. Cass followed them. "We'll have such fun while we await her."

There was no mistaking the disappointment on Julian's face. Cass's heart dropped. He was obviously eager to see Penelope.

Julian quickly recovered, however, and smiled at his hostess. "Of course. That reminds me, Lady Worthing. I have some friends in the area, and I'd be ever so grateful if I might invite them over for a visit. Their country house is only a few miles' ride from here."

Cass gulped.

Lucy tugged at the neck of her gown. "Friends of yours, you say? Wh-who might they be, Captain Swift?"

Julian's smile was wide. "Lord Owen and Lady Cassandra Monroe."

CHAPTER EIGHT

"Oh, Janie, you're here. Wonderful!" Lucy nearly did a dance of joy when Jane Lowndes came striding into Cass's bedchamber later that afternoon. Cass glanced up. She and Lucy had been busily trying to decide which gown Cass should wear for the dance. That is, after they'd had a giant row about why exactly Lucy had told Julian that inviting Owen and Cassandra Monroe to the house party was a lovely idea.

"I had to," Lucy explained. "What would he have thought if I'd acted as if I didn't know you? Or if I'd made up some excuse as to why I was reluctant to invite you?"

"You're supposed to be quick with your tongue, Lucy. Now he's sure to invite Owen and we'll be ruined," Cass had pointed out.

"Inviting and arriving are two quite different things," Lucy replied. "Your brother is certain to be in London, and *you* obviously cannot come. Write Julian a letter in your own hand and tell him so. It'll be explained away easily enough."

That last idea had given Cass some hope, but the entire scheme still didn't sit easily with her.

Jane's arrival was a welcome respite from Cass's constantly swirling thoughts. "I'm here to help," Jane declared. "And to watch this debacle, of course."

Cass rushed over to her friend and gave her a hug. Jane had dark brown hair and dark brown eyes that sparkled with intelligence. She normally wore her favorite color, blue, and she was constantly pushing her silver spectacles up her nose. "Thank you so much for coming," Cass said. "I'm certain I'm going to need you."

"Are you jesting? I wouldn't miss this for all the tea in London." As usual, Jane held a book in one hand. Her reticule dangled, forgotten, in the other. She wasted no time plopping down in a chair near the window to watch the two other ladies as they dug through the wardrobe.

Lucy pulled out a soft pink gown and presented it to Cass. "This one?"

"Too demure," Cass replied, shaking her head.

Setting her book aside for a moment, Jane pulled off her gloves and stuffed them into her reticule. "What are you waiting for? Tell me all the details, your invitation was quite devoid of them."

Lucy tossed the pink gown onto the bed and tapped her finger against her chin. "I know we promised to help you next, Janie, but an opportunity we just could not resist presented itself a few days ago."

Jane arched a brow. "Opportunity?"

"Yes." Lucy nodded.

"Presented itself?" Jane asked next.

"Yes." Lucy dove back into the wardrobe and pulled out a robin's-egg-blue gown this time. "This one?"

Cass wrinkled her nose. "Too bright."

"Stop putting me off and tell me the details," Jane demanded.

Cass sat serenely on the edge of the bed, while Lucy

proceeded to tell Jane all about Patience Bunbury and Penelope's defection.

Jane's big brown eyes grew wider and wider as she listened. She pushed up her spectacles again. "So, let me see if I have the right of it. You're telling me that you've staged this entire house party as a means to get Julian to fall in love with Cass?"

Lucy nodded. "Yes."

"Only he doesn't know she's Cass?" Jane continued.

"Right," Lucy said. "Though that will be easily clarified later."

Jane blinked at Lucy. "How exactly do you see that being successful?"

"Details, Jane, details. We'll worry about that particular bit when the time comes."

Jane turned her dark gaze to Cass. "And you've approved of all this? I must say, I find it difficult to believe."

Cass pressed her hands to her cheeks, knowing she was turning an unfortunate shade of pink. "I know. I know. I've no idea what's come over me. All I know is that I do so want to spend time with Julian." She sighed.

"Oh, Cass, I can't blame you. But don't you think this will end poorly?" Jane asked.

Lucy tsked. "You should have seen how Julian looked at her when he met her at Penelope's house."

"The man just came back from war. No doubt he'd look at anything wearing a skirt in such a fashion. No insult intended, Cass," Jane replied.

"None taken." Cass scooted off the bed and took Lucy's place staring into the wardrobe. Soon, she was rummaging into the wardrobe herself to see if anything else caught her fancy.

"Oh, no. It wasn't that. He didn't look twice at *me*," Lucy continued. "He was entirely smitten with our Cass, as I always knew he would be."

Jane's dark brow arched yet again. "Then why didn't you just tell him that she was Cass?"

"Time was of the essence. He was dead set on chasing Penelope off to her house party immediately. He is obviously looking for her. He needs time alone with Cass. We must give it to them."

Jane stood and strode over to put her hand on Cass's sleeve. "You know I'd do anything for you and this is no exception. I'll play along and do whatever I can to help. I just hope you don't end up getting hurt. Or hurting anyone."

Cass smiled at her friend, but unexpected tears stung the back of her eyes. "Thank you, Jane. I'm resigned to the fact that Julian will marry Pen. But I just want to spend time with him for a bit."

Jane patted her hand and gave her a sympathetic smile. "Don't worry, my dear, if you want a few days with Julian, you shall have them."

Cass returned her smile with a weaker one. "Thank you, Janie."

"Jane, what did you tell your mother about coming here?" Lucy asked, nudging Cass aside and pulling out a soft yellow gown.

Cass scrunched up her nose and shook her head at the yellow.

Jane laughed. "Both of my parents are perfectly happy at present thinking I'm off at the Duchess of Claringdon's house party with all her eligible, titled gentleman friends. Mother sent one of the housemaids with me, but you're my chaperone officially, now, Lucy. And you've given me an excellent idea with this Patience Bunbury business, Cass. A nonexistent chaperone. I love it. I intend to implement it the moment I return. I am a fully converted Bunburyist. I merely need to think of a reason why Mother cannot meet her."

Cass and Lucy both smiled at their friend. Jane was an unrepentant bluestocking. She just happened to be the only child of a genius father who had made such sound investments for the Crown that he'd been knighted. Her mother, however, wishing her daughter was more like her and less like her cerebral pater, was beside herself in her attempts to get Janie married off. Jane had no intention of doing anything of the sort. No doubt her mother had been overcome with glee when Jane had announced that she actually *wanted* to go to a *ton* house party.

Jane returned to her seat and smoothed her hands over her skirts. "By the by, what is Upton's part in this scheme?"

Cass and Lucy exchanged an uncomfortable look. "We haven't told Garrett," Lucy admitted.

Jane poked out her cheek with her tongue. "Whyever not? He's usually up for a good ruse."

Lucy pulled a peach-colored gown from the wardrobe and presented it to Cass for her consideration. "He's too good. He'll want to tell the truth."

Jane laughed. "Upton?" She rolled her eyes. "Whatever do you mean? The man is a profligate rake and an accomplished gambler, hardly someone who would be mistaken for a man of the cloth. Besides, I imagine that in order to be an adequate rake and gambler, one must have to tell a few fibs now and again."

"Hmm. That's a good point, Jane," Lucy said.

"No!" Cass gulped. "Don't tell Garrett. And might I remind you that *I* want to tell the truth."

"Oh, no you don't. Not really," Lucy replied. "If we'd told Julian the truth that day at Pen's, he would have demanded she come downstairs and those two would be planning their engagement right now. He would have greeted you, wished he could have you, and set about doing the honorable thing and preparing for his wedding with your cousin."

"And somehow a house party is supposed to change all of that?" Jane asked, skepticism dripping from her voice.

"It's supposed to provide the *opportunity* to change all of that," Lucy replied. "Two people need time to get to know each other. If Cass and Julian had merely talked briefly at Pen's house, they would have gone their separate ways and not seen each other again until the wedding. The *wrong* wedding."

"But I already know Julian. And I certainly don't expect it to change anything," Cass argued. "And no to that gown."

Lucy tossed the peach gown on the pile with the rest of them. "Of course you know him, dear, but he doesn't know you're Cass. He only knows you're beautiful. Besides, don't worry about all of that now. Leave everything to me."

Lucy's infamous second-favorite saying. Cass glanced at Jane and shook her head.

Jane merely shrugged, drew her book up to her nose, and began reading. "As usual, I'm certain this is all to become much more complicated before it becomes simpler."

Cass sighed. "Wait until she tells you about how Julian wants to invite Owen."

Jane snapped her book shut. "Owen?"

"And Lucy said it was a lovely idea," Cass added.

The book toppled from Jane's hands. She tried to grab for it but it landed with a thud on the carpet. "You did not!"

"I'll explain it to you later," Lucy replied, flourishing a hand in the air. "Now, don't worry, Cass. Once Julian spends a bit of time in your company, he'll be questioning his commitment to Pen. Also, our little plan serves to keep him away from her so that they are unable to make it official just yet."

Cass pulled a silver gown from the cabinet. "This one!"

"Ooh, it *is* perfect," Lucy agreed.

"Yes, that one," Jane added, reaching down to retrieve her book.

Cass sighed again wistfully and looked out the window across the autumnal countryside. A forest of trees met her eyes all in various stages of turning red, and gold, and orange. The leaves had already begun to fall, turning the ground beneath them into a painter's palette of lovely colors. Cass sighed once more. How she wished she could be outside painting the quiet landscape instead of being inside in the middle of a sordid affair. She shook her head. "My aunt and uncle will no doubt disown me if they ever find out. To say nothing of what my parents will do to me. Why, they'll probably send me off to a convent."

"You should be so lucky." Jane snorted. "But don't worry. They would never be so kind as to send you to a convent. You're worth far more to them as marriageable chattel, darling. Not to mention you aren't Catholic." She laughed.

Lucy laughed, too.

Cass hugged the silver gown to her chest, heedless of the wrinkles she was no doubt inflicting upon the fine fabric. It was depressing, but true. She was worth more to her parents as an object to be traded into marriage. She'd always known that but somehow Janie saying it out loud made it real and undeniable. Her parents sending her to a convent would be the equivalent of giving away an enormously expensive jewel to charity. She took a deep breath. "Nevertheless, if my parents do find out—"

Lucy pulled the silver gown from her grasp and rang for one of the maids to press it. "Oh, Cass. How many times must I tell you to stop worrying? How would they ever find out?"

CHAPTER NINE

Cass stood on the sidelines of the dancing. Lucy had somehow managed to persuade a few neighbors to come to the dance. None of them knew Captain Swift and all of them apparently were willing to refer to Lucy as Lady Worthing. Lucy herself had come up with an outlandish tale for Julian's sake of how her husband, Lord Worthing, had gone to visit his gout-ridden mother in Bath and that's why he was not here to help his wife host the house party. Later, when they were safely alone, Cass had pointed out to Lucy that gentlemen, not ladies, were usually afflicted by gout and Lucy had simply replied, "Oh, I've always wished gout upon my mother and now she has it, by God."

All in all, Cass had to admit that despite her worries, the dance was going quite well so far. Julian had been laughing and talking with the other guests and appeared to be enjoying himself. She tried not to glance in his direction too often. He was handsome, so unbearably handsome. And the time away at war had done nothing to detract from his looks.

But it was more than that. She knew him, knew his secrets, knew his heart. In one of his letters, he'd told her how he'd sat in a ditch next to a man named Robert Covington and written a letter to his mother for him as he lay dying.

In his letter to Cass, Julian had told her that when he was thirsty and hungry and cold, it was more difficult for him to watch his soldiers go thirsty or hungry or cold. How it felt as if a little piece of him died when any of them were left behind. She'd seen him mature through his writing. She'd watched him change from a young man full of bravado and pride for his country to a seasoned veteran who'd seen far too much of the horrors of war. And even though he was careful not to share the truly awful details, Cass knew they haunted him each night. They would haunt him forever.

But she couldn't talk to him. She couldn't let him know she knew. She wasn't Cassandra Monroe, his good friend and confidant. She was Patience Bunbury, a pretty face, a stranger. She glanced at him again and recognized the faraway look in his eye. He was removed from this place, probably still on a battlefield on the Continent. A part of him would always be there. She understood that.

Jane came floating by, a plate full of teacakes in her possession. How her friend managed to maintain her figure with the amount of teacakes she consumed, Cass would never know. Jane stopped directly in front of Cass, jolting her from her thoughts. "Very well. I've been dying to get a look at this man for years. Where is he?"

Cass didn't need to ask who she meant. Cass and Lucy had been friends with Jane for the last four years and therefore she'd been hearing about Cass's devotion to Julian all that time.

Cass clasped her hands together and looked down at her fingers. "He's . . . he's over there." She motioned with her chin. "But don't be obvious about it when you look," she squeaked.

To her credit, Jane didn't move. She nibbled on a teacake. "Why? Is he looking at you?"

"Yes. No. I don't know." And then, "Don't look!"

Jane quickly stole a glance before returning her attention back to Cass . . . and her teacakes.

"That was ever so stealthy," Cass told her with a laugh. "You should be a spy for the War Office."

"I should be a great many things which my sex does not allow me to be." Jane sighed. She shifted the plate to her opposite hand. "Now. Am I correct in assuming that Captain Swift is the tall, handsome blond fellow standing over by the doors?"

Cass nodded miserably. "Yes."

Jane popped another bit of cake into her mouth. "Oh, my. I can almost see why you've been so smitten."

Cass widened her eyes. "Why, Janie, I thought you always said there are plenty of men from which to choose and I shouldn't be so set on any one in particular."

Jane shrugged. "That is true; however, even I must admit he is a fine specimen of man. You must introduce me to him. In the meantime, I am quite convinced that he should ask you to dance."

Cass laughed. "I think so, too."

Janie tilted her head in Julian's direction. "I suggest you go over and make yourself available for the invitation."

Cass immediately sobered. "No. I couldn't."

"Very well. Introduce me to him and I shall suggest it with all due haste."

"Oh, no, I—"

"Why not? We've little else to do. I daresay things are a bit dull around here without Upton to torment."

Cass pressed her fingers to her lips. Jane and Garrett had engaged in a merry war of words ever since they met at a performance of *Much Ado About Nothing* four years ago. Lucy had invited her new friend, Jane, to the theater with her. Her cousin had attended as well. The two had never agreed upon anything, though Lucy always suspected much of their apparent dislike for one another was just for show. Cass did, too. It was sweet, in an odd sort of way, that Janie was obviously missing her verbal spats with Garrett.

But Cass had to admit, she also found herself secretly wishing Garrett was in on their plan. Everything seemed so much more . . . sane when Garrett was around to temper Lucy's ludicrous schemes. The fact that Garrett had no part in this particular one made Cass that much more anxious about it.

Be bold. The words streaked through Cass's brain.

Cass let her gaze trail over to Julian where he stood alone near the doors. He appeared to enjoy watching the other couples dance. Was he thinking of Pen? Cass couldn't help but wonder. Was he pondering where his future wife was tonight? Was he hoping she would arrive in time to dance with him? Of course Cass knew Pen never would arrive. Guilt tugged at her. She bit her lip.

Be bold. The words flashed across her brain again like lightning in the night sky. Besides, she wasn't Cassandra Monroe tonight. She was Patience Bunbury. "Very well, Jane. Let's go."

Cass picked up the skirts of her silver gown and made her way deliberately toward Julian, Jane and her teacakes in tow.

The distance between them in the ballroom seemed to stretch interminably. One of the other guests stopped her to greet her with a "Miss Bunbury" and a wink. Cass replied with a shaky smile and a nod.

She straightened her shoulders. Being called Miss Bunbury also served another purpose, to strengthen her resolve and bolster her courage. She was Patience, Patience Bunbury, bold attender of parties and shameless seeker of dances with handsome gentlemen. Well, one handsome gentleman in particular.

She and Jane made their way across the room until they stood only a few paces from Julian. Cass cleared her throat and tugged at her glove. Then she reminded herself that Patience Bunbury was most certainly not a glove tugger. She let go and calmly folded her hands in front of her instead. "Captain Swift."

He swiveled around to face her. Cass caught her breath.

His smile lit up his eyes. "Miss Bunbury." He stepped toward her, closing the last bit of space between them. He bowed over her hand, lightly touching her palm, his thumb moving across her knuckles in a slow caress that sent a thrill shooting up her arm.

Bold. Bold. Bold.

"May I present my friend—"

"Miss Wollstonecraft," Jane interrupted, moving in front of Cass and curtsying, teacakes and all.

Cass had to smother her smile. She and Lucy had argued earlier with Jane about her desire to pretend to be someone she was not. "It'll be better for everyone if only Cass and I have false names," Lucy had said. "The less complicated the better."

"I don't care who it's better for. Besides, when have *you* ever worried about anything being complicated?" Jane had countered. "I want a false name, too. I don't see why you two get to make up new identities and I must be forced to be my same boring self."

"You're not boring, Jane," Cass had replied, patting her friend on the shoulder.

"Oh, you're sweet, Cass, but the fact is that the most excitement I've had in months is this mad house party and I'm not about to allow a perfectly good opportunity to pretend to be someone else go to waste."

Apparently, Jane refused to be denied.

"Miss Wollstonecraft?" Julian bowed. "You don't happen to be related to—"

"The famous author? Yes, actually. She is my aunt."

Cass elbowed her in the ribs and Jane grunted. "This is Captain Julian Swift, Miss . . . Wollstonecraft," Cass said.

"A pleasure, Captain," Jane replied.

"The pleasure is entirely mine," Julian said.

Jane mumbled something that sounded suspiciously like, "My word, he *is* handsome," just before she inclined her head toward Cass. "Miss Bunbury here was just now telling me how desperately she loves to dance. I was telling her how desperately I love to eat teacake. And to that end, I'm off to find more. Good evening, Captain."

Jane was gone in an instant and Cass was left startlingly alone with Julian. She began to tug at her glove again and stopped herself. Again.

"Do you enjoy dancing, Captain Swift?" Oh, now he was certain to think Miss Patience Bunbury was the most forward female in the country. An advantage to playacting, she supposed, the hint of a smile creeping across her lips. Lady Cassandra Monroe would never ask a gentleman if he liked to dance, but apparently Patience Bunbury would. It was freeing, actually, and quite bold, thank you very much. She just might be able to get used to this.

One of Julian's golden eyebrows arched in the barest hint of acknowledgment of her cheekiness. "I do. Or, I used to. I cannot remember the last time I danced, actually. However, I'm not particularly adept at it, I'm afraid."

"I heard the Duchess of Richmond gave a ball just before Waterloo," Cass said. "Did you attend?"

He glanced down at his perfectly polished boots. "I did not."

"Why not?" She actually knew why not, but Patience Bunbury didn't. She swallowed the lump that formed in her throat.

Julian straightened up and cleared his throat. "On the eve of battle, I fear I was not in much of a dancing mood."

"What were you doing?" Now here was something she didn't know. But as soon as the words left her mouth, Cass wished she hadn't spoken them. It was beyond rude of her to ask such a personal question. In addition to being cheeky, apparently Patience Bunbury was also a bit too forthright.

Julian slid his hands into his pockets and looked out across the ballroom as if he was surveying a battlefield. His eyes held a faraway look as if he was remembering that night. "I was writing . . . to a friend."

Cass nearly gasped. *Stay calm. Breathe normally. Patience Bunbury is not a swooner, either, nor a gasper.*

But she couldn't help herself. She had to ask. "A very close friend?"

"Yes," he said softly, a smile in his eyes. "A very close friend, indeed."

"Penelope?" That felonious little shoulder devil had definitely made her ask that.

"No." He shook his head. "That reminds me. Do you know? Has Penelope arrived yet?"

Cass could nearly kick herself for bringing up Penelope and shattering the sense of intimacy they'd shared for just a moment. Or had that only been in her imagination? Or Patience's imagination? Oh, this was already far too complicated.

She shook her head and cleared her throat. "Actually, from what I understand, Penelope planned to stop along the way to visit a few friends this time."

And there it was, her first out-and-out lie. The rest of the lies she'd allowed to rest solely on Lucy's head. Cass had been happy enough to play along with them, but now, now she was in deep, deep enough to lie directly to Julian. Cass detested herself for lying. She imagined herself telling Julian the truth, ripping away her façade and naming herself, admitting to him that she remembered the letter he'd written her that night. It rested in a shoebox tucked away in a drawer in her wardrobe with all the others, sorted by date and stained with her tears. Tears she'd shed thinking how the Battle of Waterloo just might take Julian's life. But she couldn't tell him that. She couldn't say a word. She was already trapped in the lie.

"I do hope Penelope arrives soon. I must speak with her," Julian added.

Cass bit the inside of her cheek and kept her eyes focused on a spot on the parquet floor behind him. Of course the man wanted to speak with his future wife. No doubt he wanted to get their wedding plans under way immediately. Cass's heart wrenched. "I'm certain Penelope is looking forward to seeing you, too, Captain Swift." That was another lie and it was bitter on Cass's tongue. Pen wasn't looking forward to it at all. In fact, she'd fled from him. Pen not only didn't seem interested in marrying Julian, she didn't even want to see him. She was a coward.

"Seeing as how Miss Monroe is not here, would you do me the honor of dancing with me, Miss Bunbury? I shall do my best not to tread upon your feet."

Cass looked up at Julian and melted. He'd asked her to dance. This was why she'd come over here, after all. But now that she'd secured the invitation, she was a bit hesitant. Why? Because she was frightened that Julian would look into her eyes and know her? Because she was worried that she'd say something that would give her away? Or because she'd never danced with Julian before and she wished that for their first dance that he would know who she truly was.

"I should like that very much," she heard herself reply. He took her hand and led her onto the floor just as a waltz was beginning to play. Thank heaven for the waltz. Lovely dance, that.

It was true. Julian was not exactly, ahem, the best of dancers. She hadn't quite expected him to be as proficient as, say, the dandies, but the effect was quite the opposite of . . . graceful. Ah, well. The man was good at many other things. She could easily forgive him this. He'd been at war for seven years, after all, not perfecting his waltz. She swept along in his arms as best she could, gazing up into his eyes, and pretending all the while that he knew she was Cass and they were betrothed. Oh, she knew it was fruitless and cruel to her heart to play such a dangerous game of pretend, but she couldn't keep herself from it, even if she wanted to.

"You are an excellent dancer, Miss Bunbury," Julian said.

There it was, the reminder that he didn't know she was Cass. "Thank you. And you are . . . er . . ."

"Not?" He smiled at her.

"Oh, no. I wouldn't say—"

"Don't worry. No one has ever accused me of being an excellent dancer. Or a proficient one, for that matter. My sister taught me this dance two nights ago in the event I might need to know." His grin widened. "I consider it a victory that I have kept your feet from harm."

"It's an honor to dance with you, Captain." Cass concentrated on memorizing the broad muscles in his shoulders with her fingertips, the sound of the scratch of the wool of his coat beneath her gloves.

"I'm afraid there is not much opportunity for dancing in the army. Perhaps I should have attended the Duchess of Richmond's ball after all."

Cass closed her eyes, allowing herself to be momentarily distracted by his cologne. She'd never forget that clean scent, not as long as she lived. It had been burned in her memory seven years ago on her sixteenth birthday when he'd got close enough to—

"What was that?" Good heavens, she'd completely lost the thread of the conversation and she was distinctly aware of the fact that Julian had just asked her a question of some sort.

"I asked how long you've known Lady Worthing."

"Oh, Lucy? I've known her for—"

His brow furrowed. "Her name is Lucy?"

"Yes, why?"

"It's just that—" He shook his head. "Never mind. My apologies. I interrupted you. You were saying?"

"I've known her since I was a child." Warning bells sounded in Cass's brain. She couldn't admit that she and Lucy had been neighbors. He might begin asking questions about who her parents were and where they lived. She had to change the subject. Immediately.

"How is Daphne?" she asked in a rushed voice.

"My sister? How do you know her—"

"Oh, I, that is, Lucy mentioned her name to me. She's your younger sister, is she not?" Cass smothered her groan. She was a complete fool. She'd gone straight from one untenable subject to another. Lying was entirely too complicated for her. *Blast. Blast. Blast.*

"Yes, Daphne is in London with my mother at present."

"Is she old enough to have made her come-out?" Pretending as if she didn't know that Daphne was nineteen might just make her lies sound more convincing. Never mind the fact that Cass herself had been at the girl's come-out ball, sneaked some champagne with the younger woman, and then nearly fell into a giggling fit later when she and Daphne found themselves hiding behind a potted palm in the conservatory trying to elude rude (and smelly) Lord Montelroy, who seemed entirely too intent upon asking both of them for a dance.

"Yes, she came out last Season," Julian replied.

"And has she made a match?" Cass asked next, also pretending she didn't know all too well that Daphne was entirely unimpressed with the entire crop of London's finest.

"Not yet," Julian replied.

"Not to worry. There's still hope for her. I've been out five Seasons now." Cass winced. If they hadn't been dancing, she might have clapped her hand over her mouth. Cass had been out for five Seasons but Patience Bunbury . . . apparently, Patience had been out for five Seasons as well.

The dance was quickly coming to an end, but Cass took a deep breath. She needed to stop talking about people they knew and Seasons and age. She needed to steer the conversation back to Julian. It was much safer that way. She'd come this far, been this bold. She might as well ask Julian another question. A question she'd always wanted to ask and could never quite explain why she hadn't. Strangely, pretending to be someone else somehow finally gave her the opportunity to ask it.

"May I ask you something, Captain Swift?" Cass said, relieved that her voice didn't crack.

He inclined his head, an inquisitive look on his face. "Of course, Miss Bunbury."

She dared to meet his gaze. "What was the worst part of being in the war?"

His eyes narrowed briefly. His lips thinned nearly imperceptibly, but he did not hesitate. "Learning just how inexplicably unfair life is." He hadn't even paused. The answer had rolled off his tongue as if he answered that particular question daily. Perhaps he did.

Cass merely nodded. Life *was* unfair. That was the truth.

CHAPTER TEN

Julian strode into his guest chamber. He untied his cravat and yanked it from around his neck. He pulled open the front of his shirt and rubbed his throat. He could breathe again. Finally. Wearing a uniform had been his habit for the last seven years. Since he'd been back to England, to Society, he'd been forced to borrow some of his brother's clothing and that included the stifling cravats. How long would it take before he got used to them again?

He took a sip of the brandy he'd requested from a footman before he came up to his room. Brandy was one thing he had missed about England. Not that the brandy didn't come from France. But he'd never drunk any of it while he'd been there.

His thoughts turned to the night that had just ended. Miss Bunbury. Patience. He couldn't get her visage out of his mind. She was beyond gorgeous, any man's dream. But her quiet, calm demeanor had surprised him. He'd wondered at it. Many ladies of his acquaintance were talkative, always going on and on about fripperies and parties. His sister adored a party. Daphne never wanted to sit still. Penelope had certainly never seemed capable of sitting long enough to write a letter, let alone a long or meaningful one. In fact, the only female he'd known who seemed as quiet and contemplative as Miss Bunbury was . . . Cassandra.

Miss Bunbury had asked him what the worst part of war was. He'd been asked that question countless times. On the parcel riding back to England, on the mail coach to London, even in town when a few people had recognized him before he'd left for the house party. He usually answered with his normal, nonchalant, "I'm merely glad to be home."

No one could understand the hell that was war. Not truly. They wanted their sordid details and the thrill of talking to a seasoned soldier. But no one truly wanted to know what it was like, the smell of wet warm blood, the dirt, the sounds of screams, and the fear that became so entrenched in your soul, you had no idea where it ended and where you began. No one wanted to hear about that. So he gave them the answer they wanted, a calm reassurance that there was life after war. Survival. That's what he represented to his fellow countrymen. He was playing a role and he must continue to play it.

But when Patience Bunbury had asked him, all deep blue eyes and quiet resolve, he'd done something completely unexpected. He'd actually told her the truth. The worst part of war—the very worst—was learning how deeply unfair life was. Truly learning it. Was it fair that David Covington was dead? The young man's body buried in foreign soil while his mother sobbed for him? David was an only son. Death shouldn't have come for him. Was it fair that Julian had watched men die of infection, disease, thirst? Watched as they went mad from heat? Written letters to their mothers or their wives attempting to skim over the horrific details of their last moments on earth? No. None of it was fair. And it never would be. Least of all the fact that he, a second son, an unnecessary person, was still alive and well while his brother was now in danger.

Much to his dead father's chagrin.

His thoughts turned to Donald and Rafe. They were lost in France, captured by the enemy, more than likely dead. Over the years Julian's heart had hardened to hearing news of death. It was a hazard of his occupation after all. But it could not, would not happen to his brother, his big, strong, noble brother. Donald must live to fulfill their father's expectations, to make their mother happy, to carry on as the Earl of Swifdon, as he was always meant to.

And Rafe. A few years younger, plenty more rash, a great deal more rakish, and hell-bent on causing trouble, the young man had run off to war the moment he'd had a chance. He'd been a solider, but his penchant for slipping in and out of places quickly, quietly, and unnoticed had earned him a spot as a spy. And he was a hell of a spy. Julian could only imagine that Rafe had been captured trying to save Donald, and that thought tortured Julian. He took another sip of brandy, swallowed hard, and stared into the fire that crackled in the hearth across the room.

Yes. Life was unfair. Fate sometimes made mistakes.

CHAPTER ELEVEN

"Ah, Lord Berkeley. I'm so glad you are here," Lucy gushed as she ushered the viscount into the foyer the next morning.

Cass stood next to Lucy, beaming at the viscount. "It's good to see you, my lord."

"Thank you for inviting me, Lady Worthing." Lord Berkeley winked at them both and bowed. "And it's lovely to see you again, Miss Bunbury."

Cass smiled and curtsied to Lord Berkeley. She'd always liked him immensely. Tall and handsome and blond, Lord Berkeley was a great deal like Julian actually. No wonder she felt so at ease in the viscount's company. Yes, indeed. He looked a great deal like Julian as well. Only whereas Julian had gray eyes, Lord Berkeley's were sky blue. The viscount wore dark trousers, a sapphire-blue waistcoat, a white shirt with a perfectly starched white cravat, and black top boots. He was ever so dapper and appeared to be in high spirits today.

Not to mention, it seemed Lord Berkeley had lost his stutter. Perhaps it was because he was no longer attempting to court Lucy. Last summer in Bath, the two had had a bit of a failed romance. But Lord Berkeley was obviously still great friends with Lucy, and clearly up for a bit of fun. He'd agreed to participate in this madness, hadn't he?

"Thank you for your gracious invitation. I've been looking forward to it all week," Lord Berkeley said to Lucy.

"Now in addition to calling me Lady Worthing and Cass Miss Bunbury, Miss Jane Lowndes is here and she has decided to be Miss Wollstonecraft," Lucy informed him.

The viscount arched a blond brow. "Wollstonecraft?"

"Yes. She's the niece of the author. In her head, that is."

Cass elbowed Lucy and blushed at Lord Berkeley.

"What?" Lucy asked, her innocent look firmly ensconced upon her face. "Didn't he ask Derek to write letters to me pretending they were from him last summer? If anyone is up for this little farce, it's our Lord Berkeley here."

It was true. Poor Lord Berkeley had been so overcome by his stutter that he'd gone to Derek and asked him to help him write letters with which to woo Lucy. He'd chosen Derek because Lucy had indicated how much she enjoyed her banter with the duke. Derek had agreed until he'd inconveniently realized he was writing letters to the woman he himself loved.

Lucy smiled at Lord Berkeley. "I can only say I'm sorry the party is not larger, so we might introduce you to some eligible young ladies." She said to Cass, "Christian here is quite interested in finding a nice young woman and settling down to have an inappropriate amount of children. He told me so himself."

"Lucy!" Cass pressed her palms to her burning cheeks. Not only was Lucy using Lord Berkeley's Christian name—which just so happened to *be* Christian—she was mentioning his future children. "You must be the most improper duchess in the history of improper duchesses."

"Which is exactly how I like it," Lucy replied with another smile for Cass.

"I did, indeed, say that," Lord Berkeley interjected, bowing. "But in an effort to change the subject and spare poor Lady Cassandra any more embarrassment, let me say that I look forward to meeting Captain Swift and enjoying myself at the house party."

"Excellent." Lucy clapped her hands. "Now, don't worry that Garrett isn't here." Lucy put her arm through Lord Berkeley's, drawing him farther into the house while Cass followed behind them.

"Yet." Berkeley added with a firm nod.

Cass's head snapped up. "Pardon?"

"He's not here yet," Berkeley replied.

Still smiling, Lucy shook her head. "Oh, no, he's not coming. I thought you knew."

Berkeley shrugged. "That's not what he said to me this morning."

Cass gasped. Her hand flew to her throat.

Lucy stopped walking. She dropped Berkeley's arm and turned to face him. "This morning? You spoke to Garrett this morning? In person?"

Berkeley straightened his cravat. "Yes. We spoke before I left his house. He said he planned to come along as soon as he was able. Seems he had a few business affairs to attend to first."

Lucy's face was quickly turning a mottled shade of red. "You were at Garrett's house this morning?"

"Yes. It was on the way. I decided to stop and see if he would like to come over with me."

Cass resisted the urge to sink to the floor. Where was that elusive magic wand when one had need of it? Of course Lord Berkeley would stop to visit Garrett. Whyever would Berkeley assume that Lucy's own cousin wasn't invited to her house party? Oh, this was no good. No good at all.

Lucy quickly recovered herself. "Oh, well, that's wonderful. It'll be lovely to have him. I haven't seen Garrett in several weeks, actually."

Berkeley smiled approvingly.

Lucy looped her arm through the viscount's again and they continued their stroll across the foyer. Cass followed in their wake, frantically tugging at the ends of her gloves and considering the possible scenarios over and over again in her mind, all of them equally horrifying and with sufficiently appalling endings. *What would Patience Bunbury do?*

Lucy stopped at the foot of the staircase where a footman patiently waited. She faced Lord Berkeley. "Henry here will take you up to your rooms, my lord, and see that you are settled."

Lord Berkeley bowed again and made to follow the footman away. "Thank you, Your Grace, er, my lady," he replied.

He had barely taken two steps up the staircase when he turned back to face Lucy. "I nearly forgot. I saw someone else you both know while I was visiting Upton."

Cass was still frantically attempting to think of a way they might evade discovery by Garrett. She was barely paying attention. "Someone else?"

Lucy echoed the same words.

"Yes, he arrived at Upton's house just as I was leaving."

Cass perked up and turned to face Lord Berkeley.

"Wh . . . who? Who?" Lucy sounded like an anxious owl. Her eyes were also nearly as wide as the fowl's. Cass was half expecting her head to swivel.

Lord Berkeley smiled at Cass. "Why, none other than your very own brother, Lady Cassandra. Lord Owen Monroe."

CHAPTER TWELVE

"What would Patience Bunbury do?" Cass murmured to herself as she paced in front of the windows in the blue drawing room. How had the entire charade gone from tenuous to catastrophic in a matter of mere hours? She should have known this plan would never stand up to scrutiny . . . and the inclusion of several other people. The old Cass would have wrung her hands and asked Lucy what to do next. The new Cass, ahem, Patience, was determined to figure out a way to handle this.

"About what?" Lucy asked. As usual, she was doing several things at once. At present she was busily going over the evening's dinner menu while picking out swaths of fabric for the new table linens the housekeeper planned to order.

Cass turned to face Lucy with wide eyes. "What do you think? Garrett and Owen!"

"Garrett won't be an issue." Lucy went back to perusing the menu. "I don't think pickled beets sound good at all. Do you, Jane?"

Jane sat on the sofa in the center of the room wearing a light blue day dress. She pushed her spectacles up her nose and glanced up from her book. "Not at all." She shuddered.

"Apparently, Mother adores them. Why am I not surprised?" Lucy rolled her eyes and drew a line through the pickled beets.

"Forget the pickled beets!" Cass tossed her hands in the air. "I must think. Garrett *will* be an issue. Lord Berkeley says Garrett knows we're over here. He's not stupid. He must have guessed we're up to something, especially if Berkeley told him about the false identities. It's not possible Garrett is going to stay away."

"I'm afraid she's right, Luce," Jane replied. "I've little doubt Upton will be over here the minute he can put his horses to."

Lucy waved her quill in the air as if brushing away the matter. "Garrett doesn't scare me one bit. We'll just tell him something to keep him quiet."

"Something? What something? And what about Owen?" Cass viciously tugged at her gloves.

"Stop it, Cass. You're going to ruin that perfectly lovely kid leather. And as for Owen, there's absolutely no reason why he would come here. Lord Berkeley was quite certain he hadn't mentioned the party to Owen." She turned back to face Jane. "What do you think about pears?"

"Pickled pears?" Jane asked, wrinkling her nose.

"No. Just pears," Lucy replied.

Jane shrugged. "As long as they're not pickled, I've no objection."

Cass stopped pacing and pinched the bridge of her nose, fighting the urge to throttle both of them. "It's not that simple. I think we need to go to Garrett, find him, tell him what's going on, and secure his promise to help us."

This time Jane didn't look up from her book. "Best of luck with that." She snorted.

Lucy tapped her quill against her cheek. "Actually, Cass may have a point. It may be a problem if Garrett just barges in here and begins asking questions."

At her friends' silence Jane looked up to see them both staring at her. "What are you looking at me for?"

"You have to do it, Janie," Cass began.

Jane snapped her book closed and let it fall to the cushion beside her. "You must be jesting."

"No. I'm not. It has to be you." Cass resumed both her pacing and her glove tugging in front of the fireplace.

"Why me?" Jane asked.

"Because Lucy cannot leave her own house party, and Garrett won't listen to her in any case."

"Oh, thank you, Cass," Lucy said.

"You know it's true," Cass replied.

Jane's eyes were wide. "And you think he'll listen to *me*?"

Cass flew over to the sofa and kneeled at her friend's feet. "Don't you see? You have the best chance of convincing him, Jane. You're so good at arguing your point and you're so clever and wise and—"

Jane smiled at her and patted her cheek. "Don't think I don't know that you're merely attempting to flatter me in order to get me to do your bidding."

"Yes. I am," Cass agreed, nodding. "But it's true."

Jane tugged Cass by the hand and pulled her up to sit next to her. Then she crossed her arms over her chest. "I truly have no earthly idea what you think I might possibly say to Upton of all people to get him to agree to go along with any of this."

"You must at least try, Janie. Won't you try, for me?" Cass asked, batting her eyelashes at Jane innocently.

"It is your turn," Lucy added, abandoning the menu. "I seem to remember the last time such a mission came up, I was forced to go to Derek's town house in Bath and tell him that Cass was sick."

"Yes. And look how that ended," Jane replied. "With you married to him."

"Don't be ridiculous," Lucy replied. "It's not as if *you're* going to marry Garrett."

Jane nodded once. "Precisely why I should not be the one to go. Thank you, you've proved my point."

"Janie, don't listen to her, you may marry Garrett if you wish," Cass replied with a small laugh.

Jane tossed her hands in the air. "I do not have any intention of marrying Upton. For heaven's sake, I—"

Cass put up her hands in a conciliatory gesture. "I'm only jesting, Jane. Please. Please try. I'll have Lucy's coach put to for you. Go over there, visit him, see what he's up to. Try to find out if he truly intends to come over here. Oh, and ask him to convince Owen to stay away, too, if you please."

Jane breathed hard through her teeth. "If I go over there, I'm going to confess to everything and bribe him to keep silent. I am much more comfortable with a direct approach."

Lucy scooped up the menu again, and Cass smiled and patted Jane's hand. "Sounds divine. Use whatever means of persuasion you must."

CHAPTER THIRTEEN

Cass hugged her shawl close to her shoulders and popped open the French doors that led to the terrace. She had to get away from the group of partygoers in the house. It was a beautiful autumn evening. A bit of a chill hung in the air but the stars twinkled overhead like a row of diamonds in the black velvet sky. The smell of freshly fallen leaves whispered through the wind.

Cass glanced back into the brightly lit house. It was all so unreal. Like being trapped in a play. Everyone was calling her Miss Bunbury. She'd nearly begun to believe that was her name. With every mention of the false name, all she could think about was how she was a liar. She had to get out of there, and just breathe.

She strolled out into the night and gazed up at the stars. Then she followed a few of the stone steps down into the gardens. There were candles there, sprinkled throughout the pebbled pathways. Cass made her way to her favorite stone bench and sat down. She leaned back and took a deep breath, and then another. In addition to the leaves, the crisp air smelled of burning logs. The light wind ruffled the curls at her temples.

She squeezed her eyes shut and imagined . . . How would everything be in two weeks' time? Surely, this entire farce would be over by then. Would Julian and Pen be planning their wedding? Would Julian hate Cass for her duplicity? She shook her head and took another deep breath.

"I do hope I'm not interrupting anything." The deep male voice wafted on the cool breeze.

Cass started, and her eyes flew open, but she already knew who it was. She'd memorized his voice. Julian was standing there, not ten paces away, crushing out a cheroot beneath his boot.

"Oh, no, Ju . . . Captain Swift, not at all."

He strode closer. The candlelight highlighted the deep planes of his cheeks, glinted off his steely gray eyes. "May I?" He gestured to the bench.

Cass gulped. "Of course."

He slid onto the bench next to her, bracing his palms on the cold stone. The warmth of his body so near her own sent a shiver down her spine. There was that scent again, too, clean and strong and . . . Julian.

"Enjoying this fine weather?" he asked, shaking her from her thoughts. And just as well. Surely, he'd be suspicious if he found Miss Patience Bunbury sniffing at his coat, not that she hadn't considered it.

Cass straightened her shoulders and pulled her shawl tight. "Yes. I felt it was entirely too warm in the house just now. I do so love the outdoors."

"I do, too," Julian said. "Especially in the country. I've been waiting years to sit outside at night like this in the English countryside."

Cass nodded. *I know.* He'd mentioned it in his letters. She'd memorized them, knew each of them by heart. *"My fondest dream is to sit under the stars in the country, breathe the fresh air, and not worry about death and destruction and war."* That particular bit had been in a letter he'd written to her perhaps two years ago. It had been winter.

"The war must've been awful for you," she ventured. Of course it had been awful for him. Cass knew that. But Patience didn't. Or would she guess? *Excellent. Patience is a nitwit.*

Julian pulled his hands from the bench, braced them on his knees, and stared off into the darkened hedges. "I was one of the fortunate ones."

Cass swallowed. It still hurt to think about how close he'd come to never returning. "Because you lived?" Her voice was low, barely a whisper.

"Yes, because I came back." He paused for a moment, closed his eyes, breathed the night air. "It was not my plan."

Cass wrinkled her brow. "What do you mean?" It was not his plan? He'd never mentioned anything like that in his letters.

He opened his eyes again and shook his head. He smiled slightly but it was a smile that didn't quite reach his eyes. The one he used in ballrooms and public places where people asked him too many questions. She hated that he was using it with her. "Ah, much too grim a subject for such a festive night," he said.

"Tell me something else about yourself then," she said. She'd originally asked because Miss Bunbury wouldn't know, but the answer surprised her. What else didn't she know about Julian?

He grinned. "I'm rubbish at cards, you've already borne witness to my poor dancing skills, and I am the kingdom's most unenthusiastic hunter."

Cass blinked at him. "I didn't know that you're rubbish at cards."

He frowned.

"I mean . . . I . . . it surprises me, that's all. I thought you might have played during the war. With your men, I mean."

"The officers played, that's true, quite a lot. But I can hardly claim I won much. It was fortunate that we never played for anything valuable. Against rules, you know."

Cass closed her eyes. There *were* things about him, certain things that she didn't know, it seemed. He'd mentioned the card games with the officers in his letters. She'd always pictured him winning every hand. Now that she considered it, however, he'd never claimed as much. She dared a glance at him out of the corner of her eye. He was the man she'd loved for so long through his letters. But he was also something else, flesh and blood, real and true and sitting beside her.

"Tell me something, Miss Bunbury."

There it was again, the reminder that she was a liar. She wrapped her cloak even more tightly over her shoulders. "You've been kind enough to answer my questions, Captain Swift. I'm happy to answer one of yours."

"How are you?" His voice was soft, caring. She'd always imagined his voice like this when she'd read his letters.

She blinked and blinked again. "How . . . am I, Captain Swift?" Whatever could he mean?

"In Penelope's last letter, she told me that you'd been jilted over the summer."

Cass nearly choked. "I . . . um . . ." That was right. Pen had mentioned that she'd told Julian that Patience Bunbury had been jilted. Mr. Albatross, wasn't it? That was the reason why poor Patience needed her good friend Penelope at her side at the house party. Some friend she was, Cass thought with a bit of irony.

"I hope I haven't embarrassed you by asking the question." He gave her a small encouraging smile. It was just like Julian to ask a stranger how she was holding up. That's what Cass loved about him, his kind heart.

"No. I . . . I'm quite fine. Er, at least I will be." *Once I stop lying.* "Albus . . . er . . . Mr. Albatross. He and I didn't suit. It's for the best."

"I'm glad to hear it."

"How are you?" The words spilled from her lips more as a way to change the subject than anything else.

"Me?" There was a note of surprise in his voice.

"Yes, I'd truly like to know. It can't have been easy for you, all those years at war."

He let out a breath and ran his fingers through his hair. "It's where I belong . . . belonged. Actually, now I'm not certain where I belong."

She wrinkled her nose. "What do you mean?"

He let out a shaky laugh. "I recently learned that my brother is missing . . . in France."

She pressed a hand to her heart. "Your brother? Your brother is missing?"

"Yes. My brother is the Earl of Swifdon. He . . . he was on business in France and hasn't returned."

"I didn't know your brother was traveling," she said.

Julian furrowed his brow. "You didn't know I had a brother. How could you know he was traveling?"

She glanced away. "Oh, I . . . um. Of course not." She cleared her throat. "You said he was there on business, however. So I just assumed . . . For the Crown?"

"He . . . yes. Parliamentary business."

"And he's missing? He may be hurt?" She twisted her fingers together.

"Yes." Julian nodded.

"I'm sorry," she whispered.

"Thank you," he replied. "It's just that . . ." He looked away into the darkened hedgerow.

"Yes?" she prompted. "Please, you can tell me."

Julian groaned and dropped his chin to his chest. "I know it's selfish but I just can't help but think . . . if he doesn't come back . . . I can't . . ." He raised his head and shook it. "It doesn't matter. Forgive me for being so morose. It's unbecoming of this beautiful evening."

Cass took a deep breath, hoping he didn't see the tears shimmering in her eyes. Patience Bunbury didn't know what he would have said next, but Cass did. She knew exactly, and she longed to reach out and run her fingers through his hair, comfort him, say something to relieve his pain. But she couldn't. She clutched her shaky hands together in her lap. "I do hope your brother returns safely, Captain," was all she could offer him.

He paused for a moment, then looked up into the twinkling night sky. "May I ask you one more question, Miss Bunbury?"

Cass nodded. "Of course."

"What do you want out of life?"

She shook her head. He'd caught her off guard, surprised her. Partly because it was such an unexpected question and partly because she couldn't have imagined Julian would ask such a thing of a nearly complete stranger. But it made her nervous, too. She couldn't risk saying anything Cass might say. She must answer this question as Patience Bunbury, the woman who didn't exist. In this case, vagueness was probably best. "Oh, the same thing as most young ladies, I expect."

"Such as?" he pressed. "Forgive my impertinence, but I find since I've returned from war, I'm quite interested in knowing the answer to this question, both for myself and for others. How many people do you think truly know what they want, Miss Bunbury?"

Cass took a deep breath. That was what he was preoccupied with, the search for knowing what he wanted? Her throat clogged with tears. Julian, her Julian, had been so damaged by the war. No. He was not her Julian. He was Pen's Julian. "I don't know," she murmured. It was all she could allow herself to say. Patience Bunbury could say no more.

"So, what do you want, Miss Bunbury? Do you know?"

She glanced into the darkened foliage. *You.* Her heart screamed it.

What would Patience Bunbury say, though? "Marriage, children . . . love."

His turned his head sharply to look at her. "Love?"

She looked down at her gloved fingers. She couldn't meet his eyes. He would surely see the truth there, that they were two souls who already knew each other, knew so much about each other and had shared countless hours of secrets and thoughts. "Yes." Her voice broke on the word. "Wha . . . what do you want, Captain Swift?"

He stared at his hands and the gravel. "I want to . . ."

Cass's heart lodged in her throat. "I promise whatever you say will be held in the strictest confidence," she breathed, leaning forward, nearly on the edge of the bench. She already held many of Julian's secrets. She would never tell any of them.

He drew in a large breath. "I've had a great deal of time to think about life and what is important and I have decided that since I lived, since I returned . . ."

She nearly toppled from the bench. "Yes?"

"I want to start a fund, for soldiers, for war veterans and their families."

She tilted her head to the side, considering his words. He'd never mentioned this in his letters. "A fund?"

"Yes, especially for the injured ones, the ones who cannot work. Their lives have already been shattered by war. They deserve better than to come home to nothing."

Cass put her hand on his. "I think that's lovely."

He bent his head but did not move his hand away. "I

may not have a title, but I have friends, connections. I intend to do whatever I can to help those men."

"I'll help you, too." The words slipped from her mouth before she even had a chance to think about them. "However I can, that is."

"Thank you, Miss Bunbury." He paused for a moment. "There's one more thing, though I fear I shouldn't burden you with it."

She met his eyes then. She had to. "What's that?"

"You promise to keep it a secret?"

"Yes." She swallowed.

He gave her an intense look and for a moment, a heart-stopping moment, Cass was certain he knew her. "It's odd, but I feel as if I could tell you anything. I cannot explain it," he said. "There's only one other person on earth whom I've felt that way about."

An ache formed in Cass's chest. "Pen . . . Penelope?"

"No. My friend Lady Cassandra Monroe."

Guilt and happiness collided in Cass's belly, where guilt promptly proceeded to beat the sop out of happiness.

Cass smiled and looked away, breaking their eye contact. He didn't know her. He hadn't guessed. Oh, the guilt. *The guilt.* "I promise, Captain Swift. I won't tell your secret."

He pushed a boot through the gravel, crunching it beneath his heel. "As soon as I find Penelope, I intend to tell her I cannot marry her."

CHAPTER FOURTEEN

Cass paced in front of the windows in her bedchamber. Pacing, it seemed, was her new pastime. But if anything called for some pacing and worry, it was this latest bit of news. Julian planned to break things off with Pen? How could that be? How? Everything Cass had always known and believed seemed to be changing before her eyes. It couldn't be this easy, could it? He'd already intended to end his engagement with Pen. What did he intend to do after that? Cass hadn't had the courage to ask him. Not even as Patience Bunbury. He'd seemed so pensive, so quiet, so affected. Instead, she'd promised him his secret was safe with her and merely nodded when he'd told her he intended to break things off with Pen.

The one question she'd truly wanted to ask had died a slow death on her tongue. "Is it because of your friend Cassandra? Is that why you want to end your engagement?" But she couldn't ask that. Surely he would have wondered why she'd made that leap.

This wasn't how it was supposed to happen. Was it? Was it the answer to her prayers or the start of a nightmare? Pen? Jilted? Awful. Pen's parents would be devastated. As for Pen herself, Cass wasn't exactly certain how she would react. Her heart wouldn't be broken, that much was certain, but surely she wouldn't be pleased about being jilted by the man she'd waited seven years for. And none of this was like Julian. Julian was solid, and dependable, trustworthy to a fault. He would never hurt anyone or not hold up his end of a bargain. Something had happened to him in the last few months. He'd changed. She'd felt it in his letters but never dreamed it would be like this.

After his confession tonight, he'd quickly made his excuses and left the garden. Perhaps he thought he'd said too much to Patience Bunbury. And why had he told Patience and not Cass? He'd never hinted at anything like that in his letters to her over the summer.

And what about the news of Donald? It was unimaginable. Donald in France? Why would the earl be there? Parliamentary business, Julian had said, but that made little sense. Cass's heart wrenched at the memory of the look on Julian's face when he'd said, "If he doesn't come back . . . I can't . . ." She knew exactly what he meant. She didn't know why, he'd never said why in his letters, but she knew that Julian had always felt like the unwanted son, the unnecessary son. He felt as if he wasn't good enough to be the heir, the earl. She knew just how he felt because she'd played the same role in her family. Owen, eight years her senior, was a male, an heir. She was just a lowly female, whose only purpose lay in securing a decent match and aligning her family with another illustrious title. She'd wanted to reach out to Julian, run her fingers through his hair, comfort him, assure him that no matter what happened he could and would make his family proud. There was no possible way he could fail. As Patience Bunbury she couldn't let on that she knew anything about his deepest fears. But as Cass she could. She could and she would.

She hurried over to the writing desk against the wall

and pulled out a sheet of parchment, then she grabbed up her quill. She had a letter to write.

Thirty. Julian mentally counted off the press-ups as he did them in front of the windows of his guest chamber. Toes and palms braced against the floor, he pushed up his entire body using only the strength of his arms. Physical activity always seemed to clear his mind. He'd made a habit of doing press-ups on the nights before battles. Now that he was back in England, back in Society, he would have to do them in front of damask-covered walls on fine carpets instead of on wet, muddy, cold battlefields. Either was fine with him. As long as they still served to clear his mind.

Why had he confessed his secret to Patience Bunbury? Well, one of his secrets. He didn't even know the young woman. There was something about her, though, something besides her beauty, something that made him feel safe and content and . . . at home. It sounded ludicrous in his head even as he had the thought, but he couldn't help himself. It was true. There was something about her quiet, gentle nature, her unassuming personality, that far outshone her beauty. In her company, he felt as if he could tell her anything, everything, almost like . . . Cassandra.

Forty. He continued his exertion, his breathing coming fast and his arms burning with the strain. Normally, he welcomed the pain, tonight was no exception. It had taken him weeks to build his strength back up to be able to do this again. He gritted his teeth. Now he could only hope that Patience would keep her word and not tell Penelope what he'd said. Penelope was her friend, after all. It stood to reason that she might be tempted to tell. She'd promised him, however, and something told him she would keep that promise. But in the end, it wouldn't matter. He intended to tell Penelope himself the moment she arrived, or at the first opportunity, at least.

Something else niggled at his conscience, however. It

had been bad form to tell Miss Bunbury about his plans. The young woman had recently been jilted, after all. His confession might well have brought back those painful memories. She told him she was fine, but he had no doubt it would take a while for such a painful wound to heal. He knew all about healing wounds. Penelope had mentioned Miss Bunbury's broken engagement to him and if Penelope bothered to write, it was serious. Yes, it had been wrong of him for more than one reason to admit to Miss Bunbury that he intended to end his engagement to Penelope.

Fifty. Groaning, he let go and fell to the carpet, spent. He rolled over and scrubbed both hands across his face. Who was he? He'd once been a man who would rather take his own life than be anything other than honorable. Now, he was poised to jilt his own would-be bride.

Life. That's what it was. He'd learned the value of life lying on that bloody field outside of Waterloo. He'd learned it, and he would never forget.

A knock sounded on his bedchamber door, and Julian stopped short. He stood, strode over to the door, and yanked it open.

A footman stood at attention, two letters resting on a silver tray he held in front of him.

"I am sorry to bother you, Captain, but these arrived for you this evening."

Julian thanked the young man and flipped him a coin. The footman bowed to him. Julian pulled the letters from the tray, turned, and shut the door behind him. Recognizing Derek's bold scrawl on the first one, Julian ripped open the seal. He held his breath.

Swift,

Collin and I have arrived safely in France. Good news. We've questioned some people who heard a rumor about two Englishmen being held by the French. They think they know where the two men were taken. We're leaving in the morning to look for the camp. Don't worry. We'll be careful in case it's a trap. I'll write again as soon as I know more.

Hunt

Julian expelled his breath. Wasn't it just like Hunt to sign his letters Hunt instead of Claringdon? How long would it be before his friend got used to the fact that he was a duke? Julian smiled at the irony. He still thought of him as Hunt. How long would it be before he thought of him as Claringdon?

As for the contents of the letter, they were as good as could be expected. Hunt had a lead and was pursuing it. Julian couldn't ask for better news so soon. But, damn it. He shouldn't be here, enjoying the merriment of a country house party while God only knew what was happening to Donald and Rafe in France. *If* they were still alive, they were no doubt being held and likely tortured.

Julian crumpled the letter in his fist and tossed it into the fireplace. Wartime correspondence should be destroyed immediately.

Wait.

It wasn't wartime any longer.

Well, it was as long as Donald and Rafe weren't safe. Julian shook his head. He had to finish this nonsense with his supposed engagement and get to France to help his friends as soon as possible. Which meant no more waiting. He had to find Penelope Monroe immediately.

He turned his attention to the second letter, nearly forgotten in his grasp. He glanced down at it and sucked in his breath. It was from Cassandra.

CHAPTER FIFTEEN

Jane was ushered into the green drawing room at Garrett Upton's house the next morning. His home was nowhere near as grand as the Upbridge estate that would one day be his, but it was large and serviceable and only a few miles' ride from Lucy's house. Jane had left her maid and the groomsmen outside with the coach. This was a conversation much better held in private.

She glanced around. Upton was not yet in the room. She rolled her eyes. He was going to make her wait. Of course he was. Now how had *she* got so wrapped up in Lucy's latest scheme? She shook her head. Lucy had that way about her. The moment she got a notion in her head, she began to put it into action and the rest of them just fell into the choreographed affair that she pulled off with such aplomb. It was shocking, really.

This time, however, Jane was truly worried that Cass would end up with the bruises from this particular charade. The potential for the outcome to devastate Cass was great, something Jane doubted that Lucy had considered when she'd come up with the scheme.

Regardless, all Jane could do at this point was help,

hence her visit to Upton's lair. She had been charged with convincing Upton to either stay away or play along and she intended to accomplish her mission, one way or another.

She strode over to the wall and pulled her spectacles down her nose to get a better look at one of the portraits. Hmm. Upton. Around age twenty, she would guess. A handsome chap, she had to admit, for all that he usually drove her mad. She turned away. The last thing she wanted was to think about Upton's looks.

She took a seat on the settee in the center of the room, pulled her book from her reticule, and settled down to read. The joke was on Upton if he intended to make her anxious while she waited. As long as she had a book—and she always had a book—she didn't much mind where she was.

Her wait was not to be long, however. In the span of five minutes, Upton came strolling through the doors, his hands in his pockets, whistling as if he hadn't a care in the world. Too bad, he might be a charming chap if he wasn't so . . . Upton.

She glanced up and snapped the book shut.

His trademark nonchalant smile rested on his face. "Ah, Miss Lowndes, to what do I owe the pleasure?"

Jane gave him a long-suffering stare. "The pleasure? Really?"

He shrugged. "Would you rather I be rude?"

Jane eyed him carefully. Upton made her grit her teeth. The man was too confident by half and loved nothing better than to tease her about her bluestocking tendencies and her love of reading. In turn, she loved nothing better than to make fun of his penchant for gambling and drinking and being a general profligate scoundrel. But staring at him now, even she had to admit the picture hadn't lied. He was a good-looking man, about six feet tall, square shoulders, mahogany-brown slightly curly hair, hazel eyes that turned to dark green when he was worked up over something. Yes, Upton was handsome, which made dealing with him all that much more frustrating. Oh, ick. That was two thoughts about Upton's looks in one day. She shook her head.

"I'd rather you be honest," she retorted.

He gave her his own long-suffering stare, one that he'd no doubt perfected in her company over the years. "Let's cut to the chase, shall we, Miss Lowndes?"

She raised her chin. "By all means."

"Fine, then, I'll save you some time."

"Please do, Upton, I'm quite busy today."

He smirked at her. "Busy ripping gentlemen to shreds with your barbs or simply busy reading and educating yourself far beyond the boundaries of propriety?"

"Oh, both, Upton. I have a full day planned. Of course, you wouldn't know a thing about the joy of reading, having never finished a book in your life, but I assure you, it's every bit as taxing as gambling, drinking, and chasing ladies of ill repute. Just in an entirely different way."

He gave her a slight mock bow. "Ah, off to a fine start shredding gentlemen with your tongue. Well done. It's not even noon. But I must ask, how exactly do you know so much about gambling, drinking, and chasing ladies of ill repute?"

Her smile did not falter. "I read. A lot."

They glared at each other.

"My dear Miss Lowndes," he finally choked out. "I believe you are here because I have become aware that you, my cousin Lucy, and our good friend Cassandra are even now ensconced at Upbridge Hall at a questionable house party where Lucy and Cass are pretending to be people they are not."

Jane opened her mouth to retort. Upton held up a hand to stop her. "Allow me to finish, please."

She snapped her mouth shut.

"Not only are you doing that, but you've involved my friend Lord Berkeley in your scandalous behavior."

She opened her mouth again.

Garrett wagged a finger. "I'm not finished."

She shut her mouth.

"And finally, I happen to know that this entire scheme is one that is extremely ill-advised. Do you care to know *how* I know that?"

More glaring from Jane. She crossed her arms over her chest and tapped her slipper along the rug. "Oh, do tell. I'm on tenterhooks." She managed a fake yawn.

He continued undaunted. "Because first, you did not invite me, which means you did not want me to know about it. If you did not want me to know about it, it is because you're all doing something you should not be doing and knew I would not play along."

He paused to solicit her reaction. She merely shrugged. It would be a frigid day in Hades before she gave Upton the satisfaction of knowing he was right. About anything.

"Secondly," he continued. "Lucy and Cassandra are using assumed names, and while I admire Lucy's vivid imagination and flair for the dramatic, I can only imagine what sort of nonsense involves false names."

Jane merely rolled her eyes this time.

"Thirdly, without exactly coming out and saying as much, Lucy has intimated to me that she may or may not be with child. Lucy's never not just come out and said anything in her life. If she's being subtle, it's not true, and if it's not true, I must ask myself why she wants me to believe it's true."

Jane pressed her lips together and blinked at him. She had heard of people playing cards and keeping their faces completely blank in an effort to keep their opponent from guessing at their hand. She had tried it with Lady Hoppington upon occasion during one of that matron's infamous rounds of whist. But she'd never been quite certain if it had worked. At the moment, however, Jane so hoped she was doing an admirable job of keeping her hand secret.

"Finally," Upton continued. "*You* have arrived upon my doorstep. And seeing as how you'd rather be boiled in oil like one of the martyrs than voluntarily seek out my company, I can only assume you have been sent by Lucy to ensure my compliance with your charade or to ask that I stay away." He flashed a grin at her. "Am I right?"

Jane had whisked off her gloves to contemplate her fingernails. "Oh, are you finished? I'd stopped paying attention quite a while ago." She smiled at him tightly.

"I'm finished. Now, answer my question."

Confound it. Upton was too wise by half. The man knew exactly what they were up to. He'd been Lucy's cousin and close friend her entire life; no doubt nothing she did surprised him. Blast Cass for sending her on this doomed mission.

Jane took a deep breath and straightened her shoulders. "It is true that Lucy is hosting a house party at Upbridge Hall and that Berkeley has been invited."

Upton paced around her, making her bristle. He was too close. She could smell his cologne and it smelled . . . not unpleasant.

"What I cannot figure out," he said, "is why you're doing it. Why would you say Cass is someone named Patience Bunbury and Lucy is Lady Worthing?"

Jane turned and stared him straight in the eye. "You got one thing wrong, Upton. *I* am also pretending to be someone I'm not. Miss Wollstonecraft." She ignored his deeply sarcastic look. "As for why we are doing it . . . it's for fun. You know all about fun, Upton, don't you? Or isn't being a drunken rake much fun these days?"

He arched a brow at her. "I'll ignore that."

"Please don't."

"No matter. I intend to find out exactly what you're all up to when I arrive at the house party tonight."

Jane struggled to keep her face blank. She closed one eye and pressed a fingertip to her eyebrow. "I beg your pardon?"

"I said I intend to come over and see for myself."

"You're not invited." Hmm. Perhaps not particularly brilliant, but they were the first words that came to mind.

He gave her another long-suffering look. "Aren't I?"

"No."

"Given the fact that Upbridge Hall is my inheritance, I have a feeling the servants may well let me in the front door."

"You cannot come." Oops, her voice had gone a bit too high there. Unfortunate, that.

He paused and leaned over the back of the settee. He was far too close to breathing down her neck. And his breath was giving her . . . oh, holy . . . gooseflesh.

"Give me one good reason," he breathed.

Jane scrambled for an answer. Why indeed could the man not come to his own cousin's party being hosted in a home he would one day own? She decided it best to switch tactics. She stood and paced away from him, desperately needing to put space between them. She had to restore her equilibrium. When she'd gone a safe enough distance, she turned to face him and narrowed her eyes on him. "Why do you want to come?"

Garrett straightened and resumed his pacing. "To see what you're up to, of course, and to hopefully stop it before it gets too far out of hand."

Too late. Jane took a deep breath. Oh, this was going to get ugly. Quite ugly, indeed. There was no help for it. Desperate times . . . "Very well, Upton. What do you want to stay away? Name your price."

CHAPTER SIXTEEN

The next morning, Cass took her watercolors and palette down to the conservatory. She hadn't painted in an age. The activity always relaxed her. It was the only thing she did for propriety's sake that she truly enjoyed. She adored staring at objects, considering their lines, making them come to life on a canvas using only a brush. It soothed her, made her forget her troubles. And that's exactly what she intended, to forget everything she'd heard last night from Julian, specifically his confession that he intended to end things with Pen.

She glanced about at the lovely scene in front of her. Flowers were her particular favorite things to paint. Well, flowers and birds. But birds tended to have a pesky habit of flying away, and Lady Hoppington's half-addled parrot had said one too many inappropriate things to her. Some of them in French.

Today, Cass had chosen an orchid as her subject. The soft scent of the flower floated through the slightly humid air in the room. She'd taken a seat on a little iron bench several paces away from the plant and was happily engaged in re-creating its delicate purple petals when Julian found her.

"There you are, Miss Bunbury."

Cass nearly dropped her paintbrush. She grappled with it, caught it, and set it down on the small table she'd asked the footmen to set up next to her. She hastily smoothed her hands over her hair, hoping she didn't get any paint streaks through it. So much for forgetting her troubles.

"Good . . . good morning, Captain Swift."

He bowed to her. "I hope I didn't startle you again. I seem to have a nasty habit of doing so."

"No, no, not at all." She smiled in reply.

"May I?" He gestured to the painting.

Cass's breath caught in her throat. He wanted to see what she'd painted? Caught off guard, all she could do was nod.

Julian came around behind her and braced his hands on the back of the iron bench. The heat of his large body radiated toward her. She could smell his scent, his usual mix of soap and the barest hint of that cologne that made her senses tingle. He tilted his head, staring at the painting. "Excellent."

A small sliver of pride shot through her. "Thank you," she murmured.

"The color is perfect. Did you mix it yourself?" He sounded truly interested in her work.

"Yes. It's something I like to do."

"My sister has been known to paint. I don't think she's nearly as accomplished, however."

Cass concentrated on wiping the paint from her fingers with a bit of linen. "Daphne?"

"Yes. You didn't say. Have you ever met her?"

Cass kept her eyes trained on her hands. Cass would be a complete cake to pretend she didn't know Daphne. But Patience Bunbury didn't know her. "I'm not certain I've had the pleasure, Captain." *Liar. Liar. Liar.*

He laughed softly at that. "If you'd met Daphne, I've a feeling you'd remember her, Miss Bunbury. I love her dearly but my sister is a bit—shall I say—unconventional?"

Now that was true, though Cass had always greatly enjoyed Daphne's company. One never knew quite what one might hear when Daphne was about. She was unexpected in that way, very much like Lucy. Cass searched for something to say that would not involve more lies. "I'm certain your sister is lovely and accomplished, Captain."

He glanced back at the painting and pointed a finger. "You paint nearly as well as my friend," he continued. "In fact, this reminds me of her work."

Cass mentally cursed herself. She was an idiot. Why had she let him see her painting? She'd sent him paintings before, small bits of watercolors she'd created over the years, drawings. Anything to cheer him, anything that could be neatly folded and included in her letters to him. He'd seen her hand before. She stared up at him, her heart lodged in her throat. Had he guessed? It was an innocuous painting of an orchid but it wouldn't take much to know the lines, the texture.

"Who?" she asked, holding her breath. He'd had to have received her letter—Cass's letter—by now and read it. But he wouldn't mention it to Patience Bunbury. No, of course not.

Julian stared at the painting for a few more moments, then he shook himself. "It doesn't matter. I came here to ask for your help, actually."

She pointed at herself. "My help?"

He nodded. "Yes."

"How could I ever be of help to you, Captain Swift?" She glanced away. *Perhaps I could begin by telling you the truth.*

He straightened up and came around to the front of

the bench to face her. "I must find Penelope as soon as possible."

"I know." She could *not* look at him.

"I was hoping you'd attempt to write to her, to ask her when she intends to arrive."

Cass's mouth fell open. "Oh, I couldn't. I . . . I wouldn't know where to begin. I don't know how I'd get a letter to Penelope. She's traveling."

"Yes, I know that, but I thought perhaps you might know where she is. You mentioned that she was stopping to see friends. Do you know where? Which friends she might be visiting?"

Cass dabbed her handkerchief to her forehead. Was it hot in the conservatory all of a sudden? A stabbing headache had begun behind her right eye. "I'm not certain. I—"

"Please, won't you help me, Miss Bunbury? It's imperative I speak to Penelope as soon as possible. I'm out of options."

Cass wanted to die. Here was Julian, begging for her help. Not only could she not help him, she would be deceiving him even more if she allowed him to think that she could. But she also couldn't say no to him. She cleared her throat. "I'll see what I can do, Captain Swift."

He smiled. "Thank you."

Julian strode away and Cass busily set about putting away her painting supplies. Julian wanted her help in finding Penelope as soon as possible? Cass had to find Lucy. It was time to end this farce.

CHAPTER SEVENTEEN

Five minutes later, Cass spotted Lucy in the blue drawing room. She and Jane sat across from each other, Jane with a book in her lap, Lucy sipping tea and perusing one of her ever-present lists.

Lucy glanced up as soon as Cass came into the room. "Ah, Cass, there you are. Sit down. Jane was just telling me something I do not want to hear. You might as well hear it, too."

Cass made her way over to the settee and took a seat. "There's something I must tell you, also," Cass insisted.

"Let Jane tell us her news first," Lucy replied. "It's about Garrett."

Garrett? Was Garrett coming? Cass's plan to tell Lucy they must tell the truth could wait a moment. She nodded her assent.

"Go ahead," Lucy prompted Jane as soon as Cass was settled. "Repeat what you just said to me."

Jane took a deep breath and squared her shoulders. "Upton is coming."

Cass blinked. "He's coming?"

Lucy nodded. "That's right."

Jane nodded, too. "Yes."

Cass made a whimpering noise in the back of her throat. "But Jane, we sent you over there to keep him from coming. What happened?"

Jane sighed. "It's not as simple as it sounds, you know. Upton can be quite stubborn. He insisted. However, the good news is that he's agreed to play along."

Cass let her shoulders sag. "How did you manage to convince him to do that?"

Jane pushed up her chin. "I'd really rather not say."

Cass and Lucy eyed Jane askance.

Jane pulled her spectacles from her nose and polished them using the fabric of her gown. "Very well. I merely told him that Cass is to be known as Patience Bunbury and you are Lady Worthing and I am Miss Wollstonecraft and he agreed."

"Just like that?" Lucy asked, skepticism dripping from her voice.

Jane shrugged. "There *may* have been a bit of bribery. By the way, Luce, he doesn't believe for a moment that you're expecting a baby."

Lucy wrinkled her nose. "Harrumph."

Cass leaned her head against the back of the settee and rubbed her temples. The headache was back, stabbing at her with a vengeance. This time it carried an ice pick. "But *why* is he coming?"

Jane shrugged. "Apparently, he wants to see for himself that we're not doing anything overly scandalous or illegal."

Lucy rolled her eyes. "Oh, that's just preposterous."

"Is it?" Jane gave her a knowing look.

Lucy harrumphed again.

Cass took a deep breath. She wanted to tell her friends that Julian planned to end things with Pen but she couldn't. She'd promised Julian she would tell no one, and while she might be a liar in one way, she refused to be a liar in another. She would keep her promise to Julian.

"It doesn't matter about Garrett because I came in here to insist that we stop this charade entirely."

Lucy blinked. "Now?"

"Now?"

"What's happened?" Jane asked.

Cass took a deep breath. "Julian asked me to write a letter to Pen today, to get her to the house party as soon as possible."

Lucy's and Jane's eyes went wide.

"What?" Jane asked.

"You can't do that," Lucy said, abandoning her list.

"Of course I can't do that," Cass agreed. "But he asked me to. He needs to speak to her . . . immediately."

"Why?" Lucy blinked again.

"I cannot say." Cass squeezed shut her eyes. She refused to continue lying. Lying spread like a disease. Once you began, you had to keep at it to cover up the other lies. No, she wouldn't do it. Lucy and Jane would just have to accept the fact that she was keeping a secret from them.

"Can't say or won't?" Jane asked, placing her spectacles back upon her nose.

"Can't." Cass nodded. "And won't. Julian asked me to keep it secret."

"But he told you?" Lucy's eyes were wide.

"Yes," Cass replied.

"Oh, that's excellent." Lucy clapped her hands. "He's confiding in you. I knew this would work."

Cass rubbed her temples again. "You are absolutely mad, you know that? I fail to see how any of this is good news."

"It's good news in Lucy Hunt's head," Jane replied with a knowing smile.

"No. No," Lucy insisted. "Don't you see? If Julian is confiding in Cass, er, Patience, it means he trusts her. He's getting close to her. It's just what we wanted."

Cass groaned. "Oh, Lucy. What am I going to say to him? I can't write to Pen, and I refuse to tell him that I've done so. We must end this."

Jane retrieved her book. "What did you say when he asked?"

Cass bit her lip. "I was vague. I didn't promise anything. I pointed out that Penelope is traveling and that getting a letter to her would be difficult."

Lucy was already deep in thought, tapping her finger against her cheek. "Good. Good. For now just tell him you're trying to determine where she might be. I'll think of something."

"Didn't you hear what I said?" Cass replied. "We must tell Julian the truth. Now."

"We can't do that, not now. Not when we're so close and we're making headway," Lucy said.

"Headway?" Cass stared at Lucy as if she'd lost her mind. "What headway?"

"Why, you just said that Julian has confided in you . . . I mean, Patience," Jane pointed out.

"You truly think I should continue this madness, Janie?"

Jane wrinkled her nose, her spectacles wobbling. "I can't say I agreed with beginning it in the first place but it does seem as if we may want to allow it to play out a bit more."

Cass plopped onto the sofa, her breath leaving her in a solid whoosh. "You've both gone mad and now Garrett is apparently coming."

"That reminds me," Jane said. "Upton also wanted to know where Claringdon is while his wife is getting up to obvious trouble."

Lucy made another disgruntled noise. "As if I need a husband to keep an eye on me."

"I told him Claringdon left for the Continent," Jane said. "I think Upton's quite convinced we're in need of a man over here."

"As I said, preposterous," Lucy retorted, crossing her arms over her chest, a frown etched across her face.

"Isn't it?" Jane agreed.

Cass sighed. "Please just tell me he didn't say anything about Owen?"

"Nothing, and Owen wasn't there," Jane replied.

"Thank God for that, at least," Lucy added.

"There's just one thing. Doesn't Upton know Captain Swift?" Jane asked.

"Yes." Lucy nodded. "They served together in the army years ago."

"He insisted he go by his own name," Jane added.

"Did you tell him Julian is here?" Lucy ventured.

Jane shook her head. "No. I left that part out. I knew he'd ask questions I couldn't answer."

"Probably for the best," Lucy said.

Cass pressed her temples harder. Her friends had gone mad, that was all there was to it. They'd gone mad and so, perhaps, had she because she was actually listening to them. "What are we going to do when Garrett asks those questions when he arrives?"

Lucy flourished a hand in the air. "You'll just have to explain it to him, Cass."

Cass sat up straight and blinked. "Me?"

"Yes, you," Lucy replied.

"Why me?" Cass asked.

Lucy rolled her eyes. "He'll play along if you ask him to."

Cass stared back at her. "What? Why do you say that?"

Lucy expelled her breath. "I thought it had been obvious for quite some time now. Are you telling me you truly don't know?"

"Know what?" Jane narrowed her eyes on her friend.

"That Garrett's been madly in love with Cass for an age, of course."

CHAPTER EIGHTEEN

Madness, it seemed, was ever so difficult to extract oneself from, Cass decided. Garrett arrived after dinner. The small party was playing cards in the gold drawing room. When a footman announced her cousin, Lucy excused herself. She rushed out to the foyer where she apparently spoke with Garrett. By the time he swept into the room to join the others, he had a wide smile on his face and a twinkle in his eyes. Cass said a silent prayer.

Garrett played his role to perfection. He greeted the room's occupants with a friendly zeal and called everyone by their assumed names with decided aplomb. He clapped Lord Berkeley on the back and seemed positively delighted to call Lucy Lady Worthing. Cass watched him warily, still praying.

When he came to the table where she was playing cards with Jane, he bowed over Cass's hand. "Miss Bunbury, a pleasure."

"Mr. Upton."

"Miss Wollstonecraft." He nodded to Jane. "You're looking quite scholarly this evening."

Jane narrowed her eyes on him but merely replied with a tepid, "Mr. Upton."

Cass glanced at her. It was completely unlike Jane to remain silent at one of Garrett's barbs and she rarely gave him the honor of putting *mister* in front of his name. *Upton* was usually as much as she could manage.

Garrett nodded to both ladies and continued his tour of the room. Cass watched him carefully. He greeted Julian with a handshake. "Glad to see you made it home, Captain."

Julian stood and clapped Garrett on the back. "Glad to be home, Upton."

Garrett soon settled down at a game himself. Cass watched him for a different reason this time: any sign of his supposed love for her. Lucy must be mad. Why, Garrett had shown her nothing but brotherly concern her entire life. She'd never once got the notion that he felt anything other than friendship. Lucy, however, was quite convinced, and once Lucy was convinced of something, there was no dissuading her from it.

Jane had quickly excused herself from the room, not saying a word, obviously not even interested in giving her opinion on the ridiculous matter. Lucy had gone on to emphasize to Cass how certain she was and assured her that she had nothing to worry about as long as she had a talk with Garrett herself. He would do anything for her.

It didn't make Cass feel any less uneasy. She wasn't about to use Garrett for her purposes. No. Garrett was her friend, and she would ask him the truth. It was high time she became more forthright. And there was no time like the present.

Cass excused herself from her card game and made her way to the library. She sat at the writing desk in the corner and took out a sheet of parchment and a quill.

She quickly scribbled a note for Garrett. Then she found a passing footman and asked him to deliver it posthaste.

Garrett arrived minutes later. He strolled into the room looking handsome and friendly and smiling as usual. She'd always liked Garrett a great deal. Just like his cousin, he was fun and funny and friendly and loyal. He was a wonderful man, but certainly not someone she could see herself falling in love with. She hoped Lucy was wrong and that Garrett did not have feelings for her. She would never want to hurt her friend by refusing him.

He bowed to her. "Miss Bunbury," he said, a grin on his face.

Cass returned his smile. "Please, sit," she offered, patting the chair next to her.

Garrett made his way over and took a seat.

"How is Aunt Mary?" Cass asked, referring to his mother. She was officially Lucy's aunt, not Cass's, but Cass had spent last summer with the lovely woman in Bath and referred to her as Aunt Mary now, too.

"Busy and active as ever," Garrett replied.

"I'm glad to hear it. Please give her my best." Cass paused, then clutched the arms of the rosewood chair in which she sat. "Thank you so much for coming, Garrett. And for . . . you know?"

He grinned at her. "Of course I came. Though I must admit, I'm hoping you'll give me an explanation for your recent name change. Dare I guess it has something to do with the appearance of one Captain Swift?"

Cass bit her lip and glanced away. "Yes. It does."

"Ah, how did I know? And is he not the same man you've been in love with for many years?"

Garrett didn't seem the least bit jealous saying those words. Surely Lucy was wrong. Besides, Garrett had known Cass was in love with Julian since she'd met him.

She nodded. "Yes. Yes, he is."

Garrett narrowed his eyes on her. "Then, why, pray tell, would you want him to think your name is Patience Bunbury? And forgive me for asking another rather obvious question, but hasn't he met you before?"

Cass tugged at her gloves. She might as well buy new gloves, these were hopelessly stretched. "The reason for the name change is quite a long story, but it turns out he didn't remember me. Or how I look, at least. It's been many years."

Garrett's grin widened. "I see. As for the long story, it's one involving Lucy, I'm sure."

"Yes. It was Lucy's idea."

Garrett stretched his long legs out in front of him and sighed. "Again, how did I know?"

"That's why I asked you here, Garrett. Will you please continue to play along, without an explanation? For now?" She waited a moment. "For me?" That last part made her wince.

"I'd already told Miss Lowndes I would. Didn't she report back?"

"She did. But now that you're here, I just wanted to make certain. Between the two of us."

Garrett nodded. "Don't worry. I will not go back on my word. I'm not certain what you all are up to, but I do want to caution you, Cassandra. Be careful. Lucy can get the best of us into schemes we'd rather not participate in. Lord knows she's done it before."

"I'm far gone into this one, I'm afraid," Cass replied, still tugging on the ends of her gloves.

"You're feeling a bit guilty, aren't you?" Garrett's voice softened.

Cass let her hands fall into her lap. "Yes. I am, ever so much. I feel just awful." She was treating Garrett as if he were the priest and she, the confessor. But it was so freeing to admit how dreadful she felt about all the lies.

He patted her on the back. Nothing but a brotherly pat, she was certain of it. "There, there," he said. "It's not easy to say no to Lucy."

"What am I going to do?" Cass shook her head. "I don't know why I ever agreed to it. Lucy introduced me to Julian as Patience and I didn't correct her and— Oh, he is going to hate me when he finds out."

"Have you thought about telling him the truth? Just coming out with it?" Garrett asked.

Cass nodded frantically. "It's all I can think about. Oh, Garrett, do you know what it's like to feel such guilt?"

Garrett was silent for a moment. Cass raised her head and looked at him. He sat up straight and stared off into the fireplace. "Yes," he replied simply. "I learned all about guilt. Twice."

Cass turned to him. "Twice," she echoed in a whisper.

"The first time was when I was eleven years old, and my uncle looked at me with hate in his eyes."

Cass gasped. "Because Ralph died?"

Garrett nodded.

Ralph was Lucy's older brother. He'd died when he was nine years old and Lucy was seven. Both children had had fever but only Lucy had recovered. Garrett's father was next in line for the inheritance of the earldom, which meant, as an only son, Garrett would eventually inherit the title and properties meant for his dead cousin. Lucy had often spoken about how angry and bitter it had made her father.

"I'm so sorry, Garrett. I cannot imagine how awful that would be," Cass said quietly.

Garrett shook his head. "The second time was on a battlefield in Spain. And that, that was much, much worse."

Cass sucked in her breath. Lucy had once alluded to something horrible that had happened to Garrett during the war, something that had made him come home and never return. He'd been injured, somehow, or at least that was what everyone had assumed. He'd been in the army then, met Derek Hunt and Julian at that time. But Cass had never heard the details about what happened and she was too shy to ask. She stared at him, trying to screw up the courage to ask now. But she just couldn't. If Garrett wanted to share that story, he would. She waited with bated breath. Oh, why couldn't she be Patience Bunbury right now? Patience would be bold enough to ask.

He glanced back at her and the solemn, serious look on his face was quickly replaced by his irrepressible grin. "Yes, Cassandra. I know a great deal about guilt and here is my advice."

She scooted forward until she sat on the edge of her seat, staring at him, waiting for his words. "Yes?"

"If there's any way you can dispel it, do so, as quickly as possible." He looked her in the eye. His hazel eyes had turned a dark mossy green. "Otherwise, it will destroy you."

Cass nearly fell out of her seat. Garrett, fun-loving, happy Garrett, she'd never seen him like this. But something told her he was quite serious and quite right. "You think I should tell Julian the truth?"

"At your first opportunity," Garrett breathed.

Cass nodded. "I know. You're right. I want to. I—"

Garrett narrowed his eyes on her. "But you're not going to, are you?"

Cass bit her lip and glanced away. "You don't know how much I want to." She couldn't look at him. If she weren't such a coward, she would have asked him what happened in Spain. If she weren't such a coward, she would ask him if he felt something other than brotherly love for her. If she weren't such a coward, she would tell Julian the truth. In fact, if she weren't such a coward, she never would have allowed herself to be trapped in this untenable position to begin with.

"Thank you, Garrett," was all she said. "I truly value your advice."

He nodded.

She took an unsteady breath and searched her mind for something simple to say to restore their usual lighthearted camaraderie. "Tell me, what did Jane promise you to get you to agree? Lucy and I are absolutely on tenterhooks to find out."

Garrett's grin returned in full force. "She promised me that she would keep her mouth shut and not barb me during the house party. I'd say that's worth any amount of playacting. In fact, I wasn't entirely certain I was coming, but I couldn't pass up such an opportunity."

CHAPTER NINETEEN

Julian had been standing with his back against the cool marble wall in the corridor outside the library wondering where he might find Miss Bunbury. He'd already checked the terrace and the conservatory with no luck. The library door swung open and Garrett Upton strode out of the room.

Julian narrowed his eyes on Upton. He'd have to question the chap later about his possible involvement with Cassandra. Why did that thought make him jealous? But his next thought made him jealous, too. Was Miss Bunbury in the library? Had she been speaking to Upton privately?

Julian strode over to the door to the library and stepped inside.

It was dark in the room. Only a brace of candles stood on a small table in the far corner. He squinted, adjusting his eyes to the dimness.

"Miss Bunbury?" he ventured.

"Yes," a small voice answered.

She was here. She had been speaking to Upton. "Seems you and I are drawn to the same locations. I do hope you are not beginning to believe I am following you. Though I must admit that I was seeking your company this evening." He smiled at her.

He could see her now. Sitting on the settee in the center of the room, she smiled back at him. "I believe you, Captain Swift."

"Do you mind if I join you?" he asked.

"Please do." She gestured to the open space next to her.

He made his way over and sat beside her. "Did I see Mr. Upton leaving the room a few moments ago?"

The unspoken question hung in the air. *What were the two of you doing in here together?*

"Yes, we spoke briefly." It looked as if she'd winced. "I do hope you don't think it overly forward of me to have been speaking alone to a man in the library," she murmured. "But we seem to be doing the same thing ourselves now, aren't we?"

Julian clenched his jaw. She was right. And he had no cause to judge her or doubt her intentions when he was forcing his company upon her now as well. For all he knew, that's what Upton had done. Why was Upton making him jealous all of a sudden? "Do you know him? I mean, have you met him before?" What in God's name had made him ask that question?

She shook her head. Was that another wince? "No. He'd just come in here looking for a book to read before bed. I think he left because he didn't want to disturb me." She glanced away.

"I do hope I'm not disturbing you," Julian said.

"Not at all," Miss Bunbury replied. "I just wanted to be somewhere a bit more quiet for a few moments. I don't much like large crowds."

"Neither do I."

"I know."

He squinted at her. "What was that?"

She cleared her throat. "Oh?"

"I want to apologize to you, Miss Bunbury," he continued.

She turned to look at him. "Whatever for?"

"For burdening you with my secret last night. It was extremely ill-mannered of me. I apologize."

She bit her lip. "Captain Swift, I haven't written to Penelope. I—"

He nodded. "I understand. I shouldn't have asked you to. Another attempt to burden you with my problems. Please accept my apology."

She smiled at that. "No need to apologize, Captain. And I do hope you believe that I have no intention of telling anyone . . . what you told me about Penelope . . . or your brother."

"Thank you for that, Miss Bunbury. You are very kind. Especially given that it may have been difficult to hear of a broken engagement, considering your circumstances. As for my brother, I . . ." His thoughts flashed back to the letter from Cassie, the one she'd sent last night. Apparently, she was not in the country. She'd returned to London for some reason. She said she looked forward to seeing him and she'd heard that Donald was missing and might be in danger. Julian wasn't certain how she'd found out.

"I know you're worried, Julian," her letter had read. *"I know you love him, you miss him, and I pray that he comes back safe and sound. But I also know that you're thinking you can't do it, fill his shoes if it comes to that. And I want you to know that you can. You will. I have every confidence in you."*

Cassie, as always, had got right to the heart of his deepest fear and she'd reassured him. It was just what he'd needed to hear, right when he'd needed to hear it. And it had come from Cassie. Cassie, whom he missed.

Cassie, whom he'd yet to see since he'd returned. She was more than a friend. She was . . .

In love with another man. Possibly Upton. That's why Upton was making him so blasted angry this evening.

"You needn't explain, Captain Swift," Miss Bunbury said, rousing him from his thoughts. "May I ask you something? Something a bit . . . forward?"

He inclined his head and grinned at her. "I think it's only fair."

She took a deep breath. "What made you decide you do not want to become engaged?"

She'd surprised him. He remained silent for a few moments before answering. "The truth is, Miss Bunbury, I pray you do not think me a scoundrel, but I find myself thinking quite a great deal about another lady."

Cass couldn't breathe. Another lady? Had she heard him correctly? Julian was in love with another lady. Another lady. Not Pen. Could it be? It had to be . . . her. Cass! Who else could it be? He'd never mentioned anyone else in any of his letters. She struggled to keep her face blank. "I don't think you're a scoundrel at all, Captain Swift." Her stays were cutting into her lungs. She felt hot, cold, dizzy. "I understand, actually. My parents have been pushing me to marry gentlemen I don't want to for years."

"Ah, so you do understand?" he replied.

"More than you know," she whispered.

"Please don't mistake me. I've absolutely nothing but respect for Miss Monroe. It's just that . . . We don't know each other very well—at all, really, and there's . . . someone else, whom I've come to know quite well. Through her letters . . ."

Cass closed her eyes, fighting back tears. It *was* her. It was. And now she would have to tell him the truth and only hope that he didn't hate her. She would tell him her name, fall to her knees and beg him to forgive her. But first, she had to be certain. "Does this woman know you, you . . . care for her?"

Julian cracked a smile. "Actually, no. Not yet. I haven't told her anything. I felt it best to end my affiliation with Penelope first."

Cass nodded. That was so like Julian, ensuring he did the correct things in the correct manner.

He leaned forward and braced his elbows on his knees. "And now, I'm not certain that I'm going to tell her."

Cass's brows snapped together. Not certain? Why wasn't he certain? "You do not expect the lady to return your affection?"

Julian let his head fall into his hands and scrubbed one fist through his burnished hair. "No."

Cass stopped breathing. "No?" she echoed.

"I attempted to visit her when I was in London. And I learned . . . I discovered . . ."

Cass's heart was nearly thumping out of her chest. It was painful. "What?" The word was barely a whisper.

Julian shook his head. "It seems she's in love with another man."

CHAPTER TWENTY

Cass swallowed and swallowed again. Tears burned the backs of her eyes. She couldn't breathe.

It wasn't her.

He wasn't talking about her. He couldn't be. She hadn't seen him in London, not as Cass, and she obviously wasn't in love with another man. Julian couldn't possibly think that about her. She'd never mentioned it in her letters, and her parents weren't in London. They couldn't have been the ones to tell him such nonsense. No. No. Julian was talking about someone else entirely, some other woman. Some other woman he cared about and had been writing to, all the time he'd been writing to her solely as a friend. A woman he'd never seen fit to mention to her. Cass was going to vomit. She had to get away.

"I'm . . . I'm ever so sorry to hear that," she murmured, biting the inside of her cheek to keep from crying.

"It's all right. I shouldn't have expected that she would wait for me all these years."

"No, I . . . I don't suppose—" Her voice cracked. She didn't care if she seemed rude. She had to leave before she broke down sobbing, wrapped her arms around his ankle, told him she was Cass, and begged him to love her. That would be very, very bad form. No. Better to leave with a shred of dignity. Perhaps she might be able to see him again. Perhaps she might be able to look at him, but right now, while her heart was breaking, she had to get away. Had to.

"I'm sorry, Captain Swift, but I fear that I'm . . . unable to . . ." She stood and ran from the room. She could hear Julian's calls, asking after her health, if he might be of assistance, but she just couldn't stop. Tears streamed down her face, tears she couldn't let him see. Better to allow him to think she was mad or sick or both.

She ran out of the library, down the corridor, and up the main staircase. A few of the servants watched as she flew past. If they thought she seemed overwrought running through the halls, she didn't care. She ran up the marble staircase and down the long corridor to her bedchamber. She didn't stop until she landed squarely on her bed, where she let the wrenching sobs rack her entire body.

Cass cried for exactly ten minutes. She hugged a pillow against her face and bawled like a child whose Christmastide stocking was empty. Then she sat up, dried her eyes with a handkerchief she retrieved from her reticule, and stared. She crossed her arms over her chest and contemplated the wall. It occurred to her then. She was tired of crying. She'd cried the entire time she'd thought Julian was dying. She'd cried for hours, days, weeks. She'd cried and cried, and when she'd known he was coming back to marry Pen and would be forever lost to her, she'd cried more. And now, she realized, staring at the shadowy wallpaper in the darkness, she was quite through with crying. Patience Bunbury wouldn't cry like this, would she?

She rang for her maid. The young woman appeared in the doorway, minutes later. "Maria, please send a message to the duchess and Miss Lowndes. Tell them I must see them as soon as possible."

"Yes, my lady," Maria said, hurrying away to do as she asked.

Yes. Cass was finished with crying. She was going to take action, just what Patience Bunbury would do. She had a plan.

Fifteen minutes later, Lucy and Jane hurried into Cass's bedchamber. "What is it, dear?" Lucy asked, flying over to her bed and pushing Cass's curls back from her face to look at her.

"It's Julian," Cass replied, wiping away the last remnant of tears.

"Oh, no, what happened?" Lucy asked.

Jane watched her closely, a sympathetic look on her face. "Tell us, Cass."

Cass straightened her shoulders. "Julian told me tonight he cares for someone else. Someone other than Penelope."

Jane's brow furrowed. "Not Penelope?"

"No." Cass's voice was calm.

"Who?" Lucy asked, looking equally confused.

"I don't know. It doesn't matter," Cass replied. "I just know it's not me . . . Cass, and it's not Penelope."

"I don't understand, dear," Lucy said. "Is it Patience?"

"No."

"Who, then?" Jane asked, her hands splayed upward in a question.

"I don't know," Cass replied. "But whoever she is, she apparently doesn't return his affection. He said so."

"He said that?" Lucy asked.

"Yes," Cass replied. "At first it made me cry. Now it's making me angry."

Jane's eyebrows shot up. "Angry?"

"Yes. Angry. Angry enough to do something about it."

Lucy's different-colored eyes scanned her face. "What do you mean?"

Cass gritted her teeth. "I mean I need a plan."

"A plan?" Jane echoed.

"Yes." Cass nodded resolutely. "When I thought that I'd be breaking up Julian and Pen, I was racked with guilt. I felt absolutely awful. She may not love him, that's true, but still, she's my cousin and they are intended for each other."

"Yes, dear, and . . ." Lucy prompted.

"Now I am without guilt. Oh, I still have guilt about lying to Julian about who I am, but I have no more guilt about taking him away from Pen. He doesn't seem to want Pen. And I know Pen doesn't want him."

"What else did he say?" Jane prompted.

Cass took a deep breath. She would not reveal Julian's secret that he intended to break things off with Pen. It was enough to tell her friends that he had feelings for someone else, some unknown woman whom Cass wanted to throttle.

"It doesn't matter. All that matters is, if Pen doesn't return his affection and this other woman is in love with someone else, why should I not try to make him love me?"

"You as Patience or you as Cass?" Lucy asked.

"Both!" Cass replied with a wide smile.

"This is so complicated." Lucy sighed, tapping her finger against her cheek.

"No thanks to you," Jane pointed out, nudging Lucy with her elbow.

Lucy gave her a mock-angry look.

Cass took a deep breath. "As long as Julian intended to marry Pen for love, I knew I couldn't be with him, not really. But now, nothing is standing in my way. I feel no guilt whatsoever fighting for Julian with this unknown lady."

Lucy squeezed her hand. "What do you plan to do, Cass?"

Cass pushed herself into an upright position. "Why, I'm going to be bold. You taught me that, Luce."

Lucy and Jane exchanged worried glances.

Jane searched Cass's face. "What exactly do you intend to do?"

Cass let a giant smile spread across her face from ear to ear. "I plan to test the depth of his devotion to whoever this woman is. I plan to fight for him. I plan to seduce Captain Julian Swift."

CHAPTER TWENTY-ONE

Cass came down to dinner the next evening in the lavender gown. She'd spent the entire afternoon with her maid, lowering the bodice, taking up the sleeves, adding a little turquoise pendant, and generally making the concoction all but indecent. As a result, her ample cleavage, which she'd never quite appreciated before, was pushed up and out to its full advantage. Garrett raised both eyebrows in obvious shock when she walked into the room, but her gaze was solely on Julian.

Julian's gray eyes studied her and widened. Then he shifted in his chair as if he was uncomfortable. Perfect. She smiled to herself. He obviously liked what he saw, exactly what she'd wanted. She didn't have long to contemplate the matter, however, before Lucy hurried over to her. "May I speak with you in the corridor?"

Cass didn't have time to object. Her friend nearly dragged her out of the room, all eyes upon both of them.

Once in the cool, marble hallway, Lucy studied her from top to toe. "What are you wearing?"

Cass shrugged. "Just a gown."

"Don't shrug. You may pop out." She gestured to Cass's bosom.

Cass gasped. "I cannot believe you said that."

Lucy lifted both brows. "I cannot believe you're *wearing* that. You're not the Cass I know."

"No, I'm not," Cass agreed in a whisper so the passing servants wouldn't overhear. "I told you, I'm bent upon seduction."

Lucy shook her head. "Be that as it may, Captain Swift just asked me a few moments ago whether I thought he should return to London in search of Penelope or was I quite certain she was indeed on her way."

Cass shrugged. "What did you tell him?"

"I told him I was quite certain she was on her way, of course, but he's getting more and more difficult to stave off."

Cass laughed. "Oh, *now* you're worried. Really? Aren't you the one who has said all along not to worry?"

Lucy narrowed her eyes on her friend. "You're not worried?"

Another shrug. "Not really. Not any longer. Did you seat me next to Julian as I asked?"

Lucy nodded. "Of course I did."

"Excellent. Then let's eat." Cass stepped around Lucy and made toward the door.

Lucy put her hand on Cass's shoulder to stop her. She narrowed her eyes again. "Who are you?"

Cass flashed her a bright smile. "Don't you recognize me, Lucy? You created me. I'm Patience Bunbury."

Cass swept into the dining room. The moment she entered the room, all eyes were upon her again. She boldly strode over to Julian's side to sit at the empty seat next to him. "Captain Swift." She nodded to him.

He stood until she sat and helped her push in her chair.

Excellent. He was certain to get a good view of her décolletage from above. He looked a bit uncomfortable again when he resumed his seat. "Good evening, Miss Bunbury."

The service began soon after, and Cass kept the conversation moving at a brisk clip, talking about things like the weather, the delicious food, and last evening's card games. Every now and again, Julian's eyes dipped to her chest. A little thrill shot through her. She'd never before used her feminine wiles so blatantly, but tonight, tonight she was exceedingly pleased to have them at her disposal. It was going exactly according to her plan. He winced and seemed uncomfortable each time he glanced down.

Once the last course was removed, Cass put the second part of her plan into action. "I hope you'll skip the drinks with the gentlemen this evening and take me for a stroll around the gardens before it gets too cold." Now that was *quite* bold, indeed. The art of being bold was becoming easier with practice.

"If you wish, Miss Bunbury," Julian answered easily. He offered his arm and she put hers through his. He helped her pull up her shawl. He escorted her out of the drawing room, through the corridor, and out of the French doors in the library that led to the terrace.

They silently walked down the stone steps and into the gardens before Julian turned to face her. "I must say I was a bit surprised you asked me to escort you out here tonight."

She tucked her head down. "Did you not say you enjoyed the outdoors?"

"I did. I do. Very much. But given the way you left the library last night . . ." He cleared his throat.

"I'm sorry about that," she replied. "I wasn't feeling quite well, I'm afraid."

His face reflected his concern. "I'm pleased to hear that it wasn't my company that caused you to run off. I do hope you're feeling better this evening."

"Oh, I'm feeling *ever* so much better this evening, Captain."

They strolled a bit farther until they came upon the same stone bench they'd sat upon the last time they'd been in the gardens. Cass released Julian's arm and took a seat. She patted the space next to her. If he sat there, she'd have him right where she wanted him. She leaned back and braced her hands behind her. Her chest jutted out. Perfect. She let the shawl fall away from her décolletage. Also perfect.

Unfortunately, Julian remained standing. He cleared his throat and stared off into the distance. "It's not too cold out here for you?"

"No. Not at all." Actually, it was freezing, especially since her chest was exposed, but she wasn't about to tell him that. Though no doubt he could tell by the fact that her breasts were decidedly standing at, ahem, attention.

"You . . . you look qu-quite beautiful tonight." He tugged at his cravat.

My word. Had she made Julian Swift blush? She couldn't quite tell in the scant light from the candles but she had a suspicion.

Cass steeled her resolve. Whoever this other lady was, she wasn't going to win Julian without a fight. A big fight, a fight that involved décolletage. A lot of it.

"Won't you sit, Captain Swift? It might be a bit warmer if we . . . sat close to each other."

Oh, that was scandalous. The first of many scandalous things she intended to say tonight.

He sat, though his body was rigid and he didn't look at her.

"I do hope Penelope will arrive tomorrow," he said, his voice a bit unsteady.

"Let's not talk about Penelope." Cass pressed her chest against his arm and leaned up, her mouth scant inches from his. He turned slowly. She looked into his eyes. He had to know she wanted him to kiss her. Didn't he? Didn't he?

She wrapped her arms around his neck and leaned up, up, up . . . She closed her eyes and let her head fall back a little. She sighed.

Julian pulled her arms from his neck and slid away from her, ensuring a good arm's length remained between them. "Miss Bunbury?"

Cass opened her eyes and blinked at him. Just like on her sixteenth birthday. She wanted to cry but she refused to. There would be no more crying. Instead she pressed her lips together and tried to look composed. "Yes."

"I . . . Frankly, you don't know how much I want to kiss you right now."

"Then why don't you?" Oh, there went Patience Bunbury's reputation. The harlot.

Julian stood and paced toward the hedgerow, scrubbing his fingers through his hair. "Because at the moment, I still have an understanding with Penelope Monroe."

CHAPTER TWENTY-TWO

Why, oh, why did Captain Julian Swift have to be so blasted honorable? That thought was topmost in Cass's mind as she wandered into the private family breakfast room the next morning, a frown on her face.

"Dear, you must look at this," Lucy said the moment Cass walked through the door. Lucy was holding a letter in her hand, her bright eyes busily scanning the words.

Jane was already there, eating a muffin. Garrett was nowhere to be seen. Cass slowly made her way over to where Lucy sat with the letter.

"Where's Garrett?" Cass asked.

"He and Berkeley were up with the sun and went for a ride. And I'm so glad because otherwise, I'd have to explain *this* to him." Lucy waved the letter again.

"What is it?" Cass couldn't muster much interest. Her thoughts remained on Julian and her failure to seduce him last night. He'd given the excuse about Penelope but Cass wondered if it didn't have more to do with the woman he was in love with. Either way, he'd been decidedly uninterested.

Jane wiped her mouth with her napkin. "Why do you look so glum, Cass?"

Cass sighed. "Things did not go according to plan with Julian in the gardens, that's all."

Lucy breathed a sigh of relief. "I'm glad for that. When I saw you leave with him wearing that gown, I was quite certain you intended to take advantage of him. I was a bit worried for the captain, to be honest."

Cass propped an elbow on the table and rested her chin on it. "I didn't take advantage of him. I merely gave him the chance to take advantage of *me*."

Jane was doing an awful job at attempting to hide her smile. "And he refused?" She reached into the basket that rested in the center of the table and pulled out another muffin.

"I did my best, truly," Cass said. "But he reminded me that he's engaged to Pen. Or supposed to be."

"The scoundrel. How dare he?" Jane smiled.

"He doesn't even love her. She doesn't love him. Why must they continue this farce of an understanding?" Cass sighed.

"Yes, well, as to that, you need to look at this." Lucy waved the letter again.

Cass halfheartedly pulled the letter from Lucy's fingers and began to read it. It was from . . . Pen. Cass sat up straight.

"Oh, no!" She gasped, her hand falling like a leaden weight to the tabletop with a thud.

"Exactly," Lucy replied, crossing her arms over her chest.

Jane sat up straight. "What does it say?"

Cass scanned the contents, her heart beating out of her chest. She read aloud.

Darlings,

I decided I was being ridiculous hiding from Captain Swift. I need to face him and get it over with. I

*paid a call to his mother and Daphne. There, I was
informed that Captain Swift had recently left for a
house party in the country. Why, imagine my surprise when I inquired as to the location of the house
party and realized that he was at Lucy's house, of
all places!*

All three friends exchanged worried glances.

"Keep reading," Lucy said in a singsong voice.

"Yes, go on. Go on," Jane prompted.

*I think this is absolutely perfect, darlings. I have
some important news to share. I'll tell you all about
it after I arrive. Look for me on Wednesday afternoon. I simply cannot wait to see you both.*

Cass gulped. Wednesday afternoon? It was Wednesday morning.

"What do you think her 'important news' is?" Jane
wanted to know.

"Who cares about that?" Cass nearly shrieked. "Do
you know what this means?"

"It means Penelope is on her way here as we speak,"
Lucy declared, tapping her finger against her cheek.

Cass tossed the letter onto the tabletop. She searched
the room's ceiling. "What are we going to do?"

"It solves the problem of you producing her for Captain Swift, at least," Jane pointed out, taking another bite
of her muffin.

"But it presents an even greater problem," Cass moaned.
"What shall we do?"

"There's nothing to do," Jane replied. "You either have
to send Captain Swift on his way or intercept Penelope
somehow. Those are the only two choices."

Lucy snapped her fingers. "No, wait!"

Cass raised her head, a bit hopeful at Lucy's tone. "What?"

Lucy's eyes had a telltale gleam in them. She'd thought of something. "This may just be perfect."

"How could it be perfect?" Jane popped another bit of a muffin into her mouth.

"Do you intend to eat all of those muffins?" Lucy asked her.

"Perhaps," Jane replied.

"Stop talking about the muffins!" Cass nearly shouted, her anxiety rising with each moment. "What were you going to say, Lucy?"

"Yes, tell us how this could possibly go well," Jane replied, blinking at Lucy.

Lucy tapped her fingers along the tabletop. "Julian and Penelope would need to be in each other's company in order to end their agreement, correct?"

"Yes," Cass replied, narrowing her eyes at her friend.

"And if she comes here, they will be in each other's company, correct?" Lucy continued.

"Aren't you forgetting the part where Cass is pretending to be Patience Bunbury and you are calling yourself Lady Worthing? How will you explain that to Penelope?" Jane asked.

"We won't have to," Lucy replied.

"What are you talking about?" Cass asked.

Lucy shrugged. "We'll simply hide."

"Hide?" Cass rubbed her eyes.

"Hide?" Jane nearly spat out her muffin. "You have truly gone mad now."

Cass shook her head. "What do you mean, hide?"

"When Pen arrives, we can arrange for her to see Julian. They'll end things. Pen will then come in search of us and we'll ensure we're alone with her. I cannot imagine she will want to stay at a house party with her former betrothed, can you?"

"Why don't you just tell Pen that Cass is pretending to be Patience Bunbury?" Jane asked, her eyes also narrowed.

"Oh, I doubt she'd like to know that we've ruined the identity of her most valued friend," Lucy replied.

"Lucy is right about that," Cass agreed. "Besides, she asked me to tell Captain Swift she was *with* Patience not *become* Patience myself."

"I'm glad you agree with me, Cass, because—"

"Wait just a moment. I said you were right about that. I do not, however, agree with you on the rest of it." Cass shook her head. "The idea of hiding from Pen is ridiculous."

Lucy scrunched up her nose. "Why? I quite like it."

"I cannot believe I'm saying this, but I actually agree with Lucy," Jane said.

Cass bit her lip and glanced at her friend. "You do, Janie?"

"Yes, I do. Penelope has never seemed to give a toss about Captain Swift. I wouldn't be surprised if she is utterly relieved. And if you meet with her alone, you'll be able to keep her from knowing that you're pretending to be Miss Bunbury."

Cass held her breath. It all seemed too easy. "I suppose there is no harm in trying. But I must insist that if Pen is upset after speaking with Julian, we will stop this entire thing. I will not see my cousin hurt."

"Agreed," Lucy said with a nod.

Cass turned to Jane. "Will you meet her at the door, Jane? Make certain she's comfortable?"

Jane nodded. "Of course, and I'll ensure she's shown into a private room with Captain Swift immediately."

"Perfect!" Lucy declared.

Cass swallowed. It sounded perfect, but the old Cass, the unbold Cass, was already worrying about it all. Oh, what would happen if it all went terribly, horribly wrong?

CHAPTER TWENTY-THREE

After breakfast, Julian made his way into the conservatory. He needed to find his hostess to tell her he was leaving. God only knew how long it would take for Penelope to arrive. He couldn't stay here any longer after the mistake he'd nearly made with Patience last night. Patience was gorgeous, her body was perfect, her face, ethereal. The way she'd looked in that low-cut gown. Julian shuddered. When she'd asked him to walk with her in the gardens, a warning bell had tolled somewhere in the back of his mind. It wasn't a good idea to remain close with her. Their interludes at the party had shown him that he was unnaturally attracted to her. He wanted her. Badly. But only a scoundrel would kiss one lady while he was supposed to be engaged to another. No, he would not do any such thing . . . until he had broken things off with Penelope. And that wasn't likely to happen if she never arrived. He would return to London. Penelope would turn up eventually. He certainly couldn't keep chasing her across the countryside. It had been a bad idea to come here. He knew that now.

He made his way past the rows of deep green palms

and bright flowers to the center of the conservatory. One of the servants had informed him that Lady Worthing had been seen coming in here a bit earlier. Laughter reached his ears. He turned a corner around a large pear tree and came into a clearing near the iron bench. Patience was there with her watercolors set up again. Only this time she was drawing Miss Wollstonecraft and Garrett Upton. Luckily, Lady Worthing was with them.

"Be certain to paint her book," Upton was saying to Patience.

"I'd like to put my book—" Miss Wollstonecraft began.

"Ah, ah, ah," Upton replied. "Don't forget our bargain."

Miss Wollstonecraft's eyes narrowed but she snapped her mouth shut.

Lady Worthing burst out laughing. "Now this is positively delicious."

"What are you reading this time, Jane?" Upton asked. "How can you stand all those books that end happily?"

"The good end happily and the bad, unhappily. That is what fiction means, Upton," she retorted.

"Mr. Upton," he replied with a grin.

Julian watched them closely. It appeared the four of them were close friends, indeed. Miss Wollstonecraft opened her mouth to reply. Not wanting to eavesdrop on their conversation, Julian stepped into the open space and cleared his throat.

All four of them turned to face him. Patience met his gaze and quickly looked away, turning her attention back to her painting.

"Ah, Captain Swift. Good to see you. We have some wonderful news for you," Lady Worthing called, motioning for him to come closer.

Julian made his way over to the little group. "What's that?"

"Why, your intended will be arriving this afternoon. I

received a letter from Penelope this morning saying as much," Lady Worthing replied.

Julian closed his eyes, relief flooding him. Lady Worthing was correct. He couldn't have asked for better news. "I am glad to hear it," he replied. He glanced at Patience, her pretty blue eyes clouded, but still she didn't look at him. Damn. He'd hoped it wouldn't be awkward between them but it was. Of course it was. She'd wanted him to kiss her last night, and he'd refused her. And blast it if she didn't look beautiful today in a pretty yellow gown with tiny flowers embroidered upon it. She looked just like one of the blooms in the conservatory, as if she belonged here.

"May I?" he asked, motioning toward the painting she was working on.

Patience nodded.

Upton stood and made some excuse about needing to see to his horse, something about the animal's hoof. Lady Worthing and Miss Wollstonecraft quickly made their excuses as well, and within a few moments, Julian found himself completely alone with Patience in the conservatory. He wondered at the others' simultaneous abrupt departures. Had Miss Bunbury told them what had happened between them last night? Surely not. At least, he hoped not.

He drew in a breath and made his way behind her to look at the painting just as he had the other day. The work was clearly not finished but Patience had done a remarkable job of it so far. Miss Wollstonecraft's pretty face was outlined in blue. Her spectacles and book were both there. Patience had managed to capture a certain look on the woman's face, partly mischievous, partly intelligent. Upton was there, too, sitting next to her. She'd rendered him nearly lifelike, even down to the slight curl of his hair that Julian had not noticed before.

"It's striking," he said quietly.

"Thank you."

"You all seem to be quite friendly. Even Upton."

She hesitated. "I'm . . . I'm quite close with Lucy and Jane."

He nodded. "I'm close with Derek Hunt, the Duke of Claringdon. Do you know him?"

Patience closed her eyes briefly. "Who hasn't heard of the famous Duke of Decisive?" she murmured.

Julian laughed softly at that. "Yes, he is that. He's gone to the Continent at the moment. He's looking for my brother and our good friend Captain Cavendish." Why was he telling her all of this? Miss Bunbury probably didn't care, but anything to keep the conversation from the awkwardness of last evening. "The rest of my friends seem to have died in the war, I'm afraid."

She searched his face, looking as if she wanted to say more, but instead she pressed her lips together and set about putting her brushes away and gathering up her canvas. "I hope the duke finds your brother. Are you close to him?" she asked. "Your brother, I mean."

"Not as close as I'd like to be," Julian answered simply. It was true.

"I . . . I'm quite sorry to hear that," Miss Bunbury said.

"I am, too. As soon as I speak with Penelope, I intend to go in search of Donald and Rafe."

Miss Bunbury went pale. She pressed her hand to her throat. "You're going back to the Continent?"

"Yes."

"But . . . but you nearly died. You cannot put yourself in such danger again." She reached for him. Her hand grasped his sleeve. Her fingers were shaking.

Julian moved his hand to cover hers. "Your fingers are cold."

"I know." She didn't break their eye contact.

Julian squeezed her fingers with his, willing heat to

return to her hand. He studied her face. Her reaction had been so genuine, so intense. If he didn't know any better, he'd think she had tears in her eyes. Miss Bunbury was quite sensitive, it seemed, sensitive and caring. Could it be that she'd developed such a *tendre* for him in only a few short days?

"I cannot allow my brother and friend to remain missing. The only reason I didn't go with Hunt to begin with was because my orders would not allow it and I felt I owed it to Penelope to speak with her first. But I must go look for my brother as soon as possible."

Miss Bunbury glanced away. "So, you'll be leaving as soon as you speak with Penelope?"

"Yes."

She turned back and met his eyes. Her bottom lip trembled. "I wish you well, Captain. Penelope will be here soon."

CHAPTER TWENTY-FOUR

Cass, Lucy, and Jane spent the next two hours in the up-stairs drawing room nervously waiting for Penelope to arrive. Cass stared out the window that faced the front drive, her insides a roiling mess of nerves. She still wasn't certain at all that this Penelope business was a good idea or a valid plan. However, Jane's endorsement of it had given her a bit of hope. Still, it worried her.

Adding to her worry was the news that Julian intended to leave for France as soon as he spoke with Penelope. Her heart ached. She'd just got him out of harm's way, and he intended to put himself back into it? It was a nightmare. Julian was too honorable and steadfast to do anything but search for his brother and Captain Cavendish, but it felt as if someone large was sitting on her chest every time she thought of him returning to the Continent. The war might be over, but France was hardly safe at the moment. She'd read in the papers, there were bands of rebels and spies still roving about. Paris itself was extremely dangerous as the treaty was being negotiated. What was Donald even doing there? He was an English earl. He had no business in France. Unless . . .

"She's here!" Lucy shouted, pulling Cass from her thoughts.

Cass glanced out the window. Lucy was right. Penelope's coach was making its way down the long drive.

"Now," Lucy declared, nodding at Jane.

Jane returned the nod and made her way to the door. "Leave everything to me," she said, just before slipping away.

Cass wrung her hands. "Oh, Lucy, what if—"

"No. No. I won't hear any what ifs," Lucy said. "Where is the selfsame young lady who was bent on seduction last night? I want to see her back, if you please?"

"But what if—"

Lucy gave her a stern stare, and Cass shut her mouth with a pop.

The wait was interminable. Cass was back to her old habits, pacing in front of the windows, and tugging at her gloves. Lucy, seemingly impervious to the tension of the situation, sat down and began going over yet another list, this one from the gardener, something about the flowers that were to be planted in the gardens in the spring. More than half of an hour passed before Jane returned, Penelope herself close on her heels.

Cass eyed her cousin. She didn't look sad. She wasn't crying. Didn't even have a discontented look on her face. In fact, she was . . . smiling.

Jane, however, looked as if she'd just had an encounter with an extremely unpleasant ghost. Her face was white as milk.

"Cass!" Penelope rushed forward and pulled her cousin into her embrace.

"P-Pen. Good to see you," Cass managed, all the while eyeing Jane suspiciously. Jane shook her head and glanced down at the rug.

Pen greeted Lucy just as enthusiastically and then

plopped onto the settee. The three other ladies flocked around her.

"What? Er . . . when d-did you get here?" Cass managed.

"Oh, I'd say it's been close to an hour since, wouldn't you, Jane?" Pen asked.

"Yes, a good long while now," Jane agreed, nervously fidgeting with her spectacles.

Pen looked about the room. "Do you have any tea, Lucy? I'm quite famished."

Lucy nodded. With a look that could only be called confused on her face, she rang for tea.

"And what have you been doing?" Cass asked. That was it. She had to be blunt. She couldn't endure the suspense.

"Why, Jane showed me into one of the drawing rooms and I spoke with Captain Swift."

Jane plucked at her neckline. "Yes, indeed."

"I did think it only right to see him first, don't you agree, Cass?" Pen continued.

"Oh, yes. Yes, of course." Cass watched her cousin in horror, waiting for the next words past her lips. "And . . . ah, how did it . . . go?" She winced. So did Lucy. So did Jane.

"That's what I came up straightaway to tell you. Didn't I, Jane? I said, 'I must see Cass immediately and tell her.' Didn't I, Jane?"

Jane nodded. "Yes. Yes, you did."

Cass and Lucy exchanged alarmed looks.

"What happened?" Lucy burst out, just as the butler entered the room with the tea tray.

Several excruciatingly silent minutes passed while the butler set up the tea service before Lucy dismissed the man and took over herself. She cleared her throat. "You were saying, Penelope?"

"Oh, yes. I had the most clever idea."

Jane's face remained milky. She refused the tea Lucy offered her.

"And what was that?" Cass managed to ask in a calm voice. At least she hoped it was calm. Frankly, she felt as if she were on the verge of a hysterical fit. She took a sip of tea.

Pen dropped three large lumps of sugar into her teacup and stirred it rapidly. "Why, I told Captain Swift that my name was Patience Bunbury."

It took the better part of five entire minutes for Cass to stop coughing. Now she was quite certain one or both of her lungs would never be entirely the same again.

"Are you quite all right, Cass?" Pen asked, flying to her side, concern etched across her features.

"Oh, I . . . yes, yes. Quite all right," Cass managed to choke out. "Did you say you told Captain Swift you're Patience Bunbury?"

Pen nodded happily. "I most certainly did."

"But, ah, aren't you supposed to be at her house party?" Cass continued. It was all so confusing.

Pen fluttered a hand in the air. "I suppose so, but no matter."

"Did he . . ." Cass cleared her throat again. "Did he ask you where Penelope Monroe was?"

The catlike grin remained on Pen's plump face. "He did not."

Cass glanced at Jane, who nodded. "That's right. He didn't."

"I'm telling you, it was a brilliant idea," Pen continued. "Ever so clever of me, I daresay."

Lucy pressed a fingertip to her temple. "Tell me, Penelope, though I'm certain it should be obvious, why exactly did you think telling Captain Swift that you're

Patience Bunbury was a—how did you put it?—clever idea?"

Pen smiled widely. "Why, of course it's perfect, don't you see? It was obvious to me the moment he saw me that he didn't recognize me. It has been seven years, after all. I decided that I'd tell him I was Patience and that way, perhaps, we might be able to get to know each other a bit better. To be quite honest, I'd intended to break things off with him up till now. That was the news I mentioned in my letter. But seeing him again made me feel a bit sorry for the chap. I mean, he doesn't like hunting or fishing or any of the things Father likes. I think he's quite cerebral and dull to be honest."

Jane clapped her hand over her mouth and then raised her eyes toward the ceiling.

Pen kept talking. "But I had to admit when I saw him again that he is exceedingly handsome, and he did almost die. I would hate to toss him over without giving him a chance. I realized pretending to be Patience was perfect once I saw him. Pretending to be Patience for the remainder of this house party will give me the chance to get to know him and ask him some questions, without all the pressure of supposedly being engaged."

Cass and Lucy exchanged glances. Then they lifted their eyes to Jane. "What did Captain Swift say when Penelope introduced herself as Patience Bunbury?"

Jane tugged on the fabric near her throat again. "He . . . uh . . . he said he'd very much like to see Lady Worthing as soon as she has a free moment."

Penelope took a large gulp of tea and looked around expectantly at all of them. "Who is Lady Worthing?"

CHAPTER TWENTY-FIVE

"I must go with you, Lucy." Cass paced in front of the windows in Lucy's bedchamber.

Somehow the three friends had managed to finish their tea with Penelope and send her off to her rooms. They'd given her some thin excuse about Lady Worthing being another guest at the party. Then, they'd quickly retreated to Lucy's bedchamber to plan their next move.

"I'm not certain that's a good idea, Cass," Jane warned.

"Did Julian seem angry?" Cass asked, biting her lower lip.

"Angry? No. It was a bit more like . . . confused."

"No doubt he's confused." Lucy tapped her finger against her cheek.

"No, Lucy. Stop it," Cass said.

"Stop what?"

"Stop thinking whatever you're thinking. You're coming up with an even more ludicrous scheme than the last one, and I won't have it. It's time to tell the truth. I'll go with you to see Julian. I'll be honest with him. It's time."

Lucy shook her head. "But if you tell him the truth, he'll know you're Cass."

Cass pressed a fingertip to her temple. "Yes. I know. That's the point."

"Are you going to tell him that Penelope is really Penelope, too?" Lucy asked.

Cass straightened her shoulders and firmed her resolve. "I'm going to tell him everything. He deserves the truth. This has all gone on long enough."

In the end, Lucy relented, perhaps only because she couldn't think of anything more outlandish to do to extricate them from their present predicament. Perhaps because Jane had chimed in and agreed with Cass that it was time to tell the truth. Perhaps it had been a mix of both, but at any rate, Lucy sighed and said, "Very well, let's get this over with."

They made their way downstairs to the blue drawing room and sent Jane in search of Julian to tell him that Lady Worthing was waiting there to speak with him.

As they waited, Cass and Lucy both sat staring out the window.

"What if we—" Lucy offered.

"No." Cass shook her head.

"But I could—" Lucy said.

"Absolutely not," Cass replied.

Lucy opened her mouth to try again, no doubt, but the door cracked open and Julian strolled inside. Cass took a deep breath.

Lucy stood to greet him, a shaky smile on her lips. "Captain Swift."

"I want to know one thing," Julian said, eyeing them both with a look that was a mixture of confusion and suspicion. Cass's heart dropped. Here it was. Julian might well hate her in just a few short moments.

Lucy swallowed audibly. "Yes, Captain Swift?" She bowed her head.

Julian nodded toward Cass. He crossed his arms over

his chest and tapped his booted foot on the rug. "Why is Penelope Monroe claiming to be you?"

Cass had to sit. That was all there was to it. Never in her wildest imaginings of how this conversation would go did she think it would happen this way. She blindly searched for the arm of the chair behind her and dropped into place, the breath whooshing from her body as she landed.

Lucy recovered much more quickly. "Whatever do you mean, Captain Swift?"

Julian's brows were arched. "I mean, I met with Penelope not an hour ago in this very room and she told me her name was Patience Bunbury."

Lucy blinked at him, her mind obviously whirring with ideas. She placed a hand to her throat. "She did?"

"Yes, she did." Julian tapped his boot again.

Lucy cleared her throat and inclined her head. "And did you ask her why she did that?"

Julian stopped the tapping. "No. In fact, I was so shocked I pretended I didn't know who she was. But why would she say such a thing?"

Lucy's voice was high and thin. "I'm not sure, Captain Swift. Are you quite certain the lady in question was, in fact, Penelope?"

"I'm quite certain she was not Patience as I've already met Patience." He motioned toward Cass again. "And she looked very much like my memory of Penelope Monroe. A bit older, to be sure, but she hasn't changed much."

Cass fought her nod. No, Pen hadn't changed much. But Cass was stricken dumb. She couldn't talk, could only listen as Lucy rapidly answered Julian's questions and asked him her own. How had this happened? It was madness.

Lucy straightened her shoulders and lifted her chin. "I have yet to see Miss Monroe today, Captain Swift." Cass winced at the new lie. "But I assure you, I intend to go in search of her immediately and get to the bottom of this."

Lucy swept up her skirts and headed for the door, obviously in a rush to leave before she had to come up with an even more elaborate story.

"Miss Bunbury, will you please keep Captain Swift company while I find Miss Monroe?"

Cass opened her mouth to protest but shut it again when she saw the look on Julian's face. As if he . . . wanted her to stay. "Of course," she murmured lamely.

Moments later, the door shut behind Lucy, and Cass screwed up her courage. Now was the time. Finally. She could not allow this farce to continue a moment longer. Julian would only hate her all the more for it later. Not to mention the fact that only the truth would serve to explain all of this once Pen appeared.

"Captain Swift, I—"

"I'm glad Lady Worthing left us alone," Julian said, crossing over to the settee and sitting next to Cass.

Cass blinked. "You are?"

"Yes. Quite." He smiled at her. "I'm not certain what Penelope is up to, but her lying to me like that has just served to reinforce my decision to end things with her. She's not the same girl I knew in my youth."

Cass nearly whimpered. She glanced away. "I suppose she'll have a good explanation."

"What possible explanation could she have for impersonating another woman? It makes no sense. It's positively mad."

That was it. The tiny bit of courage Cass had screwed up drained from her soul in that instant. She couldn't tell him. Not now. Oh, she was a horrible coward.

"You didn't . . ." Her voice wavered. "You didn't have a chance to break things off with her?"

His laugh was scornful. "How could I when she was

telling me she was someone else entirely? It was laughable." He narrowed his eyes. He turned to face Cass. "You don't suppose she discovered my intentions? That she lied to me to keep me from saying what I meant to?"

Cass went hot and cold. Oh, God. He was questioning whether she'd kept his secret. "She didn't hear it from me, Captain." She hung her head. There at least was one truth in the midst of all the lies.

He paced across the rug, his arms folded behind his back. "No. No, of course she didn't. And even if she suspected, it is still mad to pretend you're someone else in order to keep from hearing bad news."

Cass could only nod. The lump of guilt and regret in her throat was choking her. She couldn't utter a word.

"As soon as Penelope returns I intend to confront her. She took me by surprise before. I didn't know what to say. I thought perhaps Lady Worthing might know why she was acting so strangely."

Another nod from Cass. "That is probably best."

"I will tell her that our engagement is off. And then . . ."

Cass glanced up. "And then?" She swallowed hard. "France?"

"Well, yes . . . But first, first I intend to find you, Miss Bunbury, and kiss you senseless."

CHAPTER TWENTY-SIX

The plan was put into motion quickly as most of Lucy's plans were. Julian was asked to remain in the blue drawing room. Pen was informed that her intended had recognized her after all and would like to speak with her again. She was a bit disappointed, but she readily agreed to meet with him once more. She took off to the blue drawing room, escorted by one of the housemaids.

As soon as Pen was on her way, Lucy motioned to Cass and Jane. "This way."

"Why?" Cass replied, her brow furrowed. "Where are we going?"

"We must go to the gold drawing room. It's next to the blue one. We'll be able to hear their conversation if we pin our ears to the wall."

"Oh, Lucy. That is horrid. We cannot do that," Cass said, frowning at her friend.

"What?" Lucy shrugged. "It's not as if I enjoy eavesdropping. I am forced to. We must know what they say to each other so we can keep our own stories straight. Besides, you told me yourself that you didn't tell him you're

Cass yet. If you're so worried about all of this, why didn't you tell the truth when I left the room?"

"Because I'm detestable." Cass moaned. "I'm detestable and so is eavesdropping."

"I don't disagree with you, about the eavesdropping bit," Jane said. "But Lucy's right again. We have to know if they discuss Patience and if Captain Swift tells Penelope he's already met her."

"We are abominable!" Cass replied. "We are all going straight to hell for everything we've done this week."

This time Jane shrugged. "I am already destined for that warm place. I'll see you both there. We'll drink brandy and curse and have a marvelous time."

Lucy laughed. Cass shook her head.

Five minutes later, Cass stood in the gold drawing room, her ear pressed against the damask wallpaper right alongside her friends'.

Julian's voice drifted to them. "Penelope?"

"Captain Swift."

"I don't know why you impersonated Miss Bunbury and it probably doesn't matter. The fact is that I came here to find you, to tell you that we cannot possibly marry."

Cass held her breath. *What will Pen say? What will she say?*

"You're telling me we cannot marry?" Pen's voice was surprisingly unanimated.

"Yes. I'm sorry." Julian's voice was a bit less harsh. "Truly."

A tiny bit of laughter floated through the wall. "Oh, Captain Swift. You are funny. I actually had come here to tell *you* we cannot marry."

Cass, Lucy, and Jane all turned wide eyes to one another. Cass clapped her hand over her mouth, then quickly pressed her ear tighter to the wall to hear the rest.

"You . . . did?" was Julian's reply.

Pen sighed. "Yes."

"Why?" Julian asked.

"I was hiding from you, to be honest," Pen replied. "I finally decided I had to find you and tell you the truth."

Julian's voice moved farther away. He must be walking or pacing. "That's why you weren't in London when I arrived?"

"I was there, just hiding," Pen admitted.

This time they both laughed.

"May I assume then that you are not angry with me and won't be asking your father to call me out?" There was a smile in Julian's voice.

Another sigh from Pen. "I cannot say my parents won't be disappointed, but I've every confidence I can convince Father not to kill you. You've survived the war, Captain Swift, one bullet to the chest is quite enough. Don't you agree?" Pen's voice sounded equally light.

"Of course I intend to speak to your parents and explain," Julian said. "I felt it imperative to speak with you first, however."

"Completely understandable and commendable of you," Pen replied.

"Then we may part as friends?" Julian asked.

"As far as I'm concerned we were never anything but," Pen assured him.

Lucy, Jane, and Cass all expelled their pent-up breath at the same time. Cass braced a hand against the wall. She wanted to melt into a puddle on the floor. How? Oh, how had this worked out so well? It was a miracle to be sure.

"They're leaving," Lucy reported, her ear still pressed tightly against the wall.

"Yes, the door is definitely opening," Jane agreed, her ear back in place, too.

Cass leaped away from the wall. "I must go. How does my hair look?" She tried to pat her coiffure in place.

"What? Why?" Lucy pushed herself away from the wall and faced Cass.

"Yes. What are you talking about?" Jane asked.

Cass rushed toward the door. "Now that I know that Pen is quite all right, I must go. Julian said he was going to come looking for me, well, Patience that is, and . . ." Shyness overtook her for a moment. She stopped and bit her lip.

"And?" Lucy prompted, her eyes wide.

Cass smiled widely. "And kiss me senseless."

Lucy rushed over and pushed her toward the door. "For heaven's sake, then, by all means, go!"

CHAPTER TWENTY-SEVEN

Julian strode straight out the door of the drawing room and ran smack into . . . Owen Monroe? His old friend? Cassandra's brother? Here of all places?

"Monroe!" He clapped the future earl on the back. "Good to see you, old chap." Owen had been one year ahead of him at Eton. They'd known each other for an age.

Monroe looked as if he'd seen a ghost, something Julian was becoming more and more accustomed to when people recognized him. "Swift? By God, it's you!"

"What're you doing here?" Julian asked. "I'd sent a note over to your parents' estate but when I didn't hear back, I assumed you were in London."

"I was. I only just came out a couple of days ago. I'm looking for our hostess but apparently she's otherwise occupied at the moment," Owen replied.

They turned the corner and walked together into the study. "Yes, well, I'm certain Lady Worthing is around here somewhere. She'll turn up. Come have a drink. Let's catch up."

Julian led the way toward the study where the men of

the party had been known to lounge around and drink during the afternoon.

Monroe's brow furrowed. "Lady Worthing?"

Julian pushed open the door to the study and allowed Monroe to precede him in. "Yes, Lady Worth—"

Upton leaped up from the sofa, directly into their path, cutting off Julian's words. The man looked as if he was about to spit out his brandy. Julian hadn't seen Upton move so quickly in his life, and that included when he was being shot at on a battlefield in Spain.

"Monroe. What in the devil's name are you doing here?" Upton said. His friend Lord Berkeley remained sitting on the sofa reading a book.

Monroe narrowed his eyes on Upton. "Mother and Father sent me over here to see what was going on."

"Going on?" Julian snorted. "You make it sound as if a house party is sordid, Monroe."

"Well, I—" Monroe barely got a word out before Upton clapped him on the shoulder.

"I had no idea you came out to the country anymore, Monroe. Thought you preferred the city."

"Mother asked me to pay a visit. She's worried about Cass."

Julian sucked in his breath. "Is Cass here? In the country?"

"That's what I was hoping to find out," Monroe replied. "I was just looking for Luc—"

"Monroe. Monroe. There is time for introductions and all of that later. Come sit. Have a drink. This is a party, after all, isn't it?"

Monroe gave Upton a narrowed-eyed stare, but he took a seat near Berkeley and waited while Upton crossed over to the sideboard and poured him a drink. He took it and downed a healthy swallow. Upton handed Julian a glass of brandy as well.

A drink sounded good after his mad afternoon with his supposed future bride trying to lie to him about her identity—of all the ludicrous things in the world—who in the hell would think that was a good idea? It was beyond idiotic. Thank God he'd had the sense not to shackle himself for life to such a ninny-headed woman. However, despite Penelope's antics, she had been calm and level-headed about the end of their engagement. He didn't know why he'd been so worried about it. She obviously didn't give a toss about him and never had. She'd barely written to him or spared a thought, most likely, in the last seven years. Finding out that she had been hiding from him had been a surprise. Apparently, she was no more keen on marrying him than he was her. He could almost laugh about it, actually, if it wasn't all so ridiculous. Instead, he chalked up the entire encounter to a bit of good luck. After his near death on the Continent, he supposed it was high time for a bit of fortune.

He was free. Finally free. Free to do what he chose. And what he chose at the moment was to have a stiff drink or two or three with Upton and Monroe and then to find Patience Bunbury later tonight and finish what they'd started. Patience Bunbury was stunning and from what he could tell last night . . . quite interested. It didn't matter that Monroe was here and might know where Cassandra was. No. He refused to ask another question about her. Cassandra was in love with another man. He was going to kiss Patience Bunbury, then he was going to leave for France, in that order.

Julian hefted his glass. "To old friends!" he announced.

Monroe, Upton, and Berkeley lifted their glasses in unison. "Old friends!" they all echoed.

Julian downed a hefty portion of his drink. He settled into his leather chair and eyed Monroe. "So, tell me, how's your sister?" Damn it. He hadn't even firmed his resolve to court Patience Bunbury for five minutes before Cassandra stole back into his thoughts. Very well. He'd only ask a question or two. Perhaps find out who she was in love with. Would her brother know?

"I'm not certain," Monroe replied, taking a sip of his drink. "Mother wrote asking me to come out and see to her."

Julian furrowed his brow. "I thought you said she wasn't at your parents' estate."

"She's not. That's why I'm here." Monroe turned to Upton. "Have you seen her?"

Upton looked as if he'd just swallowed something entirely disagreeable. "Me? No. Well, I mean I've seen her before, obviously, but I—"

Why was Upton acting so bloody nervous? Was it because he was in love with Cass, too? Julian fought the urge to ask them both outright. Were Upton and Cassandra engaged? Hunt hadn't said that much, but where was she? And what was she doing? Now Julian was worried. Was Cassandra missing? Neither her brother nor Upton appeared to know where she was.

"Your sister hasn't been at this house party," Julian said. "That I can assure you."

Owen looked at Upton. "She isn't? But Mother said she was with Lucy, and I—"

"You know Lucy and Cassandra. They'll turn up, eventually," Upton said. "To reunion! Drink up!"

All three other men lifted their glasses again.

"Lucy?" Julian asked. "As in Lucy Hunt? Derek's new wife?"

"Yes," Monroe replied. "She and Cass are thick as thieves, much to the chagrin of my parents."

Julian raised both brows. "Is that so?"

Upton, looking pale, stood quickly. "Monroe, old chap, perhaps I might speak to you in the corridor for a moment?"

Monroe shrugged. "I suppose."

Julian settled back in his chair. It was none of his business why they wanted to have a private word. He'd stay and speak to Berkeley. The viscount seemed like a good enough chap. Julian took another drink. Where was Cassandra?

"Old gambling debt," Upton whispered as Monroe stood, too.

"I hope we find Cass by morning," Monroe said as the two men started for the door. "Mother and Father will be here by then, and I don't want to have to explain why she's not."

This time Upton looked as if he'd just been struck by lightning.

CHAPTER TWENTY-EIGHT

Garrett swiped a pack of cards from the top of a table near the door on his way out of the study. He allowed Monroe to go ahead of him and followed him out. Thank God, Monroe had agreed to go with him. For one heart-stopping moment, Garrett had been convinced that Monroe was going to ask him what he wanted to talk about. That wouldn't have been good. Not good at all. Then, he'd mentioned his parents.

Garrett groaned. And this was why it was better to not get involved in any of Lucy's schemes.

But better to handle one problem at time.

Garrett knew three things about Owen Monroe. The man loved to drink, he loved beautiful women, and he loved to gamble. He'd gamble on anything. In fact, now that Garrett thought about it, Monroe was more the type who could be called a profligate rake—the moniker the smug Miss Lowndes was so quick to pin on Garrett at every turn. He might just point that out to her the next time she mentioned it. If Miss Lowndes wanted to see a profligate rake in action, she need look no further than Owen Monroe. He was a good man, but he did enjoy his vices.

Miss Lowndes was correct about one thing, however, and that was that Garrett enjoyed gambling from time to time as well. And while he wasn't as avid a player as Monroe was rumored to be, he was a more successful one if those same rumors were true. Monroe played for the fun of it, whereas Garrett always played to win. And this afternoon, Garrett was certain he was going to have to bet high.

"Let's go in here," Garrett said, gesturing to a door several paces down the corridor. It opened into a drawing room, an empty drawing room, thank God.

Monroe gave him an inquiring stare but good-naturedly followed him in. They both made their way to the center of the room where Garrett tossed the cards on the table that sat in the middle.

"What are those for?" Monroe asked, arching a brow.

"I'll get to that in a moment," Garrett replied. "First I must tell you something. Something you may not like. I need your promise that you won't leave this room, however, until you hear me out."

Monroe narrowed his eyes on him. "I don't like the sound of this, Upton. Not at all."

"I don't blame you. Believe me. Your promise?"

"Very well. I'll hear you out, but depending on what you say, that's all I'm willing to allow."

"Fair enough." Garrett gestured to a chair. "You may want to take a seat."

"I think I'll stand."

"Very well." Garrett paced in front of the door to the room, his hands behind his back, frantically searching his mind for the best way to explain all of this. If Monroe knew his cousin better, he might explain it all in one word: Lucy. But Monroe didn't know Lucy very well and that was the problem. This entire escapade would take more than a bit of explanation.

Deciding expediency was the best policy, he began with, "Cassandra is here."

Monroe's eyes widened and he turned to face him. "What? Where?"

"She's been here the entire time. But—"

"Why did Swift say she wasn't?" A look of suspicion crossed Monroe's face.

"Because there's something quite unusual about this house party. Something Swift doesn't know about."

"With all due respect, Upton, what the devil are you talking about?"

Garrett sighed and scrubbed his hand through his hair. This wasn't going to be easy, not easy at all. He spent the better part of the next ten minutes explaining as much about the charade as he thought Monroe needed to know. Understandably, Monroe asked a barrage of questions, and Garrett answered them one by one.

By the time it was over, Owen looked like a shell-shocked soldier on a battlefield, and Garrett was mentally exhausted. Lucy could certainly weave a complicated web when she wanted to. He'd give her that.

"I have just one more question," Monroe said, staring at Garrett as if he'd completely lost his mind.

"Yes?"

"What in God's name makes you think I'll play along with all of this even for a minute?"

Garrett took a deep breath. He knew gamblers. Gamblers couldn't say no to a bet, at least that was the wager he was willing to lay all his chips on at the moment.

He gestured to the cards scattered across the nearby table.

"I'll bet you one hand of piquet. If I win, you play along. If you win, you don't."

Monroe narrowed his gaze on Garrett and then looked at the cards. He settled his hands on his hips and expelled his breath. "This is ludicrous, Upton, you know that? We're talking about my sister here."

Garrett nodded. "I'm certainly not about to argue that point. Ludicrous is an apt word for it."

Monroe turned to look at the cards. Garrett could see the internal war he was waging reflected on his face. "Damn it, Upton. Deal."

CHAPTER TWENTY-NINE

After rushing from the gold drawing room, Cass had been unable to find Julian. Instead, she'd hurried upstairs to see Pen, who was busily packing her bags, her maid and chaperone at her side.

"I daresay this is the quickest trip to the country I've ever made," Pen said with a laugh.

"You're leaving?" Cass asked, her mouth a wide O.

Pen waved a hand in the air. "Yes. The coachman says if we get back on the road right away, we should make it home before supper. It won't be dark for a while yet."

"How was your talk with Captain Swift?" Cass asked cautiously. Oh, she hated herself for having to pretend as if she didn't know what had happened.

"It went much better than even I expected," Pen said with a smile. "We both let each other down quite easily and pleasantly."

Cass bit her lip and glanced away. "And you're . . . all right with that?"

Pen's smile was bright and genuine. "More than all right. I'm thrilled."

"You don't have to leave," Cass said.

"I know that. I want to leave."

"Because Patience Bunbury needs you?" Lucy strolled through the door, a catlike smile on her face.

Pen turned to face Lucy with a wide smile on her face. "Something like that. Oh, Your Grace, you won't think I'm hideously rude rushing off like this, will you? I just . . . I haven't felt so free in an age. I can't wait to return to London."

"Will you tell your parents that you won't be getting engaged?" Cass asked, a lump in her throat.

"Yes," Pen replied. "Captain Swift says he intends to formally tell them but I cannot wait to let everyone know I'm officially free."

Cass had to smile at her. She would never understand her cousin but Pen and Julian didn't suit. She'd known that forever.

"Your talk with Captain Swift went well, I take it?" Lucy asked.

Pen nodded. "Yes. Odd that he said he came here to find me. Getting shot must have made him a bit mad. No matter. I'm going back to London. There is a certain gentleman there I have my eye on."

Lucy laughed. "Then, by all means, go and Godspeed."

"Are you quite certain you're all right?" Cass asked. She hadn't been able to stop biting her bottom lip all day.

"You should be asking Captain Swift, not me. I'm fine. I'm relieved actually."

"What do you think your parents will say?" The bottom lip remained firmly wedged between Cass's teeth.

"No harm's done. There was never an official engagement. No one need claim to have cried off."

"But people knew you and Ju . . . Captain Swift were set to marry once he returned," Cass said.

Penelope shrugged. "I'll simply say I changed my mind. The heart is fickle, darling, don't you know?"

Cass swallowed. No, she didn't know. She didn't know at all. Her heart had never been fickle.

In the end, Pen and her entourage bundled themselves back into the coach and left in the late afternoon having only stayed at the house a few hours. Cass watched her go with Lucy and Jane at her side.

"Now that was utterly convenient." Lucy sighed. "There's no other word for it."

"All these years I've been convinced that Pen would marry Julian and then, just like that, it's over." Cass shook her head. "I almost cannot believe it."

"Believe it, because now you must explain to Captain Swift what happened. You cannot remain Patience Bunbury forever," Lucy said.

"No, I cannot," Cass agreed. But she could remain Patience Bunbury for one more night and that's exactly what she intended to do. Tomorrow morning, first thing, she would tell Julian the truth, no matter the consequences, but tonight . . . Tonight she wanted to kiss him.

Dinner was torturous. Cass sat three seats down from Julian completely unable to talk to him and nearly obscured from seeing him. Lucy had said it would be better this way. "The less chance you have to speak, the better, until you're ready to tell him."

Cass had agreed but it didn't make the three-hour meal any less excruciating. Not to mention, she had to sit there and endure her brother's glower the entire time. Owen, her big, strong, handsome, blond brother, was looking at her with murder in his eyes. Garrett had sent Cass and Lucy a note earlier telling them that Owen had arrived. Garrett had managed to get him alone and explain the entire escapade, but Owen, apparently, had only tenuously agreed to go along with the scheme, and that only because Garrett had bet him to keep his mouth shut over a hand of cards. Apparently, Upton had won.

Owen glowered at Cass the entire time. She could *feel* her brother's judgment. Luckily, he was on his third glass of wine. Lucy was doing an excellent job of keeping him in liquor and the company of beautiful women—she and Jane—both of whom Owen could not resist.

After dinner was finished, there was the interminable wait while the men drank their port and the women gossiped in the drawing room. Finally, *finally,* the gentlemen joined them. Cass didn't hesitate. She strolled up to Julian and whispered on the way out the door facing the opposite direction. "Meet me in the library."

Garrett stopped her just before she made it to the door. "There's something I must tell you. Get Lucy and meet me in the—"

"Sorry. I can't talk now."

Garrett's eyes were wide. "It's important, Cass."

"I'll find you first thing in the morning." She slipped out of his grip and into the hallway before he had a chance to say another word.

Cass hurried down the corridor and gently pushed open the door to the library, only to find Jane. Jane had obviously sneaked out of the drawing room again to read.

"Oh, Janie, you're going to have to leave," Cass said. "Julian will be here any moment."

"Sorry?" Jane glanced up from her book. "I was here first. Besides, I'm hiding from Upton. The less I see of him, the better. I'm not allowed to be rude to him, and it's sure to be the death of me."

Cass laughed. "Be that as it may, I've chosen this location as the rendezvous point for my assignation. You must leave. Please, for my sake?"

Jane rolled her eyes but quickly gathered her things and smiled at her friend as she passed by her on her way out the door. "You owe me a favor."

"Fine. Fine. Just walk faster, please. But not too fast, Garrett was in the corridor."

"Be careful, Cass." Jane's words had an ominous ring.

Cass swallowed and turned around. She pinched her cheeks to bring color to them and twirled her pink skirts and smoothed out the fabric. She touched her hand to her coiffure. Oh, where was a looking glass when one needed it?

It was funny how she felt no more guilt. Knowing that Pen had ended her engagement to Julian, being certain they both were happily done with their arrangement, it made Cass feel deliciously free. They'd both agreed and neither of them was unhappy with the outcome. Cass couldn't have asked for a better turn of events. Well, perhaps if Julian didn't fancy another lady, that would be the most ideal situation, but now that she no longer felt any guilt over damaging her cousin's engagement, she was free. Free to do exactly as she pleased. And even more free tonight because she was able to do it as Patience Bunbury. The last two times Cass had asked Julian to kiss her, he'd refused. Tonight, there would be no reason to refuse. She would have her first kiss. There would be time for recriminations and confessions in the morning. Tonight. Tonight there would be only pleasure.

Julian waited a respectable twenty minutes before slipping out of the drawing room and making his way to the library. He opened the door and took in Patience Bunbury's beauty. It felt like a bayonet to the chest. She was pretty, so pretty and sweet.

"Captain Swift," she said, turning to face him, her cheeks bright pink.

"Miss Bunbury." He inclined his head toward her.

"Would you . . . would you like to sit?" She gestured to the leather sofa.

Julian made his way over to the sofa and sat next to her. "Dinner was . . . interesting," he began.

She pushed a blond curl behind her ear. Fetching, that. Quite.

"What do you mean?" she asked.

"Don't tell me you didn't notice the way Owen Monroe was staring at you all evening?"

Miss Bunbury's eyes widened. "What? Owen? I mean, his lordship?"

"Yes. He couldn't keep his eyes off you. I confess I considered calling him out."

"Oh, no, no, no. You are mistaken. He didn't—"

Julian slid closer. "I know what I saw. And I must admit, it made me jealous as hell."

A little smile popped to her lips. "It did?"

"Yes, and you know what else?"

"What else?"

"I talked to Penelope again earlier. We ended our agreement. Apparently, she left before dinner."

"Was she . . . upset?"

"You didn't see her?"

Miss Bunbury didn't look at him. "No," she murmured.

"Once we got that nonsense out of the way about her pretending to be you, she wasn't a bit upset. She told me she'd been planning to end things with me herself." Julian laughed.

Miss Bunbury smiled again. "That's surprising." She seemed shy tonight, reticent. Why wouldn't she look at him?

He slid closer to her on the sofa. Their thighs touched, only the fabric of their clothing separated them. "Miss Bunbury?"

"Y . . . es?"

"I no longer have an arrangement of any sort with Miss Monroe."

"You do not?"

"No, I do not."

"Did she . . . give you an explanation for why she'd pretended to be . . . me?" Her voice cracked on the last word.

"She did but it doesn't matter. She obviously didn't know I'd already met you. Though why she would think I hadn't when I've been at a house party with you all week . . . I must admit I briefly believed she'd taken complete leave of her senses."

Miss Bunbury closed her eyes and nodded.

"I would like very much to kiss you now," Julian said.

A small gasp escaped her lips. "Me?"

"Patience," he breathed. Julian stared at her beautiful face. He did want to kiss her. Cassandra wasn't here, after all, and Cassandra was in love with another man. Patience was here and lovely and wanted him. He could tell by the way she looked at him, the way she touched him, the way she tipped back her head and closed her eyes, waiting for his kiss.

Julian lowered his mouth to hers. The feel of her sweet, soft lips under his made him gasp into her mouth. It was better than he'd expected. Much better.

He pulled her close, her bodice pressed against his chest. He pushed his tongue into her mouth, lust flooding through his veins, making his cock hard.

Patience kissed him back with a fervor and energy that enveloped him. She made little moaning noises in the back of her throat and she rocked against him.

His mouth slanted over hers, hot, hard, demanding. He couldn't get enough, didn't want to stop. She was gorgeous.

Only she wasn't . . . Cassandra.

Reality slammed into his gut. He pulled his mouth away and pressed his forehead to hers, breathing heavily. No. No. *Stop thinking about Cassie. This isn't the time. She loves another man.*

He clenched his jaw. What the hell was he doing, thinking about Cassie at a moment like this? He pulled Patience against him and kissed her again. Would Cass smell like this? Look like this? Be this irresistible?

He pulled his mouth away from Patience's once more, holding her by the shoulders. Damn it to hell, he couldn't get Cassie out of his mind. He shook his head as if that might serve to dislodge her. It didn't.

Miss Bunbury stared up at him with wide blue eyes . . . eyes that looked very much like his memory of Cassandra's eyes. He shook himself again. Now he was truly going mad, wanting Cassie so much that he was seeing her in a completely different woman. It wasn't just wrong. It was sick, and completely unfair to Patience.

She blinked up at him, looking entirely confused. Damn it. That was his fault. He hated himself for what he was about to say.

"I'm sorry, Miss Bunbury . . ." And then, "Patience. I thought I could do this but I cannot."

Tears filled her eyes. "I understand, Captain," she murmured.

Julian felt like a complete arse. He was a complete arse. What sort of man kissed a nice young lady like Patience Bunbury and then stopped? She didn't deserve this. She'd already been jilted by her intended last summer. Now she had to endure Julian's ungentlemanly behavior, as well. He wouldn't blame her if she hated him forever.

"God, Patience . . . Miss Bunbury. I'm a complete scoundrel. I truly didn't intend to lead you on or to hurt you. Do you have a brother? A father? I'm certain one of them will want to call me out."

Her voice was small. "Please, Captain Swift, no more apologies. You've nothing to apologize to me for. Please, just go."

Julian bowed his head, then nodded.

He glanced up at her again and rubbed his thumb against her high cheekbone, wiping away one delicate tear. "Damn me to hell. You're the most beautiful woman I've ever seen."

And that was true, but it didn't matter.

He stood and made his way to the door, then he turned back to Miss Bunbury. "I'm sorry."

CHAPTER THIRTY

Cass took her time dressing the next morning. She sent back every gown her maid presented to her. The gowns didn't matter, any one of them would have been fine. The truth was that she didn't want to face Julian. And each thing she accomplished to get ready to go downstairs and see him would bring her that much closer to her moment of reckoning. A moment she dreaded.

It was time. Finally time to face the truth and take the consequences. She knew that. It was over.

First, however, she had to find Garrett. He'd had something to tell her last night. She'd been rude to him, rushing off like that. If she'd known what was going to happen, she wouldn't have rushed. Would have lingered, actually. Oh, it had been a disaster. She'd tried to find Garrett after the debacle in the library but he was nowhere to be found and neither was Lucy. Instead, she'd gone up to bed and thought about how detestable she was. How much Julian was going to despise her once she told him the truth. Eventually, she'd fallen into an exhausted slumber, one that left her fitful and dreaming about Julian berating her for lying to him and marrying another woman.

Her worst nightmare. It was all about to come true and there was nothing she could do to stop it. She could only delay the inevitable.

She stared at her pale reflection in the looking glass. Julian had told her she was the most beautiful woman in the world last night. Hadn't that once been her dream? But he hadn't said those words to *her*. No, Patience Bunbury was the most beautiful woman in the world, Patience Bunbury, the woman who didn't exist. The reflection disgusted her. How could such a simple pretty face mask such ugliness and lies? She scrubbed her hands savagely across her face as if she could wipe away her looks, replace them with the mask of ugliness she knew she deserved after what she'd done. Julian was honorable and noble right up to the end. He'd been the one to stop, not her. Oh, no. She might have gone on kissing him all night, the lying little hoyden that she was.

She'd cried last night in front of him. That was poorly done also. But she hadn't been crying for the reason he thought. He probably believed she was sad because Patience had developed a *tendre* for him. But the truth was she'd been crying because she knew he couldn't kiss Patience because he still loved someone else, someone who was not Patience, and not Cass, someone whose eyes she wanted to scratch out.

Regardless, she must stop being a coward. She had to face Julian today. First, she'd find Garrett and see what was so urgent. Then, she'd find Julian. She would find him and finally tell him the truth. It was time. No matter what. No more hiding. No more lies.

Her maid returned with one more gown, a simple white one. "This one, miss?"

White, the symbol of purity, light, innocence, hardly a color she should wear today, sinner that she was. But if she was going to battle that devil who liked to pop up on her shoulder, she would need all the reinforcement she could get. "Yes, that one will be fine, Maria. I'm sorry I've been such a bother this morning."

She stared back at her reflection in the looking glass once more. Patience? Cass? Whoever she was. It was finally time to face the truth.

Cass had just started down the stairway when a large commotion in the foyer caught her attention. There appeared to be a great many people there, all of them raising their voices.

She hurried down far enough to see the occupants of the space and caught her breath. She braced a hand against the bannister to steady herself. There, in the foyer with Lucy, Jane, Garrett, and a half-dozen servants, stood her parents. Owen wasn't there. And neither was Julian, thank God. But . . . She leaned down to get a closer look.

Penelope was with them.

Cass's heart thumped. Danger. That's what this was. *Danger, danger, danger.* Every nerve in her body screamed at her to flee. Instead, she remained rooted to the spot, her shaking hand frozen to the bannister.

"I demand to see my daughter," her mother, Lady Moreland, said.

"Yes, where is Cassandra? Bring her here this instant," her father added.

Lucy kept glancing around nervously. "If you'd all just come into the drawing room, I'll be happy to fetch Cass and we can all discuss this like civilized adults and—"

"Cassandra? Cassandra is here?"

Cass closed her eyes slowly and swallowed. She couldn't see the person who'd just said those words but she knew him just the same.

Julian.

Julian strode forward then. Apparently he'd happened upon the scene in the foyer just as she had.

"Who are *you*?" Cass's mother demanded of Julian.

"Why, Auntie, don't you remember him? That is Captain Swift," Penelope offered.

Cass's mother's eyes went wide. "Captain Swift?"

"Captain Swift?" her father echoed.

"At your service," Julian said, bowing to them. "I haven't seen either of you in quite a long time. I don't blame you for not remembering me, Lord Moreland, Lady Moreland."

Cass's mother continued to eye him up and down before turning back to Lucy. "I want Cass here this instant," she demanded.

Jane and Garrett were obviously attempting to assist Lucy in herding the little group into the nearby drawing room. Unfortunately, they were having as much luck as Lucy was. "I told you, Lady Moreland. I'll be quite happy to go get Cass just as soon as you—"

Cass's mother narrowed her eyes on Lucy and pointed her finger at her. "I don't care if you are a duchess now, *Your Grace*." She sneered the honorific. "I will not have you leading my daughter down the primrose path with you. All this time I'd been under the impression that the two of you were at a house party together until my niece here came to my home yesterday after her carriage broke down nearby and informed me that you were both here, only a few miles away."

Julian's head swiveled toward Lucy. "Your Grace?"

Jane and Garrett groaned.

Penelope looked as she did when they were children and she'd tried to solve a particularly difficult maths equation, a cross between pure confusion and a bit of nausea.

Cass's parents both stared at Julian as if he'd lost his mind.

"Surely you recognize your hostess, the Duchess of Claringdon? Though I daresay she brings the title down a bit," Lady Moreland said.

Lucy winced and turned her head sharply to the side as if she'd been slapped.

That was it. Cass marched down the stairs. She'd been a coward for far too long. She couldn't allow Lucy to be treated with such disrespect by her parents, devil take the consequences.

"Mother!"

All pairs of eyes turned to look up at her.

"Mother?" Julian echoed the word, looking back and forth between Cass and her mother.

Cass marched down the stairs and made her way to the center of the group. "I will not allow you to speak to my friend so indecorously in her own home." Cass put her hands on her hips and glared at her mother.

"It's all right, Cass—" Lucy began, reaching out as if to soothe her.

Cass brushed her friend's hand away. "No. It's not all right. They've had weeks to get used to the fact that you married Derek and I didn't, and it's high time they began treating you with the respect due your title."

She knew that with each word, she was revealing herself to Julian. And she was still being a coward because this way, this way might be like quickly ripping a bandage from a wound, but everything would be out. Everything would be obvious.

She couldn't look at Julian but she could feel his gaze on her, watching her, piecing everything together.

"You demand that I treat this little baggage with respect?" her mother said in a voice that clearly indicated how shocked she was that Cass was standing up to her.

"Yes, and if the duke were here, he'd toss you out for being so impertinent to his bride."

"Yes, I'm about to toss you out as well," Garrett added.

Cass's mother opened her mouth to speak again but Julian intervened. He turned to Lucy. "Wait a moment. Am I to understand from this bit of conversation that you are, in fact, Lucy Hunt, the Duchess of Claringdon? Derek's wife?"

Jane and Garrett winced.

This time Penelope piped up. "Of course she is, Captain Swift. Who did you think she was? You've been staying at her house for the last week."

Julian narrowed his eyes on Lucy, who had the grace to look apologetic. "I thought her name was Lady Worthing." He continued to watch Lucy, but he addressed his remarks to the others.

"I sort of . . . invented that title," Lucy offered, biting her lip. Oh, this was not good. Lucy never bit her lip.

Julian quickly snapped his head to the side to confront Cass. "And you? You're not Patience Bunbury, are you?"

Penelope's mouth dropped straight open. "What nonsense are you talking about? That's my cousin Cass. She's been writing to you for years. Don't you remember her?"

Tears burned the backs of Cass's eyes but she held them in. She didn't have the right to cry. She didn't have the right to do anything, anything other than stand here and let Julian realize the truth. And hate her for it.

He searched her face. His eyes scoured her body from head to toe. For an aching moment, she felt his pain, his shock, his . . . anger. "Cassandra?" he whispered brokenly. "You're Cassandra?"

"Wait a moment, did she tell you she's Patience?" Penelope demanded.

Julian didn't take his eyes from Cass. "Yes." The one word echoed across the foyer, bouncing off the marble columns and slapping Cass across the face.

"Who in heaven's name is Patience Bunbury?" Cass's mother demanded next.

Penelope plunked her hands on her hips. "She's my very close friend who does not exist."

A cacophony ensued then. All of the occupants of the foyer began shouting out questions and explanations and more questions. It escalated to a thunderous boil while Cass and Julian just stared at each other, silently. Cass's chest ached. She couldn't breathe and she desperately fought against the tears in her eyes. Julian watched her with a look that could only be described as . . . disgust.

And she couldn't blame him.

CHAPTER THIRTY-ONE

Two hours later, Julian was standing on the terrace, his hands in his pockets, his shoulder propped against a large marble column, staring out into the gardens.

He sensed rather than saw Cass's approach. Then, he watched her advance out of the corner of his eye. She walked toward him slowly, quietly, deliberately.

He finally turned to face her. She was so pretty, so heartbreakingly beautiful. Cassandra. Cassie. The woman he'd been wondering about, the woman he'd been dreaming about. She and the ethereal Patience Bunbury were one and the same? It had been all he could think about for the last two hours, but still, he could hardly credit it.

He narrowed his eyes on her face. He was a fool. How could he have not known? Not guessed? She had Cassie's same flaxen hair. Cassie's same cornflower-blue eyes. He even saw Cassie in the tug of her smile and the tiny dimple that appeared. How in the hell had he not noticed that? Very well. It was true that Cassandra looked little like she had seven years ago, but still, she was there, inside this swanlike beauty. She was there. His gut wrenched.

She was there and she had been lying to him this entire time.

She stopped a few paces away from him. She pressed her lips together and swallowed. "I know I cannot offer any explanation that will make this right," she began. "But I wanted to . . . face you. And say"—she hung her head—"I'm sorry."

Julian looked up, squinted at her, and then went back to staring off into the gardens. "I have only one question."

She was fighting back tears. He'd seen it in the way she'd been blinking too rapidly, swallowing too often. He didn't want to care. If he didn't look at her, he wouldn't.

"Yes," she murmured.

"Why?" he asked through clenched teeth.

She reached for him but quickly snatched her hand away. Good thing. He wouldn't allow her to touch him. Instead, she wrapped her arms around her middle and spoke quietly. "Oh, Julian. I could try and explain it all to you. But it's just as inexplicable as I'm certain you've already guessed. If I told you why, it would merely sound as if I'm trying to blame Pen and she doesn't deserve the blame."

He pressed his lips together tightly. Cassie wasn't even going to do him the honor of explaining why she had lied to him. "I can't understand why you would lie about who you are, to me."

Cassandra blinked up into the blue sky, tears slipping down her cheeks. She was obviously losing the battle not to cry. "I'm sorry, Julian. So sorry. I just wanted to . . . spend time with you."

"And you couldn't do that as Cassandra?" he said, an incredulous look on his face.

She swallowed again. "No," she whispered brokenly.

He scrubbed his hands through his hair. "What about

all the letters, the friendship we shared? Did that mean nothing to you that you could lie to me this way?"

She swiped at her tears with the back of her hand. "I cannot explain myself. I only know that it made a little bit of sense to me at the time and . . . Oh, Julian, I'd do anything to take it back, to make it so that—"

He put up a hand. "Don't. Just don't."

"You didn't recognize me when we first met."

He closed his eyes briefly. "So it's my fault?"

"No. No. Not at all." She paced forward, then turned to face him. The tears flowed freely down her face now.

He pulled his handkerchief from his pocket and handed it to her. She took it with a small smile and a grateful sniff. "Always the gentleman," she murmured. "The perfect gentleman."

"I wasn't last night. When I kissed you . . . or Patience . . . or whoever you are. But I interrupted you. You were saying?"

Cassie took a deep breath. "I just couldn't believe you didn't know me and then Lucy told you I was Patience and . . . you have to know Lucy. She's— I'm a complete fool. I'm sorry. I never meant to hurt you."

"You let me kiss you, thinking you were another woman. That's completely—"

"Wrong?"

He groaned and scrubbed his hands through his hair again. "Among many other things."

"Julian, I know it seems mad and inexplicable, but you have to believe that I didn't mean to hurt you. I never meant for it to go this far. I wanted to tell you a dozen times. Everything I wrote in those letters, all of it, was true. That's me. I'm your friend Cassandra. Don't you remember me?" She grabbed his hand then and held it to her heart.

He closed his eyes. Her fingers were cold but her chest was warm. A tingle went up his arm. But he fought it. He mentally smashed his physical reaction to her. "I knew Cassandra from her letters." He yanked his hand from her grasp. "You're not Cassandra. I don't know who *you* are."

He turned on his heel and walked away.

CHAPTER THIRTY-TWO

"Won't you eat something?" Jane rubbed Cass's back. She gestured toward the tureen of soup the maid had brought up to Cass's bedchamber on a silver bed tray.

"I'm not hungry," Cass choked out. She was lying on her bed, wearing her white linen night rail, stoically staring at the wall in front of her. She wouldn't cry. She wouldn't cry anymore. Instead, she'd been silent. Silent and resigned, and that probably scared Jane more than if she'd been sobbing her eyes out.

"You've been like this for days," Jane said, worry laced through her voice. "You must eat something."

Cass pressed her handkerchief to her eyes. Yes. She'd been like this for four long days. Silent and inconsolable. The house party had quickly disbanded after the incident in the foyer. After Julian had left her on the terrace, she'd gone up to her rooms and asked Maria to quickly pack her bags. She'd traveled to her parents' estate and taken Jane with her. She hadn't so much as said good-bye to Lucy.

Lucy. Cass was filled with anger every time she thought about Lucy. She couldn't even hear her name without clenching her fists. According to Jane, Lucy had been writing letters every day, hoping to be allowed to come over and speak to her, but Cass steadfastly refused. She'd also refused her mother's insistence that she explain everything to her. Apparently, the afternoon Pen had left to return to London, an axle on her carriage wheel had snapped and she'd been closer to Cass's parents' estate than Lucy's when it happened. Of all the luck. After all the scheming, the entire farce had been ruined by a simple axle.

After the debacle in the foyer, Garrett had quickly returned to his home. Julian had left for London immediately, and Owen had happily returned to town as well, obviously pleased to be through with his sister's mad schemes. He'd taken Penelope with him. Their cousin was only too happy to have a ride. Dear Lord Berkeley had put a hand on Cass's shoulder and told her how sorry he was that this particular charade hadn't ended so well but he'd be honored to be invited to the next one.

That blasted carriage-wheel axle. Cass couldn't stop thinking about it. Not that it made any difference. And not that it was Pen's fault. But if only that axle hadn't snapped, if only Pen hadn't gone to Cass's parents' house that night, if only Pen hadn't told Cass's parents that Cass was, indeed, at the Upbridge estate, and if only the three hadn't traveled back together the next morning . . . Cass might have got away with it all. Well, perhaps she would not have actually got away with it, per se, but at least she'd have had the chance to try to explain it to Julian by herself, without him finding out in such a horrible manner. Then he would have known that she didn't intend to lie to him indefinitely, that she wasn't the horrible person he thought she was. Oh, who was she fooling? She *was* horrible. Loathsome, actually. The only person she could summon true anger against was herself.

And Lucy.

Lucy she would never forgive.

"Tell me again what Julian said when he left," Cass asked Jane in a shaky voice.

Jane took a deep breath. "He told Upton that he intended to return to London and was hoping for orders that would allow him to go to the Continent again."

"He's going to France," Cass said quietly.

"Upton wasn't certain where he was going, but he thinks that it has something to do with Derek."

"It does. Julian told me. Well, he told Patience. He said his brother and Captain Cavendish are missing in France. Derek's looking for them now."

"I do hope they are all careful," Jane replied.

"What else did Garrett say?" Cass asked.

Jane winced. "He said he tried to warn you on the last night of the party that your parents were coming. He said you wouldn't listen. Is that true?"

Cass nodded. "Yes." More blasted tears burned the backs of her eyes. She resolutely shook them away. She couldn't cry over this. It was all her own doing. "Did Garrett say anything else?"

"Yes, he said, 'Please go back to your old ways, Miss Lowndes. I don't know how to be in your company without your constant barrage of insults. It's quite dull, really. Not to mention unsettling.'"

That actually brought a smile to Cass's face momentarily.

"Ah, see there! I got you to smile," Jane announced. "You should have seen it when I was forced to admit to Captain Swift that I am not only *not* named Miss Wollstonecraft, I am, in fact, no relation to the family." Jane sighed.

Cass reached out and patted Jane's hand. "You're such a good friend, Janie. I'm lucky to have you."

"Yes, well, our other good friend is eagerly anticipating

my reply to her last letter. She'd very much like to speak with you."

Cass pressed her lips together. "No. I refuse to see Lucy. She's the cause of all of this. If we'd just simply told the truth and allowed Pen and Julian to see each other that first day, they would have broken their engagement and Julian wouldn't hate me right now."

"I know it's difficult for you," Jane said. "But Lucy really did think she was helping. Her heart was in the right place. It always is. You know that."

Cass clenched her jaw. "I cannot even look at her."

"All right. All right. I'll tell her."

Cass sniffed. "Thank you, Janie."

"For what it's worth, I do think she feels awfully sorry," Jane replied.

Cass groaned and rolled over, hugging the pillow to her chest. "Oh, Janie, I don't know what I'm going to do."

Jane stroked her hair. "Let's begin by you telling me where you'd like to be. We can go to Brighton or Bath. I'll travel with you. We'll make it a holiday."

Cass took a deep breath. "I want to go back to London."

CHAPTER THIRTY-THREE

Julian finished writing the letter to Wellington. He folded it, sanded it, and sealed it. Then he pushed the missive across the desk away from him and leaned back in his chair. He was staying at Donald's town house again, a place he truly didn't belong. He glanced around the room, his brother's study. Sparse, clean, functional, just like Donald.

Donald had been the perfect eldest son. The only son their father had ever wanted. And now Donald was missing.

Julian stood, walked over to the sideboard, and poured himself a drink. He downed it in one long gulp and poured another.

Warmth began to spread through his limbs, but no amount of alcohol would ever erase the memory of the screams of pain on the battlefield, some of which had been his own.

He took the second drink back to the desk and sat down again. A bit of it sloshed onto his hand. He cursed.

When he'd returned to London from the house party, his first order of business had been finding Penelope's parents and telling them that he did not intend to marry their daughter. Mr. Monroe had been quite reasonable, actually. Apparently, Penelope had already explained the entire situation to them. They didn't want their daughter to be unhappy any more than they wanted Julian to be unhappy. Penelope's parents both wished him well and told him how thankful they were that he'd returned from the war. They inquired after his mother's health as well as Daphne's. The entire experience had not been unpleasant. At least something had gone right after that disaster in Surrey.

Julian's next order of business should have been finding Cassie, but of course his plans there had drastically changed. He couldn't even think about her. Not after what she'd done. All he cared about now was finding Donald and Rafe.

He grabbed an opened letter from the desktop. He'd received it from Derek today. Julian's eyes scanned the page for the tenth time. It said the Hunt brothers had followed the trail they'd found when they originally arrived and had a good two more days to travel before they arrived at the location where Donald and Rafe had last been seen. If Donald and Rafe, were, in fact, the two Englishmen their informants had seen. It was all a gamble, but it was the only hope they had.

Julian took another drink. If Donald and Rafe were there, Derek would find them. There could be no one better to look for them, not even himself though he hated to admit it. He'd written that letter to Wellington, asking to join them, not because he didn't trust his friends to do the job, but because he bloody well couldn't sit here in a London town house and do nothing while his brother and his friend were missing and his other friends were on their trail. And the truth was, he intended to go after them with or without Wellington's approval. He'd prefer the former but as soon as he got his answer, he'd be off, one way or the other, unless Derek had already returned with news.

Yes, Julian wanted to go to find them, but if he were being truly honest with himself—and the brandy made him honest, damn it—he'd admit that he didn't want to stay in London because he'd be tempted to go see Cassie. The farther he got from her, the safer he would be.

When she'd apologized to him on the terrace, he'd been tempted, so damn tempted, to demand that she tell him who the hell she was in love with. She'd been remorseful the last time he saw her, with tears in her eyes. But her excuses made no sense. Part of the reason he'd left was because he couldn't stand to look at her, her ethereal beauty, her perfection, and know that he could never have her, not the way he wanted her.

Why had she allowed him to kiss her? Was she so evil that she thought it was a funny game? "I'm your friend Cassandra," she'd said. Some friend, a liar. The Cassandra he knew wasn't a liar.

And for one moment, one awful, perfect, wonderful, hideous moment when he'd been standing in that foyer with all those people listening to the words coming out of their mouths, he'd realized that the woman he'd lusted after so unmercifully and the woman he'd cared about for so long were in fact the same human being. It had been an exquisite torture, one that ripped his heart from his chest as he'd realized that he could never have her. Patience might have wanted him, but according to Hunt, Cass wanted someone else. And even if she didn't, it didn't matter because she was a liar, an actress, someone who couldn't be trusted.

Damn it. Who was the man she was in love with? Julian shouldn't care, but he did. He took another drink. By God, he'd rip the blighter limb from bloody limb when he found out his identity. No, he wouldn't. But he wanted to. God, he wanted to. Was it Upton? Upton had played along, hadn't he? Had they been laughing at Julian behind his back during the house party? Had they all been? Upton and Jane Lowndes and Lucy? Even Owen had somehow not deemed it fit to mention to him that his sister was trotting around a house party claiming to be someone she was not. What the hell was the matter with the lot of them?

Julian tossed the contents of his glass down his throat and made his way unerringly back to the sideboard to get another.

When the Duchess of Claringdon was ushered into his brother's study hours later, Julian wasn't entirely certain what day it was anymore. The brandy had accomplished its purpose.

"Thank you for seeing me, Captain Swift," the duchess said.

Julian bowed to her and nearly toppled over. "My pleasure, Your Grace, for it is not every day a true duchess visits me."

Lucy Hunt smiled a little. Her unusually colored eyes flashed.

"May I offer you a drink, Your Grace?" he continued, sweeping an arm wide toward the sideboard.

"No, thank you, Captain."

"More for me then," he said. Blast. Had he just hiccupped? Bad form. "Tell me, to what do I owe the pleasure?"

Pleasure might have come out a bit more like *pleather,* but no matter. She knew what he meant. He stumbled over to the sideboard and splashed the last of the brandy into his glass. Bloody hell. The bottle was empty. He tipped it upside down and shook it, then tossed the empty bottle into the air. He tried to catch it but missed. It thudded on the carpet and rolled under the sideboard. Julian kicked it into the corner and continued back to the sofa where the duchess was getting settled.

"I came to apologize," she said softly. "And to give you this." She pulled a letter from her reticule.

"Apologize for what?" Julian tried to focus his gaze on the duchess. At the moment there appeared to be two of her sitting there, weaving back and forth in a foggy haze like little duchess twins. "It is I who must apologize to you, Your Grace, for I am deeply in my cups."

A small smile twitched across her lips. "Not to worry, Captain. I completely understand. I should have warned you I was coming, but I came to apologize for my part in the duplicity played upon you at the house party. I was not certain you would see me."

"I wouldn't turn away my closest friend's wife."

"I see that I was worried needlessly." She glanced down at the letter in her hand. "But I've come to tell you something."

He clenched his jaw. "If it's an excuse for Cassie, I'd rather not hear it."

The duchess leaned forward on the sofa and spoke rapidly and earnestly. "You must listen. The entire thing was all my idea, truly. Though Cass insists you won't believe me telling you that, it's true. I swear it."

He pointed a shaky finger in the air. "With all due respect, Your Grace," pronounced *grath,* "even if it is true and it was entirely your idea, *you* were not my friend, a person whom I'd known for years and traded countless letters with. Your lying to me was far different from Cassandra lying to me."

"I completely understand, Captain," the duchess replied. "I do hope you'll believe it was all my idea, however. I am known for my schemes, as I'm certain my husband will tell you when next you meet. However, be that as it may, I can only hope you'll reconsider your feelings for Cass and that you'll—"

"That I'll what?" He took another drink and nearly missed his mouth.

"That you'll read this," she finished, offering him the letter.

He snatched the letter from her outstretched hand. "What is it?"

"It's from Cass."

Julian tossed the letter onto the couch where it slipped between the cushions. "Bah. I already spoke to her. I don't need any more of her excuses or her apologies."

"No. It's something far, far different, Captain Swift. Cass wrote it months ago when she thought you were dying."

He closed one eye, the two duchesses appearing more like one that way. "And she asked you to bring it to me now?"

"No. Quite the contrary. She'd have my head if she knew I'd brought it to you."

"If she didn't ask you to bring it, how did you get it?"

The duchess took a deep breath. "She had it with her at the house party. She brings all her letters from you with her. It was in the same box. I sneaked into her room. I know I shouldn't have, but I truly think . . . Read the letter, Captain. Please."

He narrowed his eyes on her. "If you think Cassandra will be displeased that you brought it to me, then why have you?"

"Because I think it will make a difference. And I think it's important. And"—she sighed—"the truth is that Cass already wants my head so I'm not risking much in coming here." She smiled a smile that didn't quite reach her eyes.

The duchess stood and smoothed her skirts. "I'll leave you, Captain. I hope you'll read the letter."

Julian stood, too, and watched the duchess go in a blurry haze. "Read the letter," he mumbled. "No more excuses."

And then he fell face-first onto the sofa.

CHAPTER THIRTY-FOUR

When Julian awoke the next morning, he was in his bed at Donald's house and the devil was playing the drums in his skull. He sat up slowly and cautiously reached for the bellpull.

The butler arrived in a matter of moments.

"I beg you, Pengree, bring me something for my head," Julian said.

"Right away, my lord," Pengree replied, swiveling on his heel and leaving the room.

Julian braced his hands against his temples and squeezed. God, why had he drunk so much brandy? He'd been an untried youth the last time he'd got so out of control with drink. Bad. Bad. Form.

The barest hint of a memory formed in his brain. Last night. The study. The brandy. The duchess. By God, Derek's little dark-haired duchess had stopped by to visit him and blast it if he couldn't remember a word that she'd said. Surely, there'd been some reason she'd come. He barely recalled trying to make out her face in the blurry haze of two bright-eyed young women who sat wavering on his sofa.

Bloody hell. It hurt to try to remember. No doubt she'd come with more excuses and lies. Or to try to tell him that Cassandra was not to blame. Rubbish, all of it. By God, he— He groaned. He'd moved his head far too quickly.

He remembered a bit about what he'd done last night, mostly ruminated about Cassie and her penchant for lying. And hadn't she played her bloody role to perfection? Even going so far as to pretend she didn't know he had a brother or a sister. Asking if they were close. It was sickening. Cassie knew damn well that he and Donald had never been close.

Pengree came hurrying back into the room with a concoction that Julian's friend Devon Morgan, the Marquis of Colton, had invented years ago when they were young men about town. It was green, it was hideous, and it worked like bloody magic. Donald had used it, too, upon occasion, and his butler obviously knew the recipe. Julian took the glass from the silver tray and stared at the vile liquid. Then he downed it in one awful gulp.

He breathed deeply, trying not to choke. "Pengree?" he finally said.

The butler stopped and turned around. "Yes, my lord."

"The Duchess of Claringdon visited me last night?"

"Yes, my lord. She was in your study for nearly a quarter hour. She asked me to check on you when she left."

Julian rubbed his temples. "And what did you find when you checked on me?"

Pengree cleared his throat. "You were, ahem, asleep on the sofa, my lord."

"Asleep?"

"In a manner of speaking, my lord."

Translation, passed out. "Did she say anything to you, Pengree? Did she leave anything?"

"No, my lord. Not to my knowledge."

Julian shook his head and then groaned again. The

green stuff didn't work quite that quickly. But he couldn't help the feeling that he was forgetting something, something the duchess had said perhaps.

"Very well, Pengree. Thank you."

The butler left the room without another word.

CHAPTER THIRTY-FIVE

"Please, Julian, please take me to the theater. It's been an age since I've had an escort." Daphne was damned convincing when she wanted to be, and unfortunately, Julian always found it difficult to say no to his little sister.

He glanced over at her. Daphne was nearly nineteen now and a grown woman. She had already survived her first Season. The change in her had shocked him. Not quite as much as the change in Cassandra Monroe but— No. That sort of thinking was entirely unhelpful.

"I'm pleased to hear that the Monroes were not angry with you for breaking off your arrangement with Penelope," his mother said from her perch on a rosewood chair a few feet away from him.

Julian let out a slight laugh. "Penelope was just as eager to be rid of me as I was of her, it seems."

"All's well that ends well," Daphne said with a bright smile. "Now, about the theater tonight . . ."

In the end, Julian agreed. Daphne seemed a bit down, not in her usual high spirits. She was sad about Donald and Rafe. Julian wanted to get her mind off her worries about them. "Very well, the theater it is."

Daphne laughed and clapped her hands.

Several hours later, as they made their way into Donald's box at the theater, Julian realized just what a monumental mistake it had been to agree to accompany his sister.

How could he have possibly forgotten that the theater just so happened to be one of Cassandra's favorite places? How many times in her letters had she regaled him with tales of going to see this play or that with her friends? It shouldn't have been a surprise when he saw her, sitting across from him in a box with her mother . . . and none other than Garrett Upton. But it was.

Garrett Upton.

Burning jealousy streaked through Julian's chest. Upton. That's who it was. It was all so clear now. Julian had had his suspicions. But now, seeing them together, he no longer had doubts. Upton had been there, at the house party, probably silently mocking Julian the entire time while his cousin and her friend played their little game with him. It had to be Upton. He was the only man other than her father and brother whom Cass had ever mentioned in her letters. Upton was always there with them. She'd even stayed at his house last summer in Bath. Another memory impaled itself in Julian's brain. Upton had been alone with Cassie in the library that night at the house party before Julian had arrived. He'd asked her about it at the time and she'd made some excuse about Upton looking for a book before bed. She had pretended she didn't even know him.

Yes, it was Upton. Julian was certain. And Upton was the heir to an earldom. Wasn't that what Cassandra had always told him her mother insisted she marry? A title. A title exactly like the one Julian did not have?

He glared across the space at the two of them. The moment his eyes met Cassandra's she dropped her gaze, put her handkerchief to her mouth, and quickly exited the box. Cassandra's mother appeared oblivious, but Upton stood and watched her go. Then he turned his stare in Julian's direction. Julian returned his look with a narrow-eyed smirk. It was a good thing Upton was on the other side of the theater or he'd smash in his bloody face.

"Excuse me a moment," Julian said to Daphne. He stood and left his own box without thinking about it, as if his legs were moving of their own accord. With ground-devouring strides, he made his way down the corridor and out into the lobby.

Cassie was standing there, shaking, a few tears in her eyes. For a moment, Julian felt as if he'd been punched in the gut. Had he made her feel this way? But then reality returned with a vengeance in the form of memories. What did he care? He couldn't trust her. Not one bit. She'd lied to him, over and over. She had only told him the truth when she'd been forced to. This entire stance of hers was probably for show. She was a consummate actress. Had she guessed he would follow her? He would do well to turn around, go back to his sister, and ignore Cassie. She deserved no less.

Then he remembered how frightened she'd looked when she heard Donald was missing in France. That hadn't been an act. She had truly cared.

"Cassandra." Her name escaped his lips of its own volition. Bloody hell. Too late.

She turned. Her eyes went wide. "Julian? Wh-what are you doing here?"

He narrowed his eyes on her. "I could have sworn you saw me in the theater."

She nodded slowly. "I did. I meant, what are you doing out here?" She gestured to the lobby.

She was trying to ask him why he'd followed her and was doing a poor job of it.

"Why are you crying?" he heard himself ask.

She glanced away. "I'm not crying."

"Aren't you?"

"Please, Julian."

He strode forward then and grabbed her by the wrist. He pulled her behind him several paces until they reached a secluded alcove in the corner. Then he spun her away from him and turned to face her. "Why are you crying?"

"I know. I don't have the right to cry about this," she said, even as a tear rolled down her nose and plopped off. She quickly pressed her handkerchief to her face.

"Then why are you?" he demanded.

"I can't help it."

"Damn it, Cassandra. You're the one—"

A bit of fire flared in her eyes, fire he'd never seen before. "I know. I know. I'm the one who misled you. I'm the one who lied. I know what I've done, Julian. I have no one to blame but myself. But I'm not lying when I say I'm sorry for it and I'd take it back if only I could."

He'd been about to say, "You're the one who loves someone else." Thank God she'd stopped him. That would have been admitting far too much, damn it. All he wanted to do now was punch his bloody fist through the nearest wall. She was standing here crying because they'd lost their friendship. As far as he was concerned, they'd lost so much more.

"You came here tonight with Upton?" he ventured.

Another slow nod. "Yes."

He clenched his fist. "Do you intend to marry him?"

She glanced away, tears streaking down both cheeks. "My mother wants me to."

He scrubbed his hand through his hair. "And you? Is that what you want?"

"Cassandra." They both swiveled around to see Upton

standing a few paces away, hands on his hips, glaring at them like a jealous bridegroom. "Are you all right?"

Cass nodded. "Yes, Garrett. I'm all right."

"No need to check on her, Upton. She's fine," Julian ground out, wishing he could bury his fist in Upton's face.

"She doesn't look fine to me," Upton replied, watching Cass carefully. "Do you need me, Cassandra?"

Julian took one menacing step toward Upton. The man needed only to say one more word. Julian had enough rage in him tonight to beat him to a bloody pulp. Cassandra brushed past Julian and stood in front of Upton, blocking him from Julian's view. She'd just saved him.

"I'm fine, Garrett. Truly. Just give me a moment."

Garrett. She was already calling him by his Christian name. Had she written him letters when he'd been gone to the war in Spain? Who wasn't she writing letters to?

"Fine. I'll wait for you over there," Upton said, moving over to the doorway that led to the row where their box was situated. Julian let his fist relax, watching the man's retreat. He'd better stay back.

Cass turned back to face Julian, brushing the tears away from her eyes with both hands. "Will you ever forgive me, Julian?" she asked in a voice that made his knees weak.

Will you ever love me, Cassandra?

He glanced away, toward the darkened corridor. "I don't think I can."

CHAPTER THIRTY-SIX

Damn Daphne and her damn penchant for wanting to be in the middle of damn Society, the middle of the action, actually. Whatever that was. And tonight, apparently, it was the Marquis of Hillborough's ball. Half of London was in the country for the autumn but the one event everyone was apparently coming back for was this blasted ball.

"Everyone will be there, Julian," Daphne had cajoled, and since Julian had yet to hear back from Wellington one way or another, he gave in to his sister's demand and escorted her to the ball.

The only good news was that Julian expected Derek back any day now. He hadn't received any letters from his friend since the last one, but Derek had been given only a fortnight in which to find the other two men. The deadline was rapidly approaching and Julian waited on tenterhooks to hear from him. Perhaps, if this mission was unsuccessful, Wellington would approve of the two of them going back together. Julian could only hope.

"Why are you so grouchy?" Daphne asked, batting her long black eyelashes at him. His sister looked positively pretty sitting across from him in the coach. She wore a light green gown. Her blond hair was pulled up atop her head, her gray eyes—the ones that mirrored his own—blinking at him curiously. She was about as tall as one of the flag boys on the battlefield, but despite her small stature, her personality was bigger than life. Daphne had always been, ahem, wild, for lack of a better term. Oh, she knew all the rules of decorum and how to be the proper daughter of an earl. Only she went about deliberately breaking those rules with aplomb.

Once, she'd run away from home and been found down by the docks a fortnight later wearing breeches and pretending to be a boy. Donald had never managed to get out of her exactly what she'd been up to and as a family they'd managed to keep the scandal under wraps, but as a result, their mother was more than glad to have one of her sons back home to help her keep an eye on the girl. It was all Mother could do, she said, to keep Daphne from sneaking out her bedchamber window at night.

Julian had finally had a chance to ask his sister what she knew about Donald's trip to France.

"Oh, come now, dear brother, I may be a female but I'm hardly stupid."

Julian had smiled at that. His little sister was even more savvy than he gave her credit for. "I had a feeling Donald was up to something when he mentioned he'd be traveling with Captain Cavendish."

"Rafe?"

"Yes. Rafe's been working for the War Office for years," Daphne replied.

"How did you know—?"

"What did I just say about not being stupid?"

Julian made a mental note not to underestimate his sister. Rafe Cavendish prided himself on his discretion and if Daphne had guessed what he was up to, she must be quite discerning, indeed.

Daphne folded her arms over her chest. "I could be just as effective a spy as Donald could be, you know. Better even, I daresay."

"If you think for one moment, I'd allow you to—"

She held up a hand. "I know. I know. I'm a lady and a young one at that. How could I ever manage to do something as dangerous as working for the War Office?" She rolled her eyes.

Julian narrowed his eyes on his sister. The girl was too intelligent by half.

"Not to worry," Daphne continued. "Donald's secret is perfectly safe with me, as is Captain Cavendish's, of course. Mama thinks they were merely carrying out some innocuous sort of parliamentary business. Nothing dangerous of course, and that's exactly what I want her to believe. Until we get word."

The two siblings exchanged glances. They both knew how dire the news might be, how serious it was. Julian nodded. Whatever else her faults, Daphne knew how to keep a secret. She also knew exactly how to get what she wanted. Two extraordinary traits, Julian had to concede. He often wondered at the type of man who would be able to get his fiery little sister to settle down to a marriage and children. Best of luck to the poor sop.

"Now, stop being so grouchy and let's enjoy the ball this evening," Daphne added.

"I am not grouchy," Julian insisted.

"Yes you are," Daphne retorted, sticking her cute little button nose up in the air. "You've been grouchy ever since you came back from the Continent."

"Yes, well, nearly dying will do that to a man."

Daphne pursed her lips. "No you don't. You don't fool me. I know you're grouchy for a reason that has absolutely nothing to do with what happened to you over there."

Julian gave her what he hoped was a bored expression. "What reason is that?"

"It's because you broke things off with Penelope Monroe," Daphne announced. "Though I cannot say I blame you. She's always been perfectly nice to me, of course, but I just never . . ." She squinted as if trying to think of the correct word to use. "I just never quite envisioned the two of you together. It didn't seem quite right, you know?"

"No, I don't know."

"Yes you do. You're just being grouchy again."

"I assure you, my mood has nothing to do with the end of my agreement with Penelope."

"Frankly, I'm quite pleased. Mama was forced to give me five pounds over it." Daphne laughed her sparkling laugh, the one that Julian had already noticed made other men's heads turn when they were out.

"Don't laugh that way. I'll have enough trouble keeping gentlemen away from you tonight."

"Oh, please." Daphne rolled her eyes once more.

Julian pulled on his gloves. "I know I'm going to regret asking this, but why did Mother give you five pounds?"

"Because I won the bet, silly."

He arched a brow. "Bet?"

"I bet Mama that when you came home you would end things with Penelope immediately. Mama said you'd be planning a spring wedding."

His brow remained arched. "Mother had that much faith in me, did she?"

"It's not that she wanted you to marry Penelope. I don't think she did, really. Though she hasn't said. It's just that she was convinced you *would* do it."

"I see. And you didn't believe I'd remain so steadfast?"

Daphne shook her head. Her blond curls bobbed against her cheeks. "Absolutely not."

"What made you so certain?"

"Because I've been around to see her cousin Cassandra grow up, dear brother." She gave him a sidewise cat-like smile. "You've seen Cassandra since you've been back, have you not?"

"Yes. I've seen her," he growled.

"Perhaps at the house party?"

Julian's gaze snapped to his sister's face. "How did you—"

"You mentioned Lady Worthing's eyes, which led me to believe that Lady Worthing is in fact the Duchess of Claringdon, which then led me to believe that Miss Bunbury might well have been Lady Cassandra. Am I right?"

Julian clenched his jaw. "It seems the entire house party was an elaborate ruse to fool me."

"I knew it! I begged Penelope to take me with her when she stopped by to visit before she left for Surrey."

"You knew about this mad ploy and you didn't think it absurd?"

"Oh, it's absurd to be sure. Though I think you'd have to know the Duchess of Claringdon to truly understand. She's a bit . . . unpredictable."

"And you didn't see fit to mention to Penelope that her cousin and friend were playacting in the country?"

Daphne plunked her hands on her hips. "And spoil the fun? I wouldn't think of it."

"You're mad, too," Julian declared, shaking his head.

"My point is that you have, in fact, seen Lady Cassandra."

"Yes."

"So I needn't explain my reasoning for why I bet Mother that you'd break things off with Penelope." Daphne smiled at him sweetly. "And I thank Lady Cassandra kindly for my five pounds."

Julian shook his head. Yes, Daphne was no longer a

cute little girl with a penchant for asking too many questions. She'd grown up to be an astute young woman who was much more thoughtful than she first appeared. Thankfully, Julian was spared more inquiry from his talkative sister when their coach pulled to a stop in front of the Hillboroughs' town house. Julian alighted first and then turned to help Daphne from the coach.

As soon as Daphne's slippered feet touched the ground, the siblings turned toward the front door.

Directly into the path of . . . Lady Moreland, Garrett Upton, and Cassandra Monroe.

Julian gritted his teeth. He glanced away but not before he caught a glimpse of her. Cassandra looked like a dream in a violet-colored gown, diamonds sparkling at her throat.

"Now this is going to be an interesting evening," Daphne said, with a wide grin on her impish little face. "An interesting evening, indeed."

CHAPTER THIRTY-SEVEN

Cass nodded a brief greeting to Daphne Swift and turned away. Thankfully, Garrett was there at her elbow to guide her toward the house. Her mother was babbling on, seemingly oblivious to the other two. There was no help for it but to stand in the receiving queue next to Julian and Daphne. She could feel Julian's eyes on the back of her neck. Or was that only wishful thinking? Perhaps he wasn't looking at her at all, perhaps he was completely ignoring her. But she couldn't ignore him. She closed her eyes. There it was, his cologne, the deliciously spicy mixture that always teased her senses.

Thank heavens the queue moved quickly at least. Unfortunately, Daphne Swift did not intend to allow them to maintain a solemn silence.

"It's lovely to see you again, Lady Cassandra," Daphne said.

Cass was forced to turn around. All of them exchanged awkward greetings. Her mother was cold and standoffish as usual.

"You, too," Cass choked out, nodding to Daphne. "Have

you had any news about your brother and Captain Cavendish?"

A flash of pain flitted across Daphne's pretty face. "No. Nothing, I'm afraid. Isn't that right, Julian?"

Julian's face was a stone mask. "Nothing. Yet."

"I do hope you hear soon and that the news is favorable," Cass added.

"Indeed," Cass's mother managed to add.

Garrett and Julian exchanged narrowed-eyed glares.

"Thank you very much, Lady Moreland, Lady Cassandra," Daphne replied.

Julian maintained his stony silence.

"My brother and I were just talking about you," Daphne added, watching Cass's face.

Cass's mother's expression was pinched, as if she'd just smelled something distasteful. Julian's eyes flared a bit but otherwise his expression did not change. Cass could only guess that he was imagining himself stepping on his sister's foot just then.

"Oh?" was Cass's only reply.

"Yes. I was just commenting to Julian that you've grown into such a beauty since he's been gone, Lady Cassandra."

Julian closed his eyes briefly; if Cass hadn't been watching so closely she might not have noticed.

"She has, hasn't she?" Garrett chimed in with a tight smile.

"Oh, yes. I was just about to say, it's a wonder she's remained unattached," Daphne added. "Isn't it a wonder, Julian?"

"Is it?" Julian ground out, a muscle ticking in his jaw.

Cass refused to allow him to see how his words hurt her. "Not such a wonder," she murmured.

"Yes, well, we do expect there to be an announcement

quite soon," Lady Moreland said, a slinky smile on her face. She beamed up at Garrett, looking like the cat who stole the cream. Cass wanted to shrink from embarrassment.

Thank heavens, the queue moved just then and she and Garrett and her mother greeted their hosts and moved into the ballroom without further comment. They made their way around the large room, greeting their friends and making small talk before Garrett asked her to dance. They left her mother with a group of her friends.

Cass danced, even though she felt as if her insides might explode. Jane was supposed to be here tonight to meet them, her new nonexistent chaperone, Mrs. Bunbury, in tow. Lucy was supposed to be coming, too. Cass still hadn't forgiven Lucy but it didn't keep Jane from trying to get the two of them together in the same room at every opportunity. What else would make Jane come out to a ball of all odious things?

Cass tried not to look at Julian, tried but couldn't help it. It seemed that every time she heard a man's deep laughter, she turned her head and found him, across the room, tall, handsome, his burnished gold hair and wide shoulders filling out his dapper black evening attire. It was like torture, knowing Julian was back, alive and well and no longer in an arrangement with Pen, but still elusively out of Cass's grasp. And who was the woman he supposedly cared for? The one who loved another man? Had she changed her mind? Given Julian another chance? Would they be announcing their engagement soon? Would Cass be able to stand it if that happened?

But the worst part, the very worst, was that she had lost him as a friend. No more sweet letters, no more long talks using their pens, no more communication at all. And it hurt. Penelope had already forgiven her, it seemed. Her cousin wasn't one to dwell on things overly long. She'd laughed off Cass's explanation of how Lucy had turned her into Patience and said something like, "Oh, my, I wish I'd been there to see that." Then she'd gone back to talking about a Mr. Sedgewick whom she had apparently developed strong feelings for over the summer and autumn. It was the first Cass had heard of Mr. Sedgewick and she secretly wondered if he, much like Patience Bunbury, did not actually exist.

Cass's mother had been furious with her. She'd nearly stopped speaking to her. But the thing that had served to soften her was Cass's spending so much time with Garrett. Lady Moreland was delighted to accompany them about, playing the role of the apt chaperone, but otherwise, making it quite clear to Cass at every opportunity that until she managed to secure a proposal from Garrett, she would not be entirely restored to her mother's good graces.

Thank heavens for Garrett. He had been lovely, appearing whenever she needed him, escorting her to events, being a steady shoulder on which to lean. He was a good, good man. For the hundredth time she wished she could fall in love with him. She felt a bit of guilt for leading him on, if, in fact, he had feelings for her, as Lucy seemed to believe. But at least she knew he was quite well informed about where her affections lay. Every time they saw Julian, Cass turned into a mess, and Garrett was there to pick up the pieces. Oh, sweet, kind Garrett. He certainly would make *someone* a wonderful husband one day. And unlike Julian, Garrett was a marvelous dancer.

"Thank you," she said as Garrett spun her around on the floor.

"Thank you? For what?" Garrett asked, his brow furrowed.

"For being there," she replied with a smile. "Whenever I need you."

"What else are friends for?" His grin was wide.

"Garrett, I—" She bit her lip. This was awkward. "Mother obviously expects you to propose and I just want to say that—"

He shook his head. "No need. I understand."

"Understand what?"

"You need me right now, and I would never leave you. I consider it part of my duty to help mitigate the unholy mess for which my cousin is responsible."

At the mention of Lucy, Cass went rigid.

"But don't mistake my help for anything other than how it is intended," Garrett continued. "Like your mother, I, too, expect you to be announcing your engagement soon."

Cass met his gaze. "But I—"

"Your engagement to Swift," Garrett finished with a sly smile.

Cass felt as if the breath had been knocked from her body. "My engagement to— Oh, I'm afraid that's impossible."

"I'm well aware that my cousin is under the mistaken impression that I'm in love with you, and at the risk of insulting you, I'm afraid Lucy is quite wrong. Though she would never admit such a possibility exists. Not that you're not lovely and accomplished, of course." He winked at her.

Cass had to laugh at that. "Would it be wrong of me to tell you that I am relieved?"

"Not any more wrong than my telling you in the first place. Now, as for your engagement to Swift, it's not impossible," Garrett said. "Improbable at the moment, perhaps, but not impossible."

Cass smiled at her friend. "Oh, Garrett. I should have taken your advice that night in the library. I should have told Julian the truth right then."

"We all make mistakes, Cassandra. Some of us are merely forced to pay more for them than others."

The dance ended then with that cryptic statement from Garrett. Cass wished she could hug her friend. If it wouldn't be unseemly, she would. He was escorting her about to help her, not because he had any intention of proposing to her, which made her feel that much more secure. She needn't worry about hurting his feelings. Disappointing Mother, however . . .

"Now, we'd best not spend more time together," Garrett said, escorting her off the dance floor. "We needn't get your mother's hopes up overly much."

"Agreed," Cass replied with another smile.

"I'll go fetch you a lemonade, and you can pretend you're enjoying yourself." Another wink from Garrett.

He left in search of the refreshment and Cass glanced around. After the dance, the ballroom had become a bit stuffy. She pulled her fan from her reticule and fluttered it in front of her face. A flash of green caught her eye. She turned her head to see Daphne Swift glance about before making a hasty exit out one of the doors that led to a corridor. Where was Daphne going? Something in Cass told her to follow the younger woman.

Cass traced Daphne's steps out of the room and around the corridor, down another long corridor, and into a drawing room at the front of the house. She watched as Daphne slipped inside, closing the door softly behind her. Cass hesitated outside. Perhaps Daphne was doing something truly private. Something Cass had no business interrupting. Did Daphne have a rendezvous with a gentleman here or—?

Cass scooted toward the door and quietly opened it a crack. She nearly rubbed her eyes. If she didn't mistake her guess, Daphne Swift was about to . . . climb out of the window. The girl had opened the pane that faced the street, and had dragged a footstool over in front of it to boost herself up. She'd just hiked up her skirts and thrown a leg over the sill.

"Daphne Swift!" Cass shoved open the door and strode into the room.

Daphne froze. Her little green backside slowly shimmied its way back inside, and she popped out onto the floor. She turned to face Cass.

"Lady Cassandra, I thought that was your voice." Daphne seemed completely unruffled after having been caught.

"What are you doing?" Cass hadn't meant to sound so forceful, or so domineering, but the sight of a young lady like Daphne wiggling out of the window had quite shocked her.

"Please don't tell on me, Lady Cassandra. I was just trying to leave."

Cass couldn't help but smile. "I can see that. Why were you trying to leave?"

"It's quite a long story that I do not wish to bore you with, but suffice it to say, I have a very good reason."

Cass shook her head. "Why didn't you just go out the front door?"

"The butler is there greeting guests. I didn't want to be seen."

Cass watched her carefully. She didn't want to pry but she also didn't want Daphne putting her reputation at risk, something the girl most certainly would have done had anyone else found her trying to escape through a window in the drawing room. "You should get back. I think your brother is searching for you. I saw him looking around just before I slipped out of the ballroom."

A small smile popped to Daphne's lips. "I thank you for the information, Lady Cassandra, but I think that if we're both being quite honest with each other, it is probably far more likely that my brother was looking for *you*."

Cass gasped and snapped her mouth shut.

"Oh, don't look so surprised," Daphne continued, an impish smile on her face. "You know it's true."

Cass cast about for something to say. "I . . . I think you ought to return to the ballroom before your—"

"Brother comes looking for you," said a deep male voice. "I quite agree."

Both ladies swung around. Julian was standing in the doorway, leaning against the jamb. He looked so handsome Cass wanted to fall to her knees. His hair was slicked to the side and his gray eyes glowed against the dark black of his evening attire.

Daphne cleared her throat. "I think you're both absolutely right. I'll just pop back into the ballroom. I promised Lord Cartwright a dance."

Daphne was gone in an instant, and Cass was left swallowing hard and staring up at Julian.

She took a deep breath and then made to move past him. "I should get back."

His hand shot out and captured her upper arm. "Wait."

Cass closed her eyes and turned her face away. "What?"

"I . . . I don't know."

Cass blinked away tears and ran her tongue over her teeth. "I didn't know you'd be here tonight. I wasn't following you."

"I know that. You needn't try to avoid me."

"I have to," she whispered.

"Why?"

For my own sanity. "Because I . . . feel guilty."

His voice was matter-of-fact. "You've already apologized."

"You won't accept my apology."

"It's not that I don't accept it, Cassie, it's just—"

Cass blinked away tears. He'd called her Cassie, the special name he used in his letters, the name no one else in the entire world called her.

"Don't," she whispered. She'd meant, don't call her Cassie, but he released her arm.

"My apologies," he said.

She turned to face him, wrapping her arms around her middle. "Julian, I . . ."

"What?"

"I don't know. I don't know what to say to you anymore. I only know it hurts. I feel as if I've lost my best friend."

"Best friend? That's what I am to you?"

"I thought so." She searched his face.

"You should go." A muscle in his jaw ticked. "Upton is probably looking for you."

She brushed past him again. She had to get out of there.

This time, his hand shot out, grabbed her shoulder and spun her around. She gasped. "Damn it, Cassie. I can't keep my hands off you." He pulled her into his arms, and his mouth swooped down to claim hers.

Cass's head tipped back and she wrapped her arms around his neck. *Yes. Yes. Yes.*

He kicked the door shut with his booted foot. His bold tongue pushed into her mouth and tangled with hers. She moaned. He pushed her up against the wall and kissed her again, again, again.

Cass forgot to think, forgot to breathe, forgot anything, everything. All she knew was that Julian was kissing her. Julian. And it wasn't a dream, it wasn't fake or false or in her imagination. It was real. The flesh-and-blood man, all hot and tall and hard and wanting, was standing in front of her, bracing her against the wall, and kissing her as if he never wanted to stop.

He cradled her face between his hands. His tongue dipped into her mouth, owned her, possessed her. She melted.

"Why are you kissing me?" she whispered against his lips.

"I don't know," he growled, just before his mouth claimed hers again.

He picked her up easily and carried her to the settee. He laid her down and covered her with his hard, hot body. Cass kicked off her slippers. She wrapped her legs around his hips, pulling her skirts up out of the way. Those blasted skirts.

Julian was unconsciously pressing against her most intimate spot. Again. Again. Again. She whimpered. His hips kept up a steady rhythm that Cass didn't even know if he was aware of. It drove her mad. The only barrier between them was his breeches. Her shift was up and out of the way and she clung to him, wanting him.

She knew so little about this. Had never kissed a man let alone done anything like this, but she'd dreamed about it. Alone in her bed all these years, she'd dreamed of Julian's body on top of hers, his lips molded to hers, his hips setting a gentle rhythm. Yes. She'd dreamed about it. But none of her dreams matched the reality of having him here, his warm skin beneath her fingertips, his insistent mouth pressed against hers, his hips moving unconsciously against her in a motion that made her want to scream his name.

Anyone might walk in on them at any time. Daphne might return, or their hostess might come in, a servant even. This was beyond dangerous, but Cass didn't care. She'd kiss him forever, let him touch her for eternity, or longer. Nothing mattered other than Julian's hands at her hips, pulling at her naked flesh, wrapping her legs around his waist tighter, groaning, kissing her. His hardness probed at her through the thin fabric of his breeches. She only wanted more, more, more.

He pulled his mouth away from hers and his breathing was harsh, ragged. He pressed his forehead against hers, and Cass fought against the urge to cry out. His hands were cradling her hips, making her crazy. She closed her eyes and pressed her forehead to his.

His mouth moved to trace her cheekbone, her temple, her ear. "Damn it, Cassie. I knew you were pretty but I never expected you to be *this* damn beautiful when you grew up."

Cass couldn't help the smile that came to her lips. "You think I'm pretty?"

"I think you're breathtaking." His mouth was back on hers. She pulled him even closer this time, her hand moving down of its own accord to trace the hard hot outline of him beneath his breeches.

He groaned and pressed himself into her hand. She rubbed him up and down. Another groan.

His mouth was on her throat, licking, kissing, sucking. She threw back her head and closed her eyes. Nothing mattered, nothing other than the feel of his hot mouth on her flesh. She wanted to feel him, touch him, taste him. He slowly moved his hand between her legs to the scorching wet flesh. Cass moaned. "Julian."

His mouth returned to her as if to silence her. He kissed her again and again, long, hard, deep. Then he sank his finger into her wet heat, and she forgot to breathe.

Julian's hot, hard finger moved inside her, and Cass wrapped her arms even more tightly around his neck. "Oh, Julian," she breathed against his mouth.

He slowly dragged his finger back and forth, back and

forth inside of her while she experienced a myriad of
emotions and feelings she'd never felt before. She pressed
her mouth against his hand. "I can't—"

"Yes," he whispered against her lips. "You can. Just let
me touch you, Cassie. I've wanted to for so long."

She didn't allow her brain to register the enormity of
those words. She was all feelings now, floating on a sea of
emotions and nerves and the most powerful lust she'd
ever experienced. He withdrew his finger and she cried
out. "Shh," he whispered against her lips.

His thumb found her then, the most delicate spot on
her body, the center of her thighs. He circled her in tiny
little movements that made her head toss fitfully against
the cushions of the sofa.

"Julian." The pressure between her legs was building, a
feeling unlike any she'd known before. His mouth continued to possess hers and his thumb kept up its gentle rhythm
on her most private spot, nudging again and again in the
most perfect location. She clenched her teeth. Her brow
furrowed. She tugged on his neck, kissing him ferociously.
"Julian!" she cried as a wave of delicious shudders racked
her body.

Cass floated slowly back to reality. Julian pulled himself
sharply away from her and cursed under his breath. Having
the warmth and heat of his body gone left her bereft. He sat
up on the sofa next to her while she scrambled to right her
skirts and clothing.

Cass sat up next to him, and touched her swollen
mouth with her fingers. Then her hand moved up to her
coiffure. Her hair was in total disarray; so were her
thoughts. She would have let him make love to her right
here in the middle of the drawing room if he'd wanted to.
She would have. She had no doubts. Even now she was a
bit disappointed that he hadn't—

"Go. Now," he ground out between clenched teeth.

She reached for him, longing to run her fingers through his burnished hair. "Julian, I—"

He blocked her hand with his arm. "Go. I don't know what the hell I was thinking."

Cass took a shaky breath. She stood on wobbly legs and smoothed her hands over her skirts.

"Go!" he demanded one last time.

She turned and fled from the room.

CHAPTER THIRTY-EIGHT

Bloody hell. Upton was here. Julian strode through the main room of the club doing his best to ignore the future earl. Right. Upton was a member of Brooks's. How could Julian forget?

The club was just as Julian remembered it. Stuffy. Smoky. Full of a lot of overfed gentlemen with too much money and too much time on their hands talking about subjects they knew little about. War, for instance.

Since the moment Julian had walked through the door an hour ago, he'd been waylaid by one chap after another, all wanting to know about his battle experiences. Every one of them had got a gleam in his eye when Julian spoke of his injuries. The vultures. All they were truly interested in was what it felt like to nearly die. He'd tell them . . . It was exactly like something you didn't want to discuss ad nauseam or, perhaps, *ever*!

Julian took a seat at a card table in the center of the next room and began a game with a few gentlemen. He didn't have long to wait before Upton came wandering over. The future earl made his way to Julian's table and stood next to him.

"What do you want, Upton?" Julian ground out, looking up at him through narrowed eyes.

Upton sat next to Julian and took his time lighting a cheroot. "Didn't think you saw me when you walked by in the other room, Swift. I tried to say something to you."

"Forgive me. I'm not in the mood for your company at present." Julian's smile was tight.

Upton arched a brow at him. "So you *did* see me?"

"Do you have a point, Upton?" Julian tugged at his cuff. The last thing he bloody well wanted to do today was trade inane banter with Upton. After his encounter with Cassie last night, Julian was in the foulest mood of his life. Daphne had told him so. She'd made it a point to inform him on their ride home that she'd never seen him more disagreeable. He was beginning to agree with her about that at least.

Damn it. He shouldn't have laid a finger on Cassandra last night, let alone all ten of them. He'd meant to tell her that they didn't need to be disagreeable with each other, instead he'd behaved like a complete animal. Touching her had been its own exquisite form of torture, the kind of torture that was worse than anything the French could dream up. It had taken every ounce of self-control he possessed to keep from ripping open his breeches and taking her then and there on the damn sofa in the middle of someone else's party. What the bloody hell had he been thinking?

He hadn't been thinking. That much was obvious. The hurt and pain in her eyes when she'd reached for him and he'd raised his voice to her had been enough to keep him hating himself for months to come. But at least he'd done the right thing, let her go. Cassandra thought he was perfect, or at least she *had* thought so. He was so damned far from perfect, he couldn't even see perfect anymore. Kissing Cassie last night, hurting her afterward with his words. That proved it. He'd made his mistake, now he had to live with it. He wasn't in the mood for Upton's recriminations. He had enough of his own.

Upton blew a smoke ring into the air. "I'll cut to the chase."

"Please do."

"Don't hurt her, Swift."

Julian ground his teeth. He wanted to punch Upton. What would happen if he did? He'd get tossed out of Brooks's on his ear. It would probably be worth it, but he didn't want word getting back to Wellington. Instead, he took a deep breath. "Don't hurt *her*? That's rich. Especially coming from you."

Upton watched him carefully. "You don't know the power you have to hurt her."

She doesn't know the power she has to hurt me. Julian lowered his voice so the others wouldn't hear. "I should have known there was something between the two of you when I saw you coming out of the library that night at the house party." He had nearly made love to Cassie on the sofa at the Hillsboroughs' party last night yet she was all but engaged to this man. What the hell was that about?

Upton narrowed his eyes on him. "What exactly are you implying?"

"Now you're escorting her around town? I expect you'll announce your engagement any day now."

Upton settled back into his chair and blew another smoke ring into the air. "If I didn't know better, Swift, I'd think you were jealous."

Julian slapped his palm against the tabletop. "You needn't have come over here to warn me, Upton. I don't intend to speak with her ever again."

CHAPTER THIRTY-NINE

The letter arrived at precisely ten o'clock that morning. The butler delivered it to Cass in the breakfast room where she was doing a positively halfhearted job of attempting to paint a chrysanthemum in a vase. Her painting looked more like a fuzzy yellow blob than the lovely fall flower, so she was happy to turn her attention elsewhere. Painting had hardly kept her from replaying her time with Julian the other night over and over again in her head. She plucked the missive from the silver tray and contemplated it for a moment before ripping it open. Daphne Swift's pretty, loopy handwriting stared back at her.

Lady Cassandra,

I must explain my behavior from last evening. Please meet me in the park at five o'clock at the head of the path near the rosebushes. I desperately need to speak with you.

L. Daphne Swift

Cass furrowed her brow. Then she reread the letter two more times. What could Daphne possibly want with her in the park? It had been quite odd that the young woman had been trying to sneak out the window at the Hillsboroughs' party, but she'd never imagined that it was due to something serious. Was Daphne in some sort of trouble? Regardless, Cass couldn't ignore such a letter. She'd always been fond of Daphne. They'd been friends. Cass would go to meet her.

Cass arrived at the park at five o'clock. Wearing her butter-yellow riding habit, she rode her own horse sidesaddle and brought only a groom with her. Just in case Daphne wished to keep the details of their meeting a secret, she thought it better not to bring her mother or a maid along as a chaperone. In fact, her mother thought she was taking a nap.

Cass stopped at the head of the path with the rosebushes. She and Daphne had ridden here together before. They'd both remarked upon how lovely the bushes were. It led off down a secluded path that ended at a small lake. It was a beautiful spot. The autumn leaves floated from the trees and crunched beneath her horse's hooves. The rain from the night before made the ground soft and smell of leaves and the upcoming winter.

Cass didn't have long to wait. Only a few minutes passed before a horse's gallop sounded on the path coming toward her.

When the rider came into view, Cass sucked in her breath. It wasn't Daphne. No. It was Julian. Her stomach leaped, did a somersault, then righted itself with a sickening lurch. She pressed her hand to her middle. She hadn't been able to stop thinking about their—ahem—*kiss*. She'd been plagued with the memories of it all day, in fact. Had been scarcely able to think of anything else. But what was Julian doing here? He'd made it quite clear that he didn't want anything to do with her.

As soon as he saw Cass, Julian drew back the reins and brought his mount to a stop. He was wearing buckskin breeches and black riding boots, a dark blue waistcoat and gray wool overcoat along with his white shirt and cravat and black hat. She wanted to look away, but she couldn't. She blushed. The memory of his mouth on hers, his hands touching her body, scalded her mind.

They both stared at each other, unblinking.

"Where is Daphne?" Julian asked, glancing around, his eyes narrowed in suspicion.

"That's a good question," Cass replied, clutching her reins as if they were her only lifeline, her fingers cramped from the effort. "Are you meeting her here, too?"

He turned his face slightly to the side as if to look down the path for his sister. "She sent me a note not fifteen minutes ago. She told me it was urgent that we meet in the park. Now."

Cass closed her eyes. She'd been duped, duped by little Daphne Swift of all people. "She wrote me a letter this morning asking me to meet her here at five o'clock."

Julian snapped his head back to face her. His features were a mask of stone. "Did you plan this with Daphne?"

Cass's mouth dropped open. "Are you serious? You honestly think I would try to trick you into—"

His face softened a bit. He held up a hand. "My mistake. Apparently, my sister thinks playing pranks is a lark. My apologies on her behalf." He swung his mount around and turned to go.

"Wait!" The word escaped Cass's lips before she had even meant to think it. She cursed herself. Why had she said that? What did she want him to wait for? What more could they say to each other after what had happened last night?

He stopped and turned back to face her. "Yes?"

"I . . ." Her voice shook. She cursed herself for that. "Would you . . . care to . . . go for a ride?"

Confusion clouded his face. He narrowed his eyes again. "With you?"

"Yes." She glanced down at her gloves where they gripped the leather reins. Oh, the devil may care if he believed she was responsible for this. Daphne had tricked them both, but now that he was here . . . she didn't want to let him go.

He maneuvered his mount back toward her and cocked his head to the side. "Where to?"

Cass smiled at him.

Minutes later, they were trotting down the secluded path past the rosebushes. They left Cass's groom behind to wait for them.

"Mother would disown me if she knew I sneaked away from the groom," Cass said softly.

"Not to mention you're with me." Julian led the way and Cass followed closely behind. "She wouldn't like that, either."

"Yes, but that's only because you are—" She stopped and glanced down at her lap.

"What?" He turned his head to look over his shoulder at her.

"Never mind." She shook her head.

He turned back to face the path but his voice drifted to her. "You were going to say *untitled,* weren't you?"

Cass tugged on her gloves and readjusted her position in the sidesaddle. "Mother has always insisted I marry a man with a title."

His voice remained clear, strong. "Like Derek?"

"Yes. She was beside herself when I refused him."

"Like Upton?"

She nodded even though he couldn't see her.

He stopped and waited for her mount to come alongside his. "You've had scores of offers, Cassie. I know from your letters. Why did you refuse them all?"

Cassie. There it was again, his nickname for her. It made her heart ache. "I refused them because I didn't love them."

His eyebrows shot up.

"What?" she asked. "Does that surprise you?"

"Yes, actually."

"I never told you that before?" she asked, trying to concentrate on maneuvering her horse around a fallen tree.

"Not in those words." He shook out his reins.

Her horse cleared the tree and Cass expelled her breath. "Why did you think I refused all my suitors?"

He gave her a sidewise smile. "I assumed none of them were good enough for you."

She laughed. "Even Derek? The duke?"

"You weren't even tempted?" Julian asked with a chuckle.

Cass sobered. "If you could see him and Lucy together, you'd know in an instant they were destined for each other. Jane and I knew right away."

Julian nodded. "I don't doubt it. How is Her Grace doing these days?"

Cass lifted her chin. "I don't know. I'm not speaking to Lucy."

Another raised brow. "You're not speaking to your closest friend?"

She glanced away. "She . . . she gave me some very bad advice."

"Lucy was the one who said you were Patience." His voice was solemn.

"Yes."

"But you could have easily corrected her that day."

"I know."

"But still, you blame her?"

They came upon the small lake then. Julian stopped, dismounted, and tied his horse to a nearby tree. He made his way over to Cass's horse and put his hands on Cass's waist to help her down. The feel of his hands on her made her insides tingle.

He lifted her easily. Once she had a sure footing on the leaf-strewn ground, he let go of her waist. She glanced away. He cleared his throat. They walked together slowly down to the water's edge.

Cass shook herself. What had they been speaking about before he touched her? Oh, yes. Lucy. "You have to know Lucy. This isn't the first time she's got me into trouble. Be bold, she always says. Look where being bold has got me."

He cracked a smile. "On an outing with a useless second son."

Cass stopped and looked up into his eyes. "Julian, please tell me you don't really believe that, that you're useless."

He bent down and scooped up a stone. He drew back his arm and skipped the pebble over the water. "But I do."

Cass pressed a hand to her throat. It ached. "You never told me that."

He skipped another stone, still staring out ahead across the water. "I suppose it's not something you write in a letter, even to a friend."

She searched his profile. "What isn't?"

His gaze searched the horizon. "That one day, when you were fourteen, your father told you that you were unnecessary."

Cass sucked in her breath. "He did not!"

"It doesn't matter."

Cass touched his arm. He didn't look at her. "It matters. Very much. To me," she said. "Please tell me he didn't say that."

Julian hefted another stone in his hand. "He used that exact word actually, *unnecessary*. By the time I was fourteen, Donald had already come of age. He'd survived childhood. He was ready to take over one day. I was no longer needed."

Cass pressed a hand against her thumping heart. "What sort of a monster would say that to a young boy?"

Julian turned to face her. "What sort of a monster would tell a young girl that she is only as good as the man who will marry her?"

"Mother said something like that to me once," she murmured. "Specifically, she said, 'It doesn't matter what a man feels about you, Cassandra, it only matters whether he will marry you.' And I set about becoming the perfect future wife, all in an effort to win my parents' approval and love." She sighed. "But my parents don't love me. Not really. I'm nothing more than a prize possession to them."

Julian's voice was soft. "I know. You told me in one of your letters. I'm sorry, Cassie."

"I told you?" She searched the ground for a stone, desperately thinking of a way to turn the subject from herself. "Yes."

"It's funny. I'd memorized everything you wrote to me," she said softly. "I didn't memorize what I wrote to you."

He jerked his head sharply to the side, a strange look on his face. "You memorized my letters?"

She blushed and bent down to get a closer look at the stones. She pushed some wet leaves away. "I know you have a scar on the underside of your chin because your first horse threw you when you were six years old."

He rubbed his chin. "That hurt. Scraped it against a rock."

She scooped up a stone and made her way tentatively to the water's edge. "I know that you were once beaten by a group of boys at Eton because you were the only one who defended a new student who'd just arrived and was frightened."

He eyed her askance. "I never said I was the only one."

She smiled. "You didn't have to. I could tell. You were the only one, weren't you?"

He folded his hands behind his back, looked down at the tips of his boots, and nodded. "Poor bastard," he whispered.

"And I know that you once gave Daphne your entire savings of spending money because she wanted to purchase a puppy that was being sorely treated by its owners."

He cracked a smile. "Daphne can be quite convincing."

"You're quite a nice brother," Cass said. She tried to skip her stone. It plopped into the water unsuccessfully.

"Owen wouldn't do that for you?" he asked.

"Oh, Owen's always been perfectly nice to me, but he was much more interested in riding and hunting and boyish pursuits. He never took much of an interest in his younger sister. Though when Lucy used to visit she always tried to get him to play with her. He wanted no part of it, of course."

"So she played with you, instead?"

"I'm afraid it was her only choice." Cass tossed another pebble into the lake, an even more dismal attempt at skipping than the last.

Julian walked over to her and handed her another stone, heat transferring from his hand to hers. "Let me show you," he said, turning her and pulling her into the recess of his arms. Cass closed her eyes. It felt so good to have his arms around her, his warmth and scent enveloping her. He took her small cold hand in his large one. "Here's how you do it. First, you must start with the correct stone. See how this one is flat?"

She glanced down at the rock in her hand. It was indeed flat. She somehow managed to nod.

He nudged her finger to the top of the stone and moved her thumb to the side. "Fling your wrist, like this. Try to keep that angle." He demonstrated the correct flip of the wrist.

Cass tried it, flinging the rock out onto the lake. The stone skipped once, twice, three times before sinking beneath the flat surface of the water.

"I did it!" She turned in his arms, a wide smile on her face, then pulled away abruptly when she realized how close they still were. She backed up quickly, putting several paces between them.

He shook his head and seemed to study the ground for more suitable stones. "You know, I remember your letters, too," he said quietly. "Let's see if I can refresh your memory about what you wrote to me."

Cass blushed and glanced down. She pushed her slipper through a small pile of leaves.

Julian folded his hands behind his back. "I know you make it your business to befriend anyone whom no one else will befriend. You're not close with Lucy and Jane for no reason."

"I love them," she admitted. "Even Lucy, when I don't want to kill her, that is."

He nodded. "I know. I also know you are exceedingly clever at sewing, singing, playing the pianoforte, and painting. Especially painting."

"I'm not proud of any of that. Mother insisted I do it." Then she smiled softly. "Well, perhaps the painting."

"You're quite good at it."

She glanced away. "Thank you."

"I still have all of the paintings you sent me. I keep them in my pack."

She turned her head to look at him. "You kept them? All these years?"

"Yes. I couldn't keep all the letters, but I kept all the

paintings. I used to look at them on days when the skies were gray and thick with smoke and stench."

Tears burned the back of Cass's eyes. She turned toward the lake so he couldn't see.

"I know you love your mother and father despite the fact that they've never been good to you," he said next.

Cass wrapped her arms around her middle. "I wrote that?"

"Not in so many words. I could tell."

She smiled at the fact that he had echoed her words from a few moments earlier. She stared unseeing across the water. "I always wanted them to love me. They seemed to love Owen just because he was a boy, an heir."

"Ah, I know all about that."

Cass stopped and placed her hand on his sleeve. "Julian . . . I meant what I said in my letter. If Donald doesn't come back." She swallowed. "You can do it. You can be the earl. You're strong enough. You're good enough."

Julian clenched his jaw. "Like Upton?"

The words stabbed Cass's heart. She turned toward the horses, still fighting tears. "We should get back."

Julian only nodded. They walked slowly to the horses, and Julian helped her remount. Using a fallen log, he hoisted himself onto his own horse.

Before they took off, Cass glanced at him. "Julian, do you think you could ever be my friend again?"

He rubbed his chin and stared off past the water. "No, Cassie. That's not what I want."

CHAPTER FORTY

Cass couldn't concentrate. She was supposed to be writing a letter to her elderly aunt Meredith. Instead, she stared off into the corner of the room, the quill forgotten in her hand. She had so much to sort out in her mind. Her outing with Julian yesterday had left her more confused than before. What did she want? What did she *truly* want? She didn't want to marry Garrett or any other man whom she didn't love. She wanted Julian. She always had and she always would. But that was obviously not to be. She'd nearly screwed up the courage to ask him who he had feelings for, but in the end she just couldn't.

Julian was still angry with her. She knew that. And what did it matter, really? He'd kissed her the other night because he was attracted to her. He couldn't help himself, but it didn't change the fact that he hated her for her lies. He didn't feel he could trust her. She couldn't hold out hope on that score. He couldn't forgive her and she had to accept that. She had to let go of her old dream. It faded before her eyes. Pen might not marry Julian, but neither would she. It was a hope she'd held for so long. So very long.

Cass shook herself from the memories and turned her attention back to the matter at hand. Regardless of what had gone on between them, she knew now that she and Julian did not have a future together, not as husband and wife. She'd been a child when she'd dreamed that dream. Now she was a woman, full-grown. Childish fantasies were best left in the past.

She had to take responsibility for her life, make her own decisions. That meant that she had to get away from her mother. That was the first order of business. As long as her mother controlled her, she would not stop pushing her toward the biggest, most noble title in every room. Cass couldn't bear that. She couldn't live the rest of her life being trotted out to social events as she got older and older. She would never marry. She knew that now.

She leaned back in her chair and combed her fingers through her hair. What did she want? Peace. She wanted peace and quiet. The barest hint of an idea skittered through her brain.

She sat up straight. She couldn't do it, could she? Oh, she'd threatened to a time or two before, but it had only been a jest, really. Hadn't it?

She tapped a fingertip against the tabletop. But it didn't have to be, did it? There were young ladies who did it all the time. It wasn't unthinkable.

She snapped her fingers. Yes. She could! She would. And her mother would have no more control over her. But first, she needed help. She stretched out her arm and dabbed the quill into the inkpot in front of her.

She needed to write two letters. Immediately.

CHAPTER FORTY-ONE

Daphne Swift and Jane Lowndes arrived at Cass's house at nearly the same time. They had both received Cass's letters and quickly made their way to the Monroes' town house. Cass had tea waiting for them. Thankfully, her mother was out paying afternoon calls and so the three young ladies were left alone.

Daphne was wearing a pretty pink dress, and her blond hair was wrapped around her head with a few ringlets dangling near her cheeks. Jane wore her usual blue with her usual book as an accessory. Daphne had the grace to look a bit guilty over her duplicitousness about meeting Cassandra in the park. Cass had to admire her for coming over to face her.

"Are you angry with me?" Daphne asked. "For luring you to the park to meet Julian?"

"No," Cass replied. "I'm not angry. But why did you do it, Daphne?"

Daphne shrugged. "I thought if the two of you spent time together, you'd realize how you feel about one another. That's what Her Grace's letter said to do."

Cass snapped up her head. "Her Grace's letter?"

Daphne nodded, her blond ringlets bouncing. "Yes. The Duchess of Claringdon wrote to me several days ago and said I must help to ensure you and Julian saw each other as often as possible while you were in London."

"Lucy wrote to you?" Cass turned to Jane. "Did you know about this?"

Jane shook her head so vigorously that her spectacles popped off her nose. She caught them in both hands and immediately scrambled to replace them. "I had no idea."

"Her Grace said I should keep it a secret," Daphne added. "Especially from you"—she nodded to Cass—"and Julian."

"Of course she did." Cass took a deep breath. "Why am I not surprised that Lucy continues to meddle in my affairs even after I stopped speaking to her over her meddling?" She poured tea into the cups.

"That's our Lucy, I'm afraid." Jane took the teacup that Cass handed to her.

Daphne sighed. "It didn't work, though, did it?"

Cass shook her head. "No. I'm afraid it didn't. In fact, your brother made it quite clear that he doesn't even want to be my friend."

Daphne's face fell. "He said that?"

"'Yes.'" Cass nodded.

"I cannot understand him," Daphne replied, accepting her teacup. "Why is he acting this way?"

Cass lifted her chin. She pulled her own cup closer. "It doesn't matter. He cannot forgive me, and I understand why. I was a fool to do what I did."

Jane took a sip of her tea. "Don't be so hard on yourself, Cass."

Cass returned her weak smile.

"I don't understand Julian these days," Daphne said, taking a sip. "How could he be like this to you?"

"I've done a lot that's difficult to forgive," Cass replied. "I don't blame him."

"I do," Daphne said. "He's being so judgmental. We all do things we ought not from time to time. For instance, I tricked you into meeting him in the park. You don't hate me, do you?"

Cass smiled at the younger girl. "No, I don't hate you, but I do contend that you owe me a favor to make up for your sneakiness. In fact, that's why I've asked you to come."

Jane tipped down her head to look at Cass over her spectacles. She gave her a wary glance. "A favor? Is that why I'm here, too?"

Cass shook her head. "No. You owe me nothing, Janie. I only wanted to beg for your assistance."

"I'll do what I can," Daphne said, "but if this is about Julian, I think you need to—"

"No." Cass straightened her shoulders. "It's not about your brother. This is about me and what I want to do. I need to take control of my own life. I've made a decision."

Jane's face scrunched into a frown. "You seem different today, Cass."

Cass smoothed her hands down her sleeves. "You mean I don't seem anxious any longer?"

Jane reached over and patted her arm. "Are you all right?"

Cass took a deep breath. "I'm perfect actually. I finally decided that I'm not going to live my life under my mother's thumb for one more minute. She'll never stop until I'm unhappily married to a man whom I don't love. I know that and I refuse to live my life according to her rules."

"I don't understand. What do you want to do, Lady Cassandra?" Daphne asked, her brow furrowed.

Cass looked at Julian's sister. "First, you must call me Cass."

"All right, Cass," Daphne answered with a smile.

Cass nodded. "Daphne, I do hope you do not take this the wrong way but you seem as if you are the type of young lady who knows how to do things you oughtn't."

Daphne blushed just a little, but then she laughed. "Oh, I understand, Cass. And you're perfectly right. Actually, I take that as a compliment."

Cass smiled back at her. "You should. I've asked you here because there's something I want to do that is going to take someone of your skill and determination to do it. I need your help."

Daphne's eyes lit. She leaned forward in her seat. "Yes?"

"I don't like the sound of this," Jane said, shaking her head at Cass.

"Be bold," Cass said. "I've been thinking about those two words. I've made mistakes, several of them. I've allowed myself to be told what to do by nearly everyone, Mother, Father, Owen, even Lucy. It's easy for me to blame all of them, to take no responsibility for the part I played in all of this." She lifted her chin. "But it's not true. It's time I stood up for myself, made my own decisions, and lived life on my own terms. I learned something being Patience Bunbury. I learned that I didn't have to be the perfect little Society miss. The world would not come to an end if I broke a rule."

Daphne waved a hand in the air. "Oh, dear, I could have told you that."

Cass folded her hands in front of her and rested them on the tabletop. "I intend for things to be different now. No more being controlled by the whims of others. I intend to see to it that I live the rest of my life in peace and quiet. I want to go somewhere where Society and all of its silly titles don't matter, a place where my parents cannot marry me off to the haughtiest title as if I'm a jewel to be sold."

Jane's eyes were wide. "Cass, I've never heard you speak like this before."

Cass nodded. "I know. High time, is it not?"

"Yes." Jane nodded resolutely. She took a small sip of her tea.

"Tell us," Daphne prompted, leaning forward in her seat. "What do you intend to do?"

Cass glanced back and forth between both ladies. "I intend to run away and join a convent. And you're going to help me."

CHAPTER FORTY-TWO

Julian tossed his gloves and hat on the table next to the front door. His outing with Cassandra in the park the other day had been absolutely frustrating. But he couldn't stop thinking about it. What did the future hold for them? How could he possibly resolve their relationship? He might be able to forgive her for lying to him but it didn't change the fact that she was in love with Upton and seriously considering marrying the man. And Upton, that fool, was warning Julian that he shouldn't hurt her? He was completely daft.

How could Cassie respond so passionately to Julian's kisses and then plan to marry Upton? It made no damn sense. Was it more of her playacting? If so, how could he have been so wrong about the girl he'd written to for years? The girl he thought he knew for so long? She'd asked him if he would be her friend. He'd been truthful in his answer. He didn't want to be her blasted friend. He wanted to be much, much more than that. Her husband. He'd stupidly said no to the question, however, closing whatever bit of the door they had left open to them. Anger had made him do it. He was a complete fool.

Nothing had changed. Nothing including the fact that if Derek returned with no news, Julian intended to go to the Continent and find his brother and Rafe even if it meant he'd die trying. In that event, at least he would finally fulfill his father's last request.

Pengree quickly swept up Julian's hat and gloves, but he was halfway to the study by then.

"I have some letters for you, my lord," Pengree announced, dogging Julian's steps.

Julian stopped and turned around. "Letters?"

The butler stopped short, too. "Yes." He handed Julian two different sealed pieces of parchment. Pengree cleared his throat. "The first one is from the Duke of Claringdon, and the second—"

Hunt? A letter from Hunt? "That'll be all, Pengree." Julian pushed open the door to the study and strode inside, ripping open the letter from Hunt as he went. Was this it, the letter that would contain Donald and Rafe's fate? Julian held his breath. His gaze scoured the few words on the page.

Swift,

I'll be returning to London Thursday afternoon. I will come to Donald's house straightaway.

Hunt

The hand that held the letter fell to Julian's side. He stared unseeing at the row of mahogany bookshelves that lined the wall. They were nothing more than a dark blur. He barely noticed the fire crackling in the hearth, the soft strains of the pianoforte playing somewhere in the house where Daphne was practicing.

Bloody hell. If Derek wasn't telling any news, he either

didn't know anything or it was bad. If Donald and Rafe were dead, Hunt would wait to tell him in person. Julian knew that. A knife twisted in his gut. He closed his eyes. It was Wednesday. He had an entire day to wait.

Tossing both letters onto the nearby desk, he scrubbed his hands across his face and finally allowed himself to think about the worst. Mama and Daphne hadn't mentioned it, either, but he knew they must have been thinking about it, attempting to prepare themselves. If Donald was dead, Julian would be the earl.

He clenched his fist, slammed it against the bookshelf. The sturdy wood didn't crack, but the books danced along the shelves. His knuckles ached. He stared at them. Blood dripped to the carpet.

Damn it all to hell. This was not the way things were supposed to be. This was not what he'd been born for. He'd never wanted the title, wasn't meant for it. His father had been quite clear about Julian's role and Julian had already failed at it once. Now. . . . If Donald didn't return . . .

Julian clamped his jaw. Thank God his father wasn't alive to see it. The old man would turn in his grave if he knew his beloved first son wouldn't live to fulfill his role as the Earl of Swifdon.

Julian stared down at Hunt's letter. *Life is inexplicably unfair.* His own words flared in his memory. That is what he'd learned in the war. He'd told Cassie that at the house party, hadn't he? So damned unfair. It had been unfair that he'd kept Penelope on the hook all these years. It had been unfair of him to develop a deep friendship with a woman knowing he would not be coming home. It had been unfair of him to live, damn it. Yet he had Cassie to thank for that.

He glanced around the study. Never had he felt his father's presence more than he did in this room today. The study of the Earl of Swifdon, his father's room, Donald's room. It was not a place for Julian.

God. This couldn't be happening. He couldn't be standing here contemplating the idea that Donald might not be coming home. Julian needed something to keep his mind off things, his fears for his brother and his constant plaguing thoughts of Cassandra Monroe.

He turned toward the door to the study. Perhaps he'd go back to the club, the boxing hall, the— His gaze fell on the second letter that Pengree had given him. It lay on the desk half covered by Hunt's missive. Julian did a double take. He slowly pulled it out and turned it around to get a good look. It was addressed to him from . . . Cassandra Monroe. He'd recognize that handwriting anywhere. He ripped open the seal, brought it closer to his face and stared at it, squinting. His brow furrowed. The date was . . . last July. How in the world—

He rang for Pengree.

The butler arrived moments later.

"Pengree?"

"Yes, my lord."

"This other letter you gave me?" He held up the letter from Cassie and waved it at the butler.

"Yes, my lord."

"Where did it come from?"

"The maids found it in the cushions of the sofa here in the study, yesterday." He motioned toward the piece of furniture in question. "Apparently, it had been wedged between them."

Julian scrubbed his hand across his forehead. "Thank you, Pengree."

"My pleasure, my lord."

The servant left the room and Julian stared at the envelope again. How did a letter from Cassandra with a date from last summer become wedged into the sofa cushions at his brother's house in London? It made no sense.

Unless . . .

The night the duchess had come to visit came back to him in a rapid vision, a haze of pictures in his mind. She'd given it to him and she'd said something about it. What? What?

With his free hand, he pressed his fingertips to his temples, as if that would help him to recall.

God. He remembered now.

She'd said she'd hoped it would make a difference. A difference about what?

He glanced down at the opened letter. His gaze scanned the page. The parchment appeared to be . . . stained with tears? He eagerly began to read.

Dearest Julian,

I've just received word that you're dying. I can hardly force myself to write that word. It's awful. It's ugly. And it breaks my heart. Yes, it breaks my heart because you're my dear friend, my future cousin, but it also breaks my heart for another reason, one you may not have guessed. I was not certain I should write this letter, but Lucy has convinced me it is necessary. And so with a heavy heart, but one that is also full of love, I put my quill to this parchment to tell you something, Julian. To tell you how desperately I love you. Not as a friend loves another friend but as a woman loves a man. I've loved you since I was a girl. I know I have. I never told you for the reason that should be quite obvious, that you are meant for Penelope. My cousin is quite dear to me and I would do nothing to hurt either of you, you must believe that. But I cannot allow you to go to your grave, dearest one, without knowing how madly, passionately, desperately I love you. I've refused all offers for some mad reason, thinking that I couldn't marry another man knowing he'll never fully have my heart, as it has always and will always belong solely to you. I can only hope this letter will reach you before you leave this earth, my love. And that after reading it, you'll know how much you have been truly loved. I will continue to write to you every day for the rest of my life, dear Julian. Whether it be in this life or the next that you shall read the letters.

Yours forever, with deepest affection,

Cassie

Julian read it twice more, just to make certain it said what he thought it said. Cassie? Loved him? And had since she was a girl? How was that possible? How had he not known? What the hell had Hunt been talking about then when he'd told him Cassie had loved another man?

Still clutching the letter in one hand, he strode over to the sofa and dropped into the seat.

Wait.

It all fell into place in one awful solid moment in Julian's mind. It slid hard into his consciousness like the loading of a musket. The way Hunt had said it, coughed and looked away. It was *him*, Julian. If Lucy had known and encouraged Cassie to write the letter to him, then it stood to reason that Lucy had told her husband. Hunt had thought he was keeping Cassie's secret when he didn't supply a name.

Blast it all. It was *him*!

Dear God. How could he not have seen this before? He'd spent his whole life wanting to change who he was, erase himself. He'd grown up an unneeded second son. Even the woman he'd been supposedly engaged to didn't want him or need him. He'd entered the army with a death wish but he was still alive.

Now because of this letter, it was finally clear to him. Cassie was the one constant, the one truth in his whole life. Cassie loved him. She always had. How could he not have seen it in her letters, all of them until now? Why had it taken this one to show him the truth? She may have lied to him but he could forgive her that sin. Her lie was nothing compared to the much greater truth of her love.

You can do it, Cassie had said. *You can be the earl. You're strong enough. You're good enough.* And he believed that now. Knew it. With Cassie's love and acceptance, he could face anything, even his deepest fears. She loved him. She wanted him. She made him feel as if he was the only man on earth. And he adored her.

He shoved the letter into his inside jacket pocket, stood from the sofa and rang for Pengree. The butler soon appeared once more.

"Pengree, have the coach put to and brought round immediately."

The butler nodded. "Certainly. Where will you be going, my lord?"

Julian turned to face the servant. "To Lady Cassandra Monroe's house."

Daphne stepped into the room, her arms crossed over her chest, a knowing look on her face. "You're too late."

CHAPTER FORTY-THREE

Julian stopped short. "What do you mean?

"She's probably already gone," Daphne replied.

Julian stared at his sister and blinked. "Cassie's not there?"

Daphne shook her head. "She was planning to leave today."

Julian clenched his jaw. A mixture of anger and fear congealed in his chest. "Where is she going?"

Daphne strode past him into the study. "I suggest you shut the door."

Pengree, a wide-eyed look on his face, quickly took himself off to summon the coach.

Julian pulled the door closed and turned to face his sister. "How do you know Cassandra is leaving?"

Daphne took a seat on the sofa and watched her brother closely. Her arms remained crossed over her chest. "I know because I helped plan her escape."

"Escape?" He took two long strides toward her and settled his hands on his hips. "What the hell are you talking about? I swear, if this is another one of your tricks like the other day in the park—"

Daphne rolled her eyes at him. "If this is another one of my tricks like the park then you'll end up in the company of one Lady Cassandra Monroe. And unless I misunderstand, that's exactly what you want this time, is it not?"

He couldn't argue with that logic. "Don't toy with me, Daphne," he warned, narrowing his eyes on her. "What's going on?"

Daphne flourished a hand in the air. "Cass wrote to me. She asked me to come over and help her. Jane Lowndes was there, too. You know, that Jane is quite intelligent. She had some wonderful ideas. Cass, I'm afraid, would make a terrible spy. A bit too high-strung for it."

Julian fought the urge to grind his teeth. "Daphne, you're making no sense. What are you saying? Where is Cassie? Why would she need to be a spy?"

Daphne laughed. "She wouldn't, silly. I only meant that she's not very adept at duplicity."

Julian snorted. "You didn't see her pretending to be Patience Bunbury."

"It can't have been easy for her," Daphne replied with a wan smile.

"Where is she, Daphne?" he said, groaning.

Daphne had the grace to look a bit contrite. "I cannot tell you that as I am sworn to secrecy."

Now he wanted to throttle her. "Fine, then, if you're sworn to secrecy, why did you bother telling me she wasn't at home?"

"She *may* not be at home. It depends entirely upon whether she's left yet. And I told you because I didn't want to see you waste your time, or a trip."

"And . . . ?"

"And nothing. I owe Cass a debt."

"I won't bother to ask what *that* means."

"Probably for the best," Daphne replied.

Julian stood in front of his sister, towering over her. He

had to get whatever information he could out of her, anything that might help him to find Cassie. "You said you helped her plan her escape. Am I to assume she's run away?"

"In a manner of speaking, yes."

He scrubbed his fingers through his hair. "I don't have time for this. Tell me where she is."

Daphne eyed him carefully. "Why do you want to know? The last I'd heard, you were angry with her. She said you refused her friendship in the park. What's changed?"

Cursing under his breath, Julian pulled Cassandra's letter from his pocket and waved it in the air. "If you must know, this is what's changed. Cass wrote me a letter months ago telling me she loves me."

Daphne's eyes grew wide. "Oh, my," she breathed. "I'd always suspected but that is . . . unexpected."

Julian shook the letter. "Now will you tell me where she is?"

Daphne stood, crossed her arms over her chest again, and paced across the carpet, obviously deep in thought. "Hmm. I have always wanted to see the two of you together but I promised Cass I'd keep her secret."

"Damn it, Daphne. I must see her. I must speak with her. Immediately."

Daphne turned quickly to face him. "If I tell you, you must agree to two conditions."

He blew out a deep breath. "Name them."

"First, you must agree not to hurt her again. I won't send you after her knowing you will upset her. She's been through enough."

"I won't hurt her. I promise," he ground out. "What's the second condition?"

"I want a favor."

He blinked at her. "What favor?"

"Ah, ah, ah. That is the complicated bit. I do not yet

know what favor I want. Specifically, I want you to *owe* me a favor. One day, when I do something I ought not, you are going to be completely on my side, no questions asked. Agreed?"

"Not a chance. Name something else."

Daphne delicately raised her chin in the air. "No. That's what I want. Those are my conditions. They are not up for negotiation."

Julian growled. "There are times when I swear I could throttle you, Daphne."

Daphne shrugged. "If you throttle me, I won't be able to tell you where Cass is. But there is absolutely no way I intend to tell you where she is until you agree to my terms."

Julian glared at her. One thing was obvious. His sister knew how to drive a hard bargain. He'd pit her against the bloody French any day. She should be in Paris negotiating the treaty. "God help me," he murmured, swearing savagely under his breath.

"Is that a yes?" She blinked at him innocently.

"Yes," he ground out. And then, "Why do I have the distinct impression that I'm going to sorely regret this one day?"

CHAPTER FORTY-FOUR

Julian pounded on the door to the Monroes' town house. The wood bounced. The portal sounded as if it might come down. When Shakespierre, the butler, appeared, Julian brushed past the much shorter man. Daphne had told him all about Cass's plans to leave for the convent. The Sisters of Perpetual Hope made their home far to the north just below the Scottish border. If she'd already left, he'd be forced to chase after her. But there was still the chance that he might be able to catch her before she left. He was counting on it.

"I must speak to Lady Cassandra immediately," Julian declared. "Is she here?"

"May I take your coat, my lord?" the butler offered.

"No, you may not. I'll wait here."

The butler raised a brow but made his way down the corridor, ostensibly to find his mistress. Julian paced the foyer. Had he found her in time? Was she here? If she'd run away, he doubted she'd have informed the butler.

Cassie's parents weren't going to like this. Not one bit. But Julian didn't give a bloody damn. Moments later, Lady Moreland came sweeping out of the back of the house, her face a mask of disapproval and anger. "Captain Swift, Shakespierre tells me you're here to call upon Cassandra."

Julian returned her harsh look. "I am."

"I'm afraid that's not possible," she replied with a tight smile.

"Cassandra's not here?" he asked, his face heating, his hands clenched into fists at his sides. If that was true, he'd leave for the convent immediately.

"I didn't say that. I said it's not possible for you to speak with her," Lady Moreland clarified.

He narrowed his eyes on her. "Why not?"

Lady Moreland pushed her nose in the air and gave him an imperious look that clearly indicated she was not amused with his failure to turn tail and run. "Perhaps if you came back another time."

She made as if to usher him out the door.

Julian didn't move. "I intend to stay here until I see Cassandra. If she's here."

One blond-gray brow arched. The lady spoke through clenched teeth. "Captain Swift, do not force me to call my husband into this."

Julian nearly laughed at that. Lord Moreland was in his sixties and quite heavy. Even though Julian was still recuperating from his war injuries, he was quite certain he could easily beat the older man in a fight, and he was more than prepared to do so if either of them tried to keep him from Cassie.

"I'm not forcing you to do anything, my lady. I'm merely stating a fact." He gave her a tight smile. "I'm not leaving until I either see Cassandra or evidence that she's not here."

Any semblance of nicety evaporated from the woman's face. She turned her head sharply to the right. "Shakespierre, fetch Lord Moreland immediately, and bring two of the footmen back with you."

Julian took a deep breath. Fine. If this was how she wanted it, this was how she was going to get it. No sixty-year-old lord and two young footmen were going to keep Julian from seeing the woman he loved.

He shot daggers at Lady Moreland with his eyes. "You might want to call the watch and the Bow Street runners while you're at it, my lady, because I'm not leaving."

Shakespierre took off into the back of the house again and Lady Moreland narrowed her eyes on Julian. "I cannot believe you're acting in such a disgraceful manner, Captain Swift, but I suppose I should not be surprised."

He placed both hands on his hips and faced her. "What is that supposed to mean?"

She crossed her arms over her chest and looked down her nose at him. "You've never had quite the *quality* that your brother does."

If she'd slapped him, she couldn't have hit her mark any better. Something told Julian that she knew that, too. But he was done living in his brother's shadow.

He glared at Lady Moreland. He refused to let her ruffle him. "And you've never had quite the pleasant kindness of your daughter, my lady. I have often wondered how you produced such an exquisite creature."

Lady Moreland gasped. "How dare you!"

Lord Moreland and the two footmen came hurrying into the foyer with Shakespierre just then. Lord Moreland was out of breath from the exertion.

"What is the meaning of this?" Lord Moreland demanded.

Julian stepped forward. "I've come to ask for your daughter's hand in marriage, my lord."

Both Lord and Lady Moreland looked as if they might faint or have an apoplectic fit, perhaps both.

"What? What? What?" Lord Moreland clasped his lapels, his jowly face turning redder by the moment.

"You've gone mad," Lady Moreland said to Julian.

Julian cracked a smile. "Is that a no?"

Lady Moreland whirled to face her husband but she addressed her remarks to Julian. "Sir, if you refuse to leave, we shall forcibly remove you from the premises."

Julian inclined his head toward both of them. "I'd like to see you try."

Lord Moreland's jowls shook. He started toward Julian with a determined look in his eye. The two footmen followed suit. The moment they laid hands on him, Julian sprang into action. The first footman received a blow to the jaw that spun him across the foyer where he lay in a heap on the rug. The second footman was a bit larger and harder to stop. He came at Julian with a bear hug around the waist. Julian pulled him up and flipped him over his back. *Thank God for all of those press-ups.* Julian spun around to face him again. The footman remained on his back, groaning and cradling his head in his hands.

Lord Moreland came at him next, though he looked no more interested in fighting him than Julian was. He quickly sidestepped the older man, twisted Lord Moreland's arm behind his back, and shoved him forward.

"This is preposterous!" Lady Moreland screamed. "Shakespierre, do something!"

Shakespierre shifted his gaze and pursed his lips. It was obvious he had absolutely no intention of engaging in a physical altercation with a man nearly twice his size, especially one who had just proven himself to be quite an accomplished fighter. Good man, Shakespierre. Good man.

"Would you like me to call Lady Cassandra?" Shakespierre offered.

"No, I would not," Lady Moreland retorted, stamping her foot. Her curls bounced along her forehead.

That was all Julian needed to hear. Cassandra was

here. "Cassie!" he called, using his loudest captain-in-His-Majesty's-army voice. "Cassie!"

"Stop it, this instant!" Lady Moreland called. "I'll have you thrown in the Tower for this ridiculousness."

"I don't care," Julian replied. And then, "Cassie!"

"Unhand me!" Lord Moreland demanded.

Moments later, Cassie appeared at the top of the stairs, wearing a high-waisted white gown with pink flowers embroidered on it and looking like an angel. She glanced about the foyer. Both hands flew to her cheeks. Her mouth was a wide O. "Julian?" she called back.

"Unhand me this instant!" her father repeated.

"With pleasure." Julian released her father's arm with a small shove and sprinted for the staircase. He ran up, taking the stairs two at a time while Cassie picked up her skirts and ran down toward him. They met at the landing in the middle. Julian picked her up and twirled her around and around.

"Why, Julian? Why are you here?"

He set her down gently and then fell to one knee in front of her. "Marry me, Cassie."

Tears sprang to her eyes. "Marry you?"

"Marry me. I read your letter, the one that you wrote when you thought I was dying. The one you never sent."

She shook her head. "How did you—"

"Lucy brought it to me."

"Lucy?"

"Yes. She thought it would make a difference and it has. Marry me, Cassie. I love you. I just didn't know you loved me until now."

She searched his face, tears running down her cheeks. "What do you mean?"

"When I first arrived in London, Hunt told me you were in love with an unnamed man. I understand now that he meant me, but I didn't realize that at the time."

She swiped at her tears. "Of course it was you, Julian. It was always you."

"And it was always you, Cassie." He stood and grasped both of her cheeks in his hands and kissed her. Her parents, who were glaring at them from the foyer, gasped.

She wrapped her arms around his neck. "I've always loved you, Julian."

"Go get him!" Lady Moreland screamed from the bottom of the stairs, her hands clenched into two red fists. She glanced about at the two injured footmen and her husband, obviously expecting them to rush up the stairs and stop the actions unfolding in front of them. None of the men looked as if they were eager to do so. Shakespierre was contemplating his fingernails.

"There is absolutely no possibility that you are going to marry Cassandra!" Lady Moreland said with another stamp of her foot.

"Hell yes, there is," Julian replied in a perfectly calm voice. "I'd like to see you try to stop me."

"How do you expect us to agree to it?" Lord Moreland demanded. He remained at the bottom of the stairs and stared up at the couple, rubbing his arm.

Julian smiled but his eyes remained fixed on Cassie. "I expect you'll agree with it because I'm about to thoroughly compromise her." He scooped Cassie into his arms and carried her down the stairs. She kept her arms wrapped tightly around his neck. He marched down to the foyer, past both of her openmouthed parents, and a wide-eyed Shakespierre.

"Did you get all that?" Julian asked the butler.

The butler nodded rapidly. "Yes, my lord."

"Good, then go tell your friends."

Julian leaned down to allow Cassie to open the door for him and then he marched outside, down the stone front steps, and directly to his carriage.

"Come back here this minute, Cassandra!" her mother shouted.

"No," Cass replied simply, a wide smile on her face.

"I . . . I . . . I intend to call my solicitor immediately," Lord Moreland called after them, his jowls no doubt shaking.

"Good, be certain to tell him the part about the compromising," Julian replied, his eyes never leaving Cassie's face.

As soon as the door to Julian's coach shut behind them, Cass turned her head to the side to look out the window and laughed. "Oh, my goodness. Did you see the looks on their faces? It was priceless. Absolutely priceless." She clapped her hands together. "I do so wish I could have captured that moment. I may paint it later."

"They'll get over it." Julian pulled her into his arms and kissed her senseless. A few minutes later when they were both able to speak again, he said, "You were about to leave for a life in the church, I hear."

Cassie bit her lip and nodded. "Daphne told you?"

"Uh-huh." He kissed her again. "Daphne told me. I forced her to. She took pity on me, I think."

"I didn't want to live without you." Cassie pressed her forehead to his.

"Thank God I found you in time. Your parents are one thing, but I would have hated to have to fight off a group of determined nuns for you. But make no mistake, I would have won."

Cassie laughed again. "Oh, I have no doubts."

He nudged her forehead with the tip of his nose. "You never answered me, you know."

Cassie shook her head. "Answered you?"

"Will you marry me?" he whispered softly against her cheek.

She threw her arms around his neck and pulled him close. "Yes. Yes. Yes! Of course I'll marry you, Julian."

"Good, because I wasn't joking about thoroughly compromising you. I'm taking you home to my bed right now."

Cassie kissed him again and melted against him. She gave him a small smile. "Drive faster."

CHAPTER FORTY-FIVE

Ten minutes later, the coach pulled to a stop in front of Donald's town house. Julian leaped from the vehicle and turned quickly to help Cass down. They walked side by side into the foyer. The moment they entered the house, Cass stopped. "What about your mother and Daphne? I'd die if they—"

"Don't worry. They left an hour ago to visit my aunt in the country for a few days, to keep their minds off Donald."

Cass let out her breath and nodded.

"Pengree, however, is a different story," Julian said. "He may well tell all the rest of the servants and then you'll be well and truly compromised. In fact, I'm counting upon it."

"No!" She stopped again, slapping at his sleeve.

He laughed and pulled her into his arms. "I'm only joking."

"Do you think my parents will come after me?" Cass breathed against his chest. "Father may call you out, you know?"

"Not if they have a brain in their heads. If they're wise they will be planning our wedding right now."

Cass shuddered. "The look on Mother's face. She was so angry. She's never going to forgive me." She paused. "But you know what? I don't care. I truly don't. For the first time in my life, I'm doing what I want to do, not what Mother wants me to do. I finally feel . . . free." She pulled herself out of his arms and twirled around in the foyer.

"I know the feeling entirely," Julian answered. "Believe me."

Julian glanced around. He'd dismissed Pengree before he left for the Monroes' house and for the moment, at least, the butler was not present. There were no housemaids or footmen around, either. Perfect.

"Come with me," he said, motioning toward the stairs.

Cass returned his wicked smile. They sneaked up the staircase and Julian led her to one of the bedchamber doors in the middle of the hall. "This is the room where I'm staying," he said.

Cass nodded and gulped. Now that they were getting close to actually doing this, she had reservations. Not about the act itself, never that. But what if she weren't skilled enough, weren't good enough, didn't please him?

Julian grasped the handle to the door and pushed it open. The large room was decorated in dark blues and golds. A huge bed dominated the center of the room. A fireplace sat at a right angle to the bed and two large leather chairs and a small table sat in front of it. Some paintings, candlesticks, and other odds and ends finished the room. Overall it was done with quite simple and refined skill. "Daphne's doing," he explained. "And Mother's."

"They have quite good taste, indeed." She strode around and touched a silver candlestick, a book lying on the table, a figurine of a lone rider on a horse.

"Forgive me, but I don't want to talk about the décor." He moved toward her and pulled her into his arms for his kiss.

Cass shivered.

Julian rubbed her shoulders and looked into her eyes. "Are you all right?"

"I think so. I will be. I'm just . . . Oh, Julian . . . I'm frightened."

He wrapped his arms around her. "Don't be, Cassie. Any time you want to stop, just say the word. I promise, we'll go slowly."

He took her hand and led her over to the curtains. He drew them and the room was plunged mostly into darkness. Next, he led her to the bed and left her standing beside it while he went over to the mantelpiece and lit two candles there. The room blossomed into a warm glow.

He walked slowly back over to her and pulled her onto the bed with him. Cass kicked off her slippers. He shucked his boots. "I'll go first," he said with a sensual smile just before he began untying his cravat.

"No. Let me." Cass smiled to herself. Where had that come from? *Be bold, indeed.*

He gave her a sensual smile, and she pushed herself up to her knees and turned to face him. Her hands went to the white fabric coiled around his throat and she slowly pulled the knot loose and unraveled it. When she was done, she tossed it to the foot of the bed.

Next, she helped him remove his claret-colored topcoat and unbutton his silver waistcoat. His shirttails were next and she helped him to pull the white fabric over his head. His chest was bared to her. She sucked in her breath. The expanse of skin was magnificent. Muscled and bronzed. He'd written her that he'd spent a lot of time out in the sun during his recuperation but she hadn't expected him to be quite this fit. His shoulders were wide and muscled, six muscles stood out in sharp relief beneath his ribs. A trail of fine hair ran in a line in the center and disappeared beneath his trousers. Her throat went dry.

Then she saw the scar, right above his heart, a jagged dark circle. She ran her fingertips along it, her eyes filling with tears. "Does it hurt you, Julian?"

"No," he breathed. "I'm mesmerized by your touch, Cassie. Please don't cry."

She let her fingers trail down to the muscles on his abdomen and heard the sharp change in his breathing. It was true. He was affected by her touch. She'd never known anything like it. She'd never felt such power before. Her tears stopped.

"Lie down," she commanded, drunk with her new strength.

Julian did as she asked. He slid back along the coverlet and propped his head on a pillow.

She let her tapered fingernail trace the outline of his rigid erection beneath his trousers and he groaned. "Cassie, I—"

"Shh," she warned. She had dreamed about this for so many nights. She fully intended to enjoy it.

She ran her fingers over the flap in his trousers and then slowly, one by one, began to unbutton the placket.

He groaned again.

Once all of the buttons were undone, she helped him move the trousers down and off his legs until he lay there fully naked in front of her. A thrill shot through her body. She'd never expected anything like it. He was magnificent, that was the only word for it. Long and lean and tall and muscled and ooh—*quite* well endowed.

"I don't want you to be frightened. I wanted to show myself to you, first," Julian whispered, sitting up and pulling her close for a tender kiss. "But if you don't let me undress you now, I think I may die."

All she did was nod. That was enough for Julian. He carefully turned her so that he could unfasten the buttons on the back of her gown. Her dress fell loose in front and

she moved off the bed to pull it from her arms and allow
it to fall in a heap at her feet. She turned back to face him,
standing in front of him clad in only her chemise, stays,
and stockings. A chill from the room made her shiver. He
immediately stood and wrapped his arms around her,
drawing her close and warming her. He was shaking,
too, but something told Cass it was for a different reason
entirely.

He bent down and scooted the fabric of her stocking
down one leg and then the next. Cass trembled. He plucked
them from her feet and threw them easily aside. Then he
turned her around and loosened the laces of her stays one
by one. It seemed to take an interminable length of time to
get out of the thing. When he was done, he turned her back
to face him. Then her chemise was gone in one large
swoosh over her head and she stood naked before him.
Watching him watch her, she plucked the pins out of her
coiffure and set them on the table next to the bed. Then she
shook her head and the entire rich mass of her blond mane
spilled over her shoulders and back.

Julian sucked in his breath. He'd never seen anything like
the perfection of Cassie's body. She was thin but not too
much so, her breasts were perfect round globes, her belly
was flat, her hips flared out and tapered down to long
beautiful legs. She looked like a goddess, just like he'd
envisioned she would, only better because she was a real
woman, standing in front of him, touching him and letting him touch her. He promised himself to go slowly, not
scare her, make it good for her.

He picked her up in his arms and laid her on the bed.
Then he followed her down and lay atop her. He shifted
his hips away so as not to frighten her with the stark evidence of his arousal. Bracing his elbows on either side of
her head, he dipped his mouth to kiss her.

Cassie wrapped her arms around his neck and kissed Julian back with such passion and longing he felt triumphant. He kissed her nose. "I love you."

He kissed her closed eyelids. "I love you."

He kissed her cheeks, her chin, her earlobe. "I love you. I love you. I love you."

She pushed her fingers through his hair. "I love you, too, Julian." Her words were a mere whisper against his lips.

He let his mouth slide down to her chin, her neck, the tip of her breast. His tongue lavished the sensitive peak. Cass groaned and arched her back.

"Shh, darling," Julian whispered. "You're gorgeous. You're absolutely perfect, Cassie. Just like I knew you would be."

"Julian, please," she whispered against his mouth.

"Wait, darling. I want to make this unforgettable for you."

His finger and thumb came up to pinch her nipple. He flicked the peak with his thumb, torturing her, while his tongue lavished the tip of her other breast. He switched, his mouth moving to the opposite breast while his thumb unerringly rubbed the opposite peak.

Cass's head moved back and forth on the pillow, her eyes tightly closed, her jaw clenched. She'd dreamed of this moment. Dreamed of it for so long and now that it was here, truly happening, it was as if her dreams were true, all of them. His mouth continued its descent, moving down her belly, touching, licking, nipping at the sensitive planes. He trailed his rough fingertips over her rib cage. His hand made its way to the juncture between her legs. He stroked there, once, twice, right in the core of her where everything had gone soft and hot and wet and wanting. "Shh," he breathed against her thigh as his hands moved around to cup her hips. His strong hands found their way beneath her thighs, up her knees, back to her hips where he cradled her in his hands.

Then his mouth was there, between her legs, and Cass stopped thinking. His tongue owned her, licked her, kissed her. She whimpered in the back of her throat. Her fingers reached down to tangle in his hair. She'd never imagined such a thing but she also never wanted it to end.

His tongue drew tiny hot circles against her most intimate spot, and the pressure and wet heat of it made Cass come undone. Her breath was ragged, releasing in sharp pants. Julian traced a finger around her hip until he inserted it into her wet warmth. She cried out and looked down at him through lust-misty eyes. "Julian," she whispered.

He returned her look with a small satisfied smile. Then he turned his attention back to her and kissed her there, again, again. Until she was mad with wanting and desperate for release. He pressed his tongue against that perfect spot, nudging it, pushing it, stroking it in just such a way that pushed her over the edge. She cried his name this time, a keening wail while his large hands held her hips steady as she came.

Julian was panting as he lifted himself up and wrapped his arms around Cass. She'd found her release. It was important to him because he would inevitably cause her pain. He held her for a moment, her heart beating wildly, the smell and taste of her still on his hands and in his mouth.

"Cass, do you know—?"

She hid her face against his shoulder. "Yes. Lucy told me a few things."

He grinned at that. "All right, then. I'll do my best not to—"

She peeked up at him. "Don't worry, Julian. I want you to make me yours in every way."

She wrapped her arms around his neck and kissed him deeply. Julian's entire body was humming with the need to release himself inside of her. *Go slowly. Go slowly. Go slowly.*

He rolled over, pulling her beneath him. "I love you, Cassie," he whispered against her temple as he positioned himself at the entrance to her body.

"I've dreamed of this for so long," she murmured.

Julian broke then. Sweat on his brow, he pushed himself only a fraction of the way inside of her. She was so tight, so tight and wet and hot. And, oh God— He clenched his teeth. Going slowly would be the death of him.

Cass moaned then and put her palms on either side of his face. "You're so handsome, so handsome, and noble and—"

"God, Cassie, don't." He groaned through clenched teeth.

"I want you," she whispered. "I want you so much. I can't stand it. I—"

She gasped. He pushed his way inside her to the hilt and the momentary flash of pain on her face made him stop and kiss her cheek, her forehead, her temple. "I'm sorry," he murmured.

"Don't stop. I'm fine," she whispered back, a smile replacing the wince. "I've wanted this for so long."

Julian closed his eyes. He braced his hands on either side of her head and pulled out and pushed back into her again, again, again. With every stroke he felt more alive. With every tilt of his hips, he felt more love. With every pulse of her heart under his, he knew it was right. This woman was his destiny, his past and his future. This is why he had lived, to come home and be loved by her. He just hadn't known it until this moment.

He opened his eyes and nudged her with his forehead, his strokes never ceasing. He wanted to wait, to make her come again. But he couldn't. The unequaled perfection of feeling her wrapped around him made him want to shatter into a thousand pieces.

"Julian, I love you," she cried, just before he exploded inside her and collapsed on top of her.

He kissed her hair and pulled her fiercely against him.

Several minutes later, Julian rolled off Cass and pulled her tight to his chest. "I'll never let you go, again."

She snuggled next to his side and kissed his shoulder. "I'll never let you go, either. What changed your mind?"

"I told you back at your parents' house. I thought you loved another man. Hunt told me so."

"But you told me"—she glanced down—"when I was pretending to be Patience, you told me you cared for another woman."

He bent his head and kissed the tip of her nose. "Yes. You."

She rose up on her elbow. "You meant you loved *me*? Cass, I mean?"

He nodded and kissed her shoulder. "Yes. It was always you, Cassie. Always. I think I knew it back when you were sixteen, but after all the years, all the letters, I was sure."

Cass lay back on her side and wrapped her arm around his neck. "I felt so torn. I didn't think I could ever be with you. It would have been a betrayal both of you and of Pen, two people I love."

"I can understand how difficult it must have been for you. Is that why you didn't send that letter?"

She took a deep breath. "Yes. I felt it would be unfair to you and unfair to Penelope. It was not until that day you came back to London that I knew Penelope didn't want to see you. But I still wasn't certain how you felt. It's funny that we never spoke much of Pen in our letters."

He nodded. "I couldn't bear it. Besides, we had plenty to write about, didn't we? I came back planning to tell her we couldn't marry. But there was another reason . . ."

The tone of his voice frightened her. "What is it, Julian?"

He grasped her arms, stared her in the eye. "The truth is that I intended to go back to work for the War Office. I meant to go back to the Continent to find Donald and Rafe, even if it meant I never returned."

"I don't understand. You were going to run away?"

"Not run away, Cassie. Die."

She gasped. "Die?"

"Yes. I felt guilty for having lived. I was meant to die in battle. I nearly did."

"Oh, Julian. No."

He nodded. "Yes. In fact, it was my father's last wish for me."

She shook her head against the pillow. "What are you talking about?"

"He told me, my last day in London, seven years ago. He told me I should die in battle. He expected it of me."

"That's sick. It's awful. He was wrong."

Julian glanced down. "Yes, well. He never thought he would need me."

Tears rolled down Cass's cheeks. "I'm so happy you lived, Julian, so very happy. I prayed for you every day. Constantly."

He pulled her tight, squeezed her close. "I know, Cassie. I know. Don't you see? You saved me. Your love, your letters, I'm here today because of you."

"I can't imagine life without you." She tightened her grip on his shoulders. "Oh, Julian. I'm so frightened of what might have happened had Lucy not given you that letter."

He squeezed her tightly. "And to think, I almost lost it."

"Pardon?"

He gently rubbed her shoulder with his free hand. "It was hidden in the sofa for a bit. I was—ahem—jug bitten."

She turned to look up at him. "Jug bitten?"

"Very well, drunk."

She laughed. "You were, were you?"

"Yes, if you must know. What did you expect? I thought you were going to marry Upton."

Her eyes widened. "I was never planning to marry Garrett. I don't love him, and he doesn't love me, despite what Lucy thought. He told me so."

"He said that?"

"Alas, I am obviously not irresistible to every man."

"It's a good thing for Upton. I'd hate to have to beat him to a pulp."

Cass shook her head. "Yes, well, he's perfectly safe, then. Besides, Daphne told you I'd planned to join the convent."

He pushed himself up on one elbow and looked at her. "Yes, and a more ludicrous notion I've never heard."

Cass shrugged. "I wanted Mother to know that she cannot just sell me like an object. I wanted to take the power away from her. I wanted control of my own life."

Julian kissed her earlobe. "Your mother will not tell you what to do ever again."

Cass closed her eyes and sighed. "Thank heavens."

"As for Daphne, it seems I've made a deal with her. She agreed to tell me your plans in exchange for my agreement to look the other way someday."

Cass raised both brows. "Are you certain that's wise, Julian? With Daphne, there's no telling what she might get up to."

His crack of laughter echoed off the walls. "Don't I know it? And to answer your question, no, it's not wise at all. In fact, it's the opposite of wise. The mere notion that

I agreed to it only demonstrates how out of my mind I was to find you." He rolled over onto his back and pulled her atop him. Then he kissed her.

Several minutes later, Cass pulled away and looked down at him. "Julian, may I ask you something?"

"Anything, my love." He pulled her close against him and buried his face in her hair.

"You said Donald was gone to the Continent . . . on business . . . Does that mean?" She glanced away. "Does that mean that he is a—"

"I'm afraid what Donald's been doing is quite dangerous, quite dangerous, indeed. Hunt will be back tomorrow afternoon and all of the details will be revealed, I fear."

"And you think Donald and Captain Cavendish . . . ?" She swallowed. "You think they may be . . . dead?"

Julian rested his chin atop her head. "I fear it. Yes, and I damn sure hope that's not the case, but now I realize, with your love, I can fulfill the duties of being the earl if I must. I can do anything with you by my side."

CHAPTER FORTY-SIX

When Owen Monroe appeared at Julian's front door the next morning bright and early, Julian wasn't entirely surprised. He'd managed to sneak Cass back to her parents' house in the wee hours of the morning, but he expected a reckoning. He just hoped it wasn't going to be down the end of Owen's pistol at twenty paces. It would be a shame to shoot Cass's brother.

Owen and Lord and Lady Moreland were just going to have to be reasonable. They didn't want a scandal. If the servants began talking, they'd be forced to allow the match. It was in their best interest to agree to the engagement as quickly as possible and begin planning the wedding.

"Mr. Owen Monroe is here to see you, my lord," Pengree intoned imperiously from the doorway of the breakfast room.

Julian didn't glance up from his newspaper. "Does he appear to be armed, Pengree?"

"My lord?" The butler's voice was inquiring.

"Does he have a pistol in his hand? Or a large bulge in the pocket of his coat?"

"My lord, I—"

Julian smiled behind the newspaper. "Never mind, Pengree. Show him in. I suppose I must take my lumps."

Pengree left then. Julian folded down the edge of the newspaper just in time to see him retreat from the room, a confused look on his butlerly face.

He returned less than a minute later. "Mr. Owen Monroe," he announced.

Owen brushed past the butler and strode into the room. Julian eyed him up and down. No apparent pistol. A good start, actually. Hmm. But Monroe was big, quite big. In fact, he'd forgotten just how big he was. Good thing Julian was adept with a pistol himself; if a duel was necessary he had no desire to challenge Monroe to a boxing match and hoped to hell Monroe didn't suggest it. Perhaps he could challenge him to a duel of press-ups.

"Care for some eggs and toast, Monroe?" Julian asked with a devilish grin on his face. He folded the paper in half and tossed it onto the table in front of him.

"No, thank you," Monroe replied quite evenly.

"Care to take a seat then or do you simply want to have a go at me right now?"

Monroe grabbed the nearest chair in front of him and turned it around. He straddled it and braced his forearms on the back of it. "What I've come to say is quite simple."

"And that is?" Julian braced his elbows on the tabletop.

Monroe looked him square in the eye. "Marry my sister or I'm going to kill you."

Julian couldn't stop his laugh. "Is that all?"

"Is that funny?" Monroe's voice took on a shade of anger.

"No, not at all. It's just that I have every intention of marrying your sister. I plan to do so as soon as possible, in fact. I'm in love with her."

"Good. I'm glad to hear it. As you know, my parents are opposed to the match but I've reasoned with them. I believe they see the—ah—merit in the idea now."

"Your parents don't approve of me because I'm a second son, but I don't give a bloody damn."

"I don't, either. I spoke with Cass before I came. She says she loves you. That's good enough for me. You and I have always been friends. I'm still not certain what that mad house party was all about but I suspect Lucy Upton, I mean, Hunt, had everything to do with it. I was forced to go along with it because I lost a bloody hand of cards to Upton."

Julian laughed aloud at that. "You lost at cards? That's why?"

"Unfortunately, yes," Monroe replied.

"She has quite the reputation for troublemaking, the duchess, does she not?" Julian asked.

"You don't know the half of it. You should have seen her as a child, a bigger tomboy you've never known. But Cass has always been devoted to her and any friend of Cass's . . ."

"Understood." Julian wiped his mouth with his napkin. "You know, Cass has told me that you and she were not particularly close. Why come here now to defend her honor?"

"We may not have been close as children, I am eight years older than she, after all, but Cass is my sister and I love her. I'll murder anyone who hurts her."

Julian gave him a knowing nod. "I feel the exact same way about my sister."

"So, we're agreed. You and Cass will marry, my parents will, however reluctantly, approve the match, and we'll all be one big happy family."

"One big happy family? I don't know about that, now, Monroe." Julian grinned at him.

Owen grinned back. "Pass the eggs, future brother-in-law."

CHAPTER FORTY-SEVEN

When Derek Hunt arrived at Donald's town house later that afternoon, he was not alone. His brother Collin was with him.

Julian glanced out the window to see them coming up the walk. His stomach sank. Perhaps he should've insisted that Mother and Daphne remain in town. They should hear this, too. However, part of him was glad that he would be able to hear it first, break it to them gently if necessary.

He took a deep breath just before Pengree came to the door of the study and announced the Hunt brothers.

Derek and Collin entered the room moments later. Both looking somber, they shook Julian's hand.

Collin took a seat on the sofa while Derek remained standing. Julian moved over to the window but remained standing, as well. The duke paced in front of the fireplace, his hands clasped behind his back. "As you might have guessed, Swift. We have news."

Collin's gaze remained trained on the rug.

Julian braced himself. He placed a hand on the back of the chair in front of him.

"We found them," Derek breathed.

Julian's heart clenched. Hunt hadn't said the one word he'd been hoping for. He hadn't said "alive."

"Rafe was badly beaten, tortured. We took him to a surgeon in Brighton. He'll make it, but he's in bad shape." Hunt eyed his friend carefully. "Very bad shape."

Julian nodded once. "I see. And Donald?"

Derek shook his head. "Rafe told us that Donald had accidentally given himself away. That's why they were captured. Cavendish did everything he could to save him." Hunt stopped, strode over, put a hand on Julian's shoulder and squeezed. "He's dead, Julian."

Julian bowed his head. He'd known it in his heart but the word was so final and heavy and difficult. *Dead.*

Julian raised his gaze to Derek's. "You found him. You're certain?"

Derek nodded once. "Yes. We brought back his body, for your mother and for Daphne. For you." He pulled his hand away from Julian's shoulder.

"Thank you for that, Hunt," Julian replied. "Mother will be grateful. So am I."

Hunt barely inclined his head. "It's the least I could do."

Collin's jaw was clenched. "I'm so damned sorry, Swift."

"So am I," Derek said. He reached inside his coat and pulled an envelope from his inside pocket. "This is for you. It's from Donald. He'd given it to one of the clerks at the War Office to deliver to you in the event . . . of his death."

Julian stared at the document unseeing. Then, he slowly pulled it from Derek's hand and made his way toward the window. Facing the street, he ripped open the seal and began to read.

Julian,

If you are reading this, then I am dead, you are alive, and you, no doubt, have many questions. The War Office asked for a volunteer. They sent word to Parliament looking for someone, someone who would bravely go off to France. I want you to know that I did hesitate. After all, I am an earl, I have no heirs, and my only brother is at war. But I knew it would be all right, younger brother. I somehow knew you would survive. Don't ask me how. I just did. You've always been a survivor and I have no doubts.

There's something I need you to know. It's quite important to me, hence, the reason I am writing this letter. I've always admired you, Julian. I know you looked up to me and wanted to be more like me, but the truth is that I've always wanted to be like you. You left for war, fought, nearly died. You showed tremendous courage and fortitude. I never had that in me. I think Father always knew it. It's not particularly dangerous to sit in the House of Lords week in and out. Well, except in August when the stink of the Thames gets to be far too much. So when the call came for a volunteer, yes, I hesitated, but in the end, I knew I had to. I am my father's son, but I am also my brother's brother. I hope I've made the Crown proud, but more importantly, I hope I've made you proud, Julian. I may have spent my life being groomed to inherit a title, but that was nothing to be proud of. Circumstances of birth are not chosen, but bravery and courage are, and those were all things you chose. The earldom is lucky to have someone as strong as you in the lead.

I heartily approve. My only regret is that I did not get the chance to shake the hand of the man you have become.

   Give my love to Mother and Daphne. As for you, I suggest you marry Lady Cassandra and see to the business of having heirs as quickly as possible.

Yours,

Donald

Julian took a deep, deep breath. His brother admired him? He'd never known it. Damn it, if only Donald were here for one moment so that he might tell him the same. Julian turned back to his two friends, fighting the sting of tears in his eyes.

"You know what this means?" Derek said in a low voice.

Julian took another deep, shaky breath. "I am the Earl of Swifdon now."

CHAPTER FORTY-EIGHT

One month later

Cass, Julian, Lucy, Derek, Jane, and Garrett all rested in the blue drawing room in the Earl of Swifdon's town house. It was Julian's town house now. He was still waiting for the official paperwork to make its way through Parliament, but he was already performing the duties of the earl. A bittersweet thing, indeed.

Donald's funeral had been a state affair. Much of the *ton* had returned from their country houses for it. It had been attended by Wellington and the Prince Regent himself.

Daphne and her mother had been beside themselves with grief, of course, but at least they had been comforted by the fact that Captain Cavendish had lived. Apparently, the poor young man was distraught for not having saved Swifdon, too. Cass had done everything she could to comfort the three remaining members of the family, but in the end she knew there was little she could do. They needed time to grieve.

The women, who were all seated on the sofa, glanced up to see Garrett and Julian exchange wary glances. They were both pacing around the carpet like caged beasts.

"Oh, for heaven's sake, you two, don't you think it's time you made up?" Cass asked.

"The silent treatment, Upton? My, my, my, what I wouldn't give to have you not speaking to *me*," Jane remarked.

Garrett gave Jane a withering look before he turned toward Julian.

"Thank you for coming to the funeral," Julian said in a gruff voice to Upton.

"I'm damned sorry about Donald, Swift. He was a good man," Upton replied.

Julian nodded. Then the two clapped each other on the back.

Cass sighed. "Oh, thank heavens. All made up."

"Yes, as long as Upton here sees fit to help me get my new bill passed in Parliament. Derek's already agreed to it. It shall be my first order of business as Swifdon."

"Already writing a new bill?" Garrett replied.

"Yes, to provide for the injured war veterans. I assume you'll have no objections."

Garrett nodded. His voice took on a serious tone. "Just tell me what you need from me and it's yours."

"Perfect," Cass said. "Thank you, Garrett."

Julian growled under his breath, clearly indicating that he didn't much care for the fact that his intended was calling another man by his Christian name.

Derek interrupted their standoff by turning his attention to his wife. He strode over to the sofa and pulled her up into his arms. He glanced at Julian. "I should have known I needed to get back to London as soon as possible when you wrote to me about a Lady Worthing and her friend Patience. As soon as you mentioned that Lady Worthing was pretty and high-spirited with different-colored eyes, I knew my wife was up to something. It could not have been a coincidence. Not when Lucy was involved."

Lucy pursed her lips and batted her eyelashes, giving her husband a completely innocent look. "At least he said I was pretty. It might have been quite awkward between the two of you had he referred to your new wife as a troll."

They all laughed.

"I told Mother she is going to get her wish, after all," Julian said to Cass, lifting her up from the sofa, too, and pulling her against him, his arms around her waist.

"What wish is that?" Cass asked, smiling.

"To see me married in a spring wedding," he replied with a smile.

"And none of these simple morning ceremonies attended by a few close friends. It's to be a grand affair, apparently."

"We can wait," Cass said.

"No we can't," Julian responded. "We'll be married as soon as the six-month mourning period has passed. Life is precious and fleeting. It's a lesson I've learned well this year."

"I'll marry you whenever you'd like," Cass replied with a laugh.

"I must say, it'll be a chore to keep my hands off you until then, my love," Julian whispered in her ear.

She leaned up and whispered back. "Yes, well. I only hope the next little earl doesn't come any earlier than nine months after the wedding."

He grinned at her.

"How is your mother?" Cass asked. The countess had retired to her bedchamber, as had Daphne.

"As well as can be expected," Julian replied. "I know planning the wedding will make her much happier. Daphne, too."

"Poor Daphne's been inconsolable," Cass replied.

"She loved Donald. She insisted on being taken to see Rafe. He's doing better but it will be quite a while before he's fully recovered."

"I look forward to meeting him," Cass replied.

Lucy came over and hugged Cass. "I'm so glad you've forgiven me, dear."

"Did I have any choice?" Cass said with a laugh, hugging her friend back. "Besides, you did redeem yourself after all."

"Yes, by delivering that letter."

"What letter?" Jane asked from her seat on the sofa.

"The letter I wrote when I thought Julian was dying," Cass replied. "The letter that told him how much I loved him."

"I made her write it, you know," Lucy said. "I'm exceedingly proud of myself."

"You should be proud of yourself," Julian added. "And I am exceedingly grateful. It did make a difference."

"I'm just so glad everything worked out for you and Captain Swift, I mean, Lord Swifdon," Jane said to Cass.

"Are you crying, Jane?" Cass asked.

"I don't cry." She raised her book to hide her face.

"Your eyes are suspiciously moist."

"Shut up," said Jane from behind the book.

Lucy smiled and turned her attention back to Cass. "I never meant to hurt you."

Cass nodded. "I know, and I shouldn't have put all the blame on you. It was my fault, too."

"No. It was my fault," Lucy insisted. "I'm the one who came up with that preposterous scheme."

"But it did sort of work," Jane pointed out.

Cass wiped at her eyes. "It did. Eventually."

"Yes, eventually," Jane allowed. "But that could be said of all Lucy's schemes."

"Oh, Cass. I promise, promise, promise, never to do anything like that to you again," Lucy said.

"Do you promise the same for me?" Jane asked with

an expectant tone in her voice, pulling the book away from her face.

"Absolutely not," Lucy replied. "Who knows what I may have to do to see *you* happily settled, Janie?"

Jane rolled her eyes. "Just don't make it too ludicrous, please."

"Duly noted," came Lucy's reply.

Derek put his hand on his wife's shoulder. "I hope you are done with your schemes, Lucy. I don't think any of us can take any more."

Lucy gave Jane a sidewise smile. "Of course. Only we must see Jane settled first and then—"

Garrett nearly spat out his drink. "Miss Lowndes is getting married?"

Jane rolled her eyes. "Of course not, you dolt. Lucy's promised to help me to stop my mother from constantly trying to trot me out and get me married."

Garrett sighed. "I suppose I should be thankful that the worst you called me was a dolt. It is nice to see you back to your normal waspishness, Miss Lowndes." He gave her a tight smile.

Jane lifted her chin and returned the tight smile. "My pleasure, Upton."

Lucy clapped her hands together. "Now that the funeral is behind us, we must next help Cass plan the wedding, of course. Then we'll see to Jane."

"And will that involve a scheme?" Derek asked his wife.

"Not necessarily." Lucy blinked at him innocently.

Derek groaned.

"Just leave me out of it," Garrett said. "Owen nearly beat me to a pulp last time."

"I cannot guarantee anything." Lucy laughed. "Some plans require a bit of help from your friends. In fact, they go best that way, I find."

"Not if the help involves a scandal," Garrett replied.

"That's not true at all," Lucy said, lifting her nose in the air. "The more scandalous, the better. That is why it is so very important to be scandalous from time to time."

"Yes, well, I'd volunteer to join the Sisters of Perpetual Hope, but I highly doubt they'd approve of my reading material." Jane shook her head and shuddered. "And the Bible is so dreadfully dull."

They all laughed. Then Jane asked, "Have you heard anything from Penelope lately, Cass?"

"The last I heard, she eloped to Gretna Green with Mr. Sedgewick."

"Who is Mr. Sedgewick?" Lucy asked.

"I have no idea," Cass replied. "I suppose we will meet him when they return."

"Are her parents beside themselves?" Lucy asked.

"They are indeed." Cass leaned her head back against Julian's chest and took a deep breath. "I suppose we should just be thankful that my parents finally came around to the idea of our marriage, darling."

"They didn't have much of a choice," Julian replied.

"Are you jesting? They came around because you're an earl now, Julian," Jane said, just before clapping her hand over her mouth. She cleared her throat. "With apologies for being so blunt."

"There is that." Julian grinned.

"It's quite nauseating really," Cass said. "Them getting their way under such awful circumstances." She shook her head.

Lucy tapped her finger against her cheek. "No matter, dear. You're soon to be a countess, whether accidental or not."

Julian pulled Cass's hand up to his lips and kissed it. "I like that. I like it very much. You are my one true love, my accidental countess."

The Unlikely Lady

CHAPTER ONE

London, April 1816

"Sir, the coach awaits you." Garrett Upton glanced up at the butler who stood in the doorway to his study. The two roan spaniels lying on either side of his chair lifted their heads and wagged their tails at the butler.

"I'll be there in a moment, Cartwright." Garrett finished sanding the letter. Then he sealed it and stamped it with the heated wax in front of him. He didn't have much time. The coach was waiting to take him to friends' wedding house party in Surrey. The Earl of Swifdon was finally marrying his bride, Lady Cassandra Monroe, after six months of grieving for the earl's older brother, Donald, had passed.

Garrett turned over the letter and stared at it. He let out a long breath. It contained what it always did, a bank draft, an inadequate message. No mention of Harold.

Garrett pushed out his chair, and the dogs scrambled from their resting spots. He stood and tossed the letter on the stack of outgoing mail. He'd worked the last fortnight to catch up with his business matters to ensure that he could enjoy the time in the countryside.

His cousin Lucy would be there. Cassandra and Swifdon. Miss Lowndes. He growled slightly under his breath. Miss Lowndes always made his blood boil, but he could stand her for a sennight, he supposed. Why Lucy insisted on remaining such close friends with that bluestocking little harridan, he'd never know.

Cartwright remained standing at attention at the door.

"Ensure this letter goes out today," Garrett said pointedly to the servant. Garrett might be the heir to the Earl of Upbridge, but the town house in Mayfair and all of its servants and contents were currently paid for due to money his mother had brought to her marriage to the second son of an earl, and an inheritance from his maternal grandfather. Garrett was a wealthy man in his own right.

"As you wish," the butler replied.

Garrett pulled on his coat that had been resting on the back of his chair. The dogs watched him intently. As he shrugged into the garment, he stared down at the letter where it rested on the top of the stack.

Mrs. Harold Langton
12 Charles Street
London

Every two weeks he sent a similar letter. He'd sent it like clockwork for the last nearly ten years, ever since he'd been a young man of twenty-one. And yes, it always contained the same contents. The bank draft, the inadequate note, and one item that was completely unseen, un-see-able.

A hefty dose of guilt.

Garrett absently rubbed one fingertip across the top of the letter and then turned and strode out the door. The dogs followed close on his heels. He made his way down the corridor and into the foyer. Cartwright scurried to open the front door for him. Placing his hat on his head, he strode out into the street where he climbed up into the awaiting carriage. He settled into the velvet seat and glanced out the window, taking one last look at his London residence.

And with that, Mr. Garrett Upton, heir presumptive to the Earl of Upbridge, was off to spend a week at a country house party in Surrey.

"Young lady, I refuse to allow you to leave this house until you answer my questions to my satisfaction." Mrs. Hortense Lowndes's dark hair shivered with the force of her foot stamping against the parquet floor.

Her daughter, Miss Jane Lowndes, fought the eternal urge to roll her eyes. She pushed her spectacles up her nose and stared at her mother calmly. If only she had six pence for every time Mother said this or some similarly dramatic statement. Her mother was treating her like a child and Jane was through with it. She had been for quite some time, actually. In fact, Jane's desire to be treated more like the twenty-six-year-old bluestocking spinster that she was and less like a girl fresh out of the schoolroom and in search of a husband was exactly why she'd invented this preposterous scheme in the first place.

Gracious. It was so difficult to be someone who didn't like crowds or people or parties when one's mother was a great lover of crowds, people, and any party. Jane's mother was pretty, kind, and meant very well. It wasn't Jane's fault that Hortense wasn't her daughter's intellectual equal. Her mother spent her days reading *La Belle Assemblee* instead of Socrates, shopping for fabric and fripperies instead of reading the political columns of the newspapers, and gossiping with her friends instead of attending the theater. It didn't make her mother a bad person, not any more than *not* wanting to do any of those dreadfully boring ladylike things made Jane a bad one. They were simply different. How many times had Jane wished that she'd been born someone who was petite and beautiful with good eyesight who loved nothing better than to attend parties? But it just wasn't her. And it wasn't going to be. The sooner her mother would accept that fact and let go of her dream of Jane marrying a gentleman of the *ton* in a splendid match, the better the two women would get on.

To date, however, Jane's mother had shown very few signs of giving in. Hence, Jane was just about to employ her secret weapon: one Lady Lucy Hunt, the new Duchess of Claringdon, also known as Jane's closest friend. Lucy had promised Jane that she would use her considerable talents with words to convince Mrs. Lowndes that Jane should be left in peace to live out her days quietly reading and studying and hosting the occasional intellectual salon and no longer be forced to attend an endless round of social events that left Jane feeling anything but social.

And to that end, Jane had employed the second-best weapon in her arsenal, her new pretend chaperone, Mrs. Bunbury. The idea had been inspired entirely by her other friend Cassandra Monroe's unfortunate incident last autumn when Cass had been obliged to pretend she was a nonexistent young lady named Patience Bunbury. It had been unfortunate only because in so doing, Cass had been forced to deceive the man she had desperately loved for the last seven years and . . . well, the entire charade had been a bit questionable there after Captain Swift had discovered Cass's duplicity. But it had all ended well enough, hence Jane's journey to their wedding festivities today and her subsequent need for a nonexistent chaperone to escort her. Jane was going to Surrey for a week to attend Cass and Julian's wedding house party and a nonexistent chaperone was the perfect companion. Jane need only settle the thing with her mother first.

"But Mother, didn't Lucy write to you and tell you all about Mrs. Bunbury?" Jane pulled on her second glove and stepped closer to the door.

Her mother nodded vigorously. "Yes, but I find it highly suspect that I've yet to meet this woman and I—"

"And didn't Lucy vouch for Mrs. Bunbury's high moral character and excellent references?" Jane continued, completely nonplussed by her mother's fretting.

The frown lines on her mother's forehead deepened. "Yes, but I cannot allow my only child to—"

"And didn't I tell you that I'm going directly to Lucy's house from here where I shall meet with Mrs. Bunbury and travel with both her and Lucy to the house party where I shall be properly chaperoned the entire time?"

Her mother opened her mouth and shut it again, reminding Jane of a confused fish before saying, "You did, but I refuse to—"

"And won't Eloise be with me the entire ride to Lucy's house?" Jane nodded toward her maid, who stood a few paces away. Eloise bobbed a quick curtsy to Jane's mother.

Her mother closed and opened her mouth a few more times. She'd apparently come to the end of her list of rebuttals. Jane knew this about her. She'd expected it. If one lobbed enough reasons at Hortense Lowndes without stopping to take a breath, one might overwhelm her with the sheer volume of logic and then . . . success was merely a matter of time. Jane could almost count the moments to her victory. One . . . two . . . three.

"I simply— I don't think—" Her mother wrung her hands and glanced about as if she'd find the answers she needed lying about the marble floor in the foyer.

Jane watched her closely. Hmm. Apparently, this particular situation called for one more volley.

Jane pasted a pleasant smile on her face. "And won't you and Father both be coming for the wedding next week, where you'll be able to see for yourself how well I've behaved and meet all the new acquaintances I've made?"

This last bit was the most important. Jane's mother liked nothing more than for Jane to meet new acquaintances, preferably of the single, titled, male variety. Of course Jane had absolutely no intention of doing anything of the sort, but her mother needn't know that.

"I shall have the opportunity to meet Mrs. Bunbury next week?" A bit mollified, her mother's face relaxed. Her shoulders had lowered and her face had taken on a bright, hopeful hue.

"Of course. Of course." Not. Jane nodded, motioned to Eloise to follow her, and made her way out the door and down the steps to the waiting coach. A footman marched behind them. Jane breathed a sigh of relief. She lived by a steadfast rule: solve one problem at a time, preferably the one right in front of you. Worry about the others later. They could wait. She'd just done an admirable job of it.

The footman helped both her and Eloise into the coach where Jane settled into the forward-facing seat and turned to look out the window back at the house. "Good-bye, Mother. See you next week." She waved a gloved hand and smiled brightly.

The coach pulled away with a jolt and Jane settled back into her seat and let out a long sigh. She was free. It would only be a matter of hours now before she'd be in the company of her closest friends, Lucy and Cass. And if that infuriating reprobate Garrett Upton just happened to be there, so be it. She'd enjoy setting him back on his heels a bit. She always did.

And with that, Jane Lowndes was off to spend a blissfully unchaperoned week in the Surrey countryside.

SECRETS OF A RUNAWAY BRIDE

"A fantastic follow-up to Bowman's dynamic debut… an enchanting, smart romance that shines with laugh-out-loud humor, delectable dialogue, smart prose, wit, and wisdom. This entertaining and highly satisfying romp is a pure joy and delight to read."
—*RT Book Reviews* (4½ stars! Top Pick!)

"A fun … yet emotionally poignant late-Regency romance which succeeds on every level." —*Kirkus Reviews*

"This was an absolutely delightful book and an author that I look forward to reading more from." —*Night Owl Reviews*

"The tale overall is incredibly charming, the writing dramatic, and the characters bold." —*Romance Reader*

"Absolutely delightful." —*Fresh Fiction*

"A sexy, quirky, altogether fun read, Valerie Bowman's *Secrets of a Runaway Bride* is everything a romance should be. Block out a few hours for this one … once you start reading, you won't be able to stop!" —Sarah MacLean,
New York Times bestselling author

"Valerie Bowman pens fabulous, sexy tales—it's no secret she's a Regency author to watch!"
—*USA Today* bestselling author Kieran Kramer

SECRETS OF A WEDDING NIGHT

"The most charming and clever debut I've read in years! With her sparkling dialogue, vivid characters, and self-assured writing style, Valerie Bowman has instantly established herself as a